"COLLISION COURSE, CAPTAIN . . ."

". . . at present acceleration, impact in seven-point-three seconds," Spock said.

"Evasive maneuvers, Mr. Sulu!"

Sulu and the navigation computer responded, and the alien ship shot by a hundred kilometers below, its lasers still drenching the *Enterprise's* shields and surrounding space in concentrated radiation.

"They apparently do not like us, Captain," Chekov commented.

"Apparently," Kirk agreed. "If this is the way everyone in this neighborhood reacts to strangers, it's no wonder all these worlds were destroyed."

"They are persistent, too, sir. The ship is returning again."

"But this will be its last run, Captain," Spock said. "It appears to be purposely inducing an overload in its primary power source. Unless something is done, all its matter and anti-matter fuel will be simultaneously converted to energy in eighteen-point-three seconds, which time will coincide with its closest approach to the *Enterprise*. If that approach is as close as previous approaches, our deflector shields will not be able to withstand the energy release."

Look for STAR TREK Fiction from Pocket Books

Star Trek: The Original Series

Final Frontier
Strangers from the Sky
Enterprise
Star Trek IV: TVH
#1 Star Trek: TMP
#2 The Entropy Effect
#3 The Klingon Gambit
#4 The Covenant of the Crown
#5 The Prometheus Design
#6 The Abode of Life
#7 Star Trek II: TWOK
#8 Black Fire
#9 Triangle
#10 Web of the Romulans
#11 Yesterday's Son
#12 Mutiny on the Enterprise
#13 The Wounded Sky
#14 The Trellisane Confrontation
#15 Corona
#16 The Final Reflection
#17 Star Trek III: TSFS
#18 My Enemy, My Ally
#19 The Tears of the Singers
#20 The Vulcan Academy Murders
#21 Uhura's Song
#22 Shadow Lord
#23 Ishmael
#24 Killing Time
#25 Dwellers in the Crucible
#26 Pawns and Symbols
#27 Mindshadow
#28 Crisis on Centaurus
#29 Dreadnought!
#30 Demons
#31 Battlestations!
#32 Chain of Attack
#33 Deep Domain
#34 Dreams of the Raven
#35 The Romulan Way
#36 How Much for Just the Planet?
#37 Bloodthirst
#38 The IDIC Epidemic
#39 Time for Yesterday
#40 Timetrap
#41 The Three-Minute Universe
#42 Memory Prime
#43 The Final Nexus
#44 Vulcan's Glory
#45 Double, Double

Star Trek: The Next Generation

Encounter at Farpoint
#1 Ghost Ship
#2 The Peacekeepers
#3 The Children of Hamlin
#4 Survivors
#5 Strike Zone

A STAR TREK® NOVEL

CHAIN OF ATTACK

GENE DeWEESE

POCKET BOOKS
New York London Toronto Sydney Tokyo

An *Original* Publication of POCKET BOOKS

POCKET BOOKS, a division of Simon & Schuster Inc.
1230 Avenue of the Americas, New York, NY 10020

ISBN: 0-671-66658-4

First Pocket Books printing February 1987

10 9 8 7 6 5

Printed in the U.S.A.

For Juanita Coulson,
whose talent and persistence
opened the door for serendipity.

Introduction

It's been a long time . . .

I first saw *Star Trek* when Gene Roddenberry apologetically introduced the two pilot episodes to a few hundred science fiction fans at the Cleveland World SF Convention a few days before the first program was broadcast.

Subsequently, I watched every episode that was aired and managed to talk about fifty friends and strangers into sending protest letters during the first "Save *Star Trek*" letter-writing campaign.

Over the years, it's gotten ever harder to resist the temptation to watch the reruns, particularly when they're showing gems like the Gary Seven episode, "Assignment: Earth," and "The Menagerie."

And now—

Well, I can only say it's been great fun these last few weeks, finally having an excuse to indulge myself in an episode a day, ostensibly for "research," and getting paid for it to boot.

Chapter One

ACCORDING TO EVEN the most conservative estimates, the Milky Way galaxy contains more than one hundred billion stars, and there are at least that many other galaxies beyond our own, beyond the reach even of warp drive. This means that for every human alive on earth at the end of the twentieth century there are twenty or more stars in our home galaxy alone, and countless billions more are spread throughout the clusters and superclusters of other galaxies, stretching to the very edge of the universe—if, indeed, an edge exists. It is therefore little wonder that, even with Federation, Romulan, and Klingon ships spreading throughout space at unprecedented rates, more than ninety-nine percent of even that one galaxy is unknown and untouched by human—or Romulan or Klingon—sensor probe. Even within the territory covered by the Federation Exploration Treaty, the unknown far outweighs the known as scout ships leapfrog over thousands of star systems in their rush to explore, to reach new horizons.

Under such circumstances, then, it is easy to go where no man has gone before. It is, in fact, often unavoidable. To survive such explorations and to return safely—that is another matter altogether.

"I fail to see the humor in the situation, Dr. McCoy."

As always, Spock's remark held neither anger nor resentment. It was simply a statement of fact, edged with the faint touch of bemused bafflement that was always present when the Vulcan science officer was dealing with less-than-logical humans.

"I know, Spock, I know," McCoy said, stepping back to give Spock ample room as the Vulcan's long, powerful fingers continued to methodically work the science station controls. "But you don't mind if we humans indulge in a good laugh now and then, do you?"

"Of course I do not mind," Spock said, most of his attention still devoted to analyzing the station's readouts for some sign of the probe that had been launched more than five minutes before. It was rapidly becoming apparent, however, that the probe was not going to reappear, either five parsecs away or five hundred, all of which struck McCoy as a fitting and somewhat amusing climax to the totally erratic behavior of the previous forty-odd probes.

"In fact, Doctor," Spock went on, still not taking his eyes from his instruments, "as you yourself have pointed out, such outbursts often seem to have a therapeutic effect on your species. It would hardly be logical for me to wish to deny you something that could improve your physical and mental well-being and hence your efficiency in performing your duties."

McCoy chuckled, still watching the display screens over Spock's shoulder. "Maybe it's just as well you *don't* ever laugh, Spock. You're already too blasted efficient. I'd hate to see what would happen if you ever developed a sense of humor. Jim and I and half the crew would only be excess baggage."

"Another example of human humor, I assume, Doctor. I find it difficult to believe that even you would look favorably on inefficiency. But if I may be allowed to—"

A shudder rippled through the *Enterprise*, momentarily shifting the deck beneath their feet. Spock, rock steady despite the movement, called up a dozen new displays on the screens.

"Another shift in field strength, Captain," he said,

"an increase of twenty-seven-point-one-six percent. I would suggest drawing back approximately ten A.U. as a precautionary measure."

"Take us back ten A.U., Mr. Sulu, warp factor three," Kirk said without hesitation. He had long since learned not to question his first officer's suggestions. "Hold steady at that position."

"Done, sir," the helmsman said, his fingers already entering the commands into his console.

McCoy, silent now as he gripped the padded handrail to steady himself, turned toward Kirk. Seated in the command chair, the captain was intent on the forward viewscreen, where the flowing ribbon of the Sagittarius arm of the galaxy overlay the distant turbulence of the Shapley Center. As they watched, the star field rippled briefly, much as the bridge itself had seemed to ripple a moment before.

"Another change in the field strength, Mr. Spock, or just the result of our motion in the field?"

"Our motion, Captain, with respect to the irregularities near the anomaly itself. The field remains steady at its new level."

"And the last probe, the one whose disappearance Dr. McCoy found so amusing—still no sign of it?"

"None, Captain."

"A malfunction in the probe itself, perhaps?"

"Unlikely, Captain. As you know, the probes are little more than powerful subspace beacons attached to impulse engines. Considering the simplicity of their design and construction, the likelihood of any vital component failing has been statistically established to be less than one in one-point-three million."

"But it is possible," Kirk persisted.

"Possible, yes, Captain, in the same sense that anything, no matter how unlikely, is statistically possible."

"Point taken. What other explanations can you suggest?"

"The most likely is that the probe is beyond the range at which it can be detected."

Kirk swung his chair to look directly at the science officer. "Out of range, Mr. Spock? I was given to understand that their signals could be picked up at a range of more than five thousand parsecs."

"Five thousand four hundred eighty, to be precise, Captain, though that is, of course, only the minimum guaranteed range."

"You're saying this—this 'gravitational anomaly' could have transported the probe more than five thousand parsecs?"

"Obviously, Captain."

"But none of the other probes has reappeared at any distance greater than five *hundred* parsecs."

"Affirmative, Captain."

"That's it, Spock? No elaboration?"

"If you wish, Captain. As you and Dr. McCoy are certainly aware, we have been unable to establish any logical pattern based on the behavior of the probes sent through the so-called anomalies. Some have not been affected at all, as if for them the anomalies do not exist. Others have vanished and emerged into normal space little more than one parsec distant, while still others have reappeared nearly five hundred parsecs away in a totally different direction. There is therefore no logical reason to assume that the range is limited in any way. The distance a probe is transported is apparently not related in any way to its entry velocity. It is more likely a result of the geometry of space itself and the manner in which it is distorted by these so-called anomalies, and that distortion appears to vary randomly from moment to moment, even to cease entirely on occasion."

"From your repeated use of the phrase 'so-called anomalies,' can I assume that your observations have suggested a more useful or more accurate term?"

"Not at all, Captain. It is only that I am beginning to doubt that these objects are indeed something as simple as anomalies resulting from surrounding areas of gravitational turbulence."

"What, then?"

"I do not know, Captain."

"But you must have some thoughts on the subject, Spock."

"Of course, Captain."

"And those thoughts are . . . ?" Kirk prompted.

"I can only say, Captain, that there is a distinct but unquantifiable possibility that they are not natural phenomena at all."

In the silence that followed, all eyes on the bridge turned to Spock. Then a short burst of laughter came from McCoy.

"An unquantifiable possibility?" McCoy said, shaking his head in mock surprise. "That isn't your Vulcan way of saying you have a hunch, is it, Spock?"

"It is hardly a hunch, as you chose to call it, Doctor. It is merely that the results of our observations so far appear totally random and therefore illogical. Past experience has led me to conclude that phenomena which appear to be illogical are less often the result of natural laws than they are the result of manipulation of those laws by intelligent but less-than-logical beings."

Captain James T. Kirk suppressed a smile as he nodded and shifted to a more comfortable position in the command chair. The thought that the anomalies were not natural phenomena had, of course, occurred to him, but, as Spock would say, he had not assigned it a high probability factor. For one thing, when the *Enterprise* had first run into one of the anomalies—run into it quite literally—the ship had been instantaneously transported more than three hundred parsecs and damaged by the effects of the surrounding turbulence. Under those conditions, everyone's priorities had centered on survival, both their own and the *Enterprise*'s, leaving little time for scientific analysis or philosophizing.

But now it was a different matter. Equipped with newly designed sensors that allowed them to precisely locate—and avoid—the strangely complex turbulence, and supplied with more than two hundred probes, they had come to study what was apparently a cluster of such anomalies discovered by a scout ship not long after the *Enterprise*'s return from the Mercanian system, where the first anomaly had deposited them so unexpectedly. Or, more accurately, they had come to study a cluster of gravitationally turbulent areas in order to determine if any or all of those areas contained at their centers the same type of anomaly that had swallowed the *Enterprise* and then spit it out three hundred parsecs away. By sending the probes through such anomalies, they had hoped to determine just where the anomalies led.

Anomalies had indeed been found in the centers of seven of the areas of turbulence so far, and forty-eight probes had been dispatched. Six had passed through the anomalies without effect, emerging on the far side with no indication of damage or change of any kind. Forty-one had reappeared at distances ranging from one to five hundred parsecs, in directions that bore no discernible correlation to anything. Two probes sent through the same anomaly within milliseconds of each other reappeared more than six hundred parsecs apart, one in the direction of the Shapley Center, the other in the general direction of Klingon territory.

In short, as Spock had said, the operation of the so-called anomalies appeared totally illogical and had thus far defied analysis. And now one of the probes had simply vanished, either transported beyond the five-thousand-parsec range of its transmitter or destroyed or . . .

"Could the disappearance be related to the shift in the field strength, Mr. Spock? The two occurrences were fairly close together."

"It is possible, of course, Captain. Without further data, however, there is no way of confirming or denying the hypothesis."

"Another probe, then, Mr. Spock?"

The hiss of the doors to the turbolift forestalled Spock's reply. A stocky man in his fifties, his tightly curling hair beginning to gray, strode onto the bridge.

His angry glower, as much as his green civilian tunic, distinguished him from the *Enterprise* personnel.

"What sort of nonsense have you been up to now, Kirk?" the man snapped, making the omission of the captain's rank sound more like an insult than an oversight.

"Welcome to the bridge, Dr. Crandall," Kirk said dryly. "What seems to be the problem?"

"The problem, Kirk, is that I was awakened only moments ago by something which, were I on a planetary surface, I would describe as an earthquake. I would like to know the cause, and I would like to know why it was not avoided, whatever it was."

Kirk turned away from Crandall toward the science officer's station. "You have the floor, Mr. Spock."

A minuscule arching of one upward-slanting eyebrow was the only change of expression as Spock turned to face Crandall. "The cause, Dr. Crandall, was an unpredicted and abrupt change in both the overall strength and the pattern of the gravitational field surrounding the so-called anomaly we are currently observing. The reason it was not avoided is that it *was* unpredicted. To the best of our knowledge at this time, such changes cannot be predicted."

Crandall, still not fully accustomed to the Vulcan's calm and rational ways, seemed to lose some of his steam.

"I see," he said. "But the ship—the ship was not damaged?"

"Not a bit," Kirk assured him. "As you know, the new sensors allow us to—"

"I know, I know," Crandall snapped. Then he glanced around the bridge, his eyes settling on the forward viewscreen. "There's an anomaly out there? A new one?"

"That's right," Kirk said. "The seventh."

"Why wasn't I called? I am, after all, an official observer, which would seem to me to mean that I should be present during all observations."

"If you will recall, Dr. Crandall," Kirk said quietly, "midway through our observations of the previous anomaly, you told us you didn't want to be bothered unless something unusual happened. 'Something downright spectacular,' I believe were your exact words."

"Something that can rattle the walls of a Constitution-class starship qualifies as spectacular in my book, Kirk. In any event, now that I am here, would anyone care to bring me up to date?"

"Of course, Doctor," Kirk said, turning away again. "Mr. Spock?"

"Very well, Captain," Spock said and then began a probe-by-probe account, complete with all particulars, of all observations since Crandall's hasty departure on the previous day's watch.

Kirk settled back to listen and to wonder once again what Starfleet Command had had in mind when they had allowed Dr. Jason Crandall to be attached to the *Enterprise* as an "official observer." True, Crandall had been in charge of the Starfleet-supported civilian labs that had developed the sensors that had been installed on the *Enterprise*, but Crandall himself, despite a doctorate in physics, was far more of a politician than a scientist. Otherwise he would never have been in charge of that or any other lab, Kirk was sure. And it had become abundantly clear after only a few days on the *Enterprise* that Crandall saw the labs—and this mission involving the sensors developed there—primarily as stepping stones to greater things, perhaps even to a seat on the Federation Science Council.

Kirk shuddered mentally at the thought. He did not naively believe that Council seats were attained purely on merit, but neither could he believe that merit and ability had no bearing at all on the matter. All current members were, at the very least, competent, some even brilliant, and the thought of Crandall bluffing or conning his way into their company was growing more disturbing each time Kirk had contact with the man.

"All right, Spock, all right!" Crandall's harsh voice cut into Kirk's thoughts. "I don't need the trajectory and serial number of every probe! All I wanted was a brief summary. Have you or have you not discovered any pattern?"

"Negative, Doctor."

"And do you fore*see* any such discovery?"

The Vulcan's eyebrows arched again, not quite as minutely as before, and his eyes flickered toward Kirk for an instant. It was, Kirk realized, as close to exasperation as he had seen Spock express in some time.

"It is impossible to foresee a discovery in the sense you seem to mean, Doctor," Spock said. "If, on the other hand, you wish to know if I *expect* such a discovery to be made, then I can only say that I have every confidence that, in time, it will be made."

"But not here and now? Not in the next few hours or even in the next few days or weeks?"

"Again, Doctor, that is impossible to say."

"Good Lord, man! I'm not asking for an oath signed in blood! All I'm asking is if you *think* you'll be able to get to the bottom of this before you run out of probes!"

"With no more data than I have at present, it would be illogical to form an opinion one way or the other, Doctor."

McCoy, who had moved away from the science station during the exchange, stifled a laugh and, when Kirk glanced at him, could only shake his head. He was obviously enjoying Crandall's frustration, all the more because he himself had so often collided with Spock's implacable wall of logic.

Then, abruptly, another shudder rippled through the *Enterprise*, not as powerful as the first but enough to send both of Crandall's hands clutching at the padded railing.

"What—" he began, but before he could get a second word out, Spock was checking his instruments and reporting.

"The field strength has decreased to zero, Captain."

"It's gone, Spock? The area of turbulence has disappeared?"

"Precisely, Captain."

"And the so-called anomaly at its center?"

"Unknown, Captain. I would suggest dispatching another probe."

Kirk considered a moment before turning to face the viewscreen again. "Take us back to within probe range, Mr. Sulu. Warp factor two."

"Warp factor two, sir."

"Any indication of renewed turbulence, Mr. Spock?" Kirk asked, his own eyes fastened to the forward viewscreen.

"None, Captain."

Finally they were once more within one hundred thousand kilometers of the anomaly, and Spock's fingers were moving unerringly across the controls of the auxiliary panel that was linked to the probes. As before, the probe would be beamed to within five thousand kilometers of the anomaly using the cargo transporter. From that point, it would proceed under its own impulse power into the anomaly.

Even so, several minutes went by before Spock looked up from the controls.

"The so-called anomaly has vanished, too, Captain."

"And what does that mean, Spock?" Crandall cut in. During the seemingly interminable wait, he had alternately stood and paced, fidgeting and frowning impatiently all the while.

"It means precisely what I said, Doctor," Spock said. "The anomaly associated with this particular area of gravitational turbulence appears to have vanished at the same time as the turbulence itself."

"What about the others? There are a dozen others nearby, aren't there?"

"There were fifteen in all, Doctor. There is no way of knowing their status without traveling to the vicinity of each and checking."

"Well, what are you waiting for?" Crandall demanded.

"Captain?"

"Your opinion, Mr. Spock?" Kirk asked.

"It would seem logical to check at least one of those we have already visited, Captain, to see if the disappearance is limited to this one anomaly."

Crandall heaved a sigh of annoyed relief. "And if *it's* gone, too, then I assume we will be heading back to the Federation. It seems to me, considering the total lack of useful results obtained so far, we have wasted quite enough time on this project. Kirk?"

"As you have said, Dr. Crandall, you are an observer," Kirk said, his tone nearly as neutral and precise as Spock's. Then, turning back to the forward viewscreen: "Lay in a course that will take us to all six previously visited anomalies, Mr. Sulu. And Mr. Spock, keep an eye on those new instruments. We don't want another unscheduled trip."

"Of course, Captain," Spock said, and a moment later Sulu acknowledged that the requested course had been laid in.

"Cautiously, then, Mr. Sulu. Warp factor two."

"Warp factor two, Captain."

On the forward viewscreen, the distant Shapley Center slid to one side and vanished as the *Enterprise* turned and aligned itself for its new destination. In a few seconds, only the scattered stars of the outer edge of the Sagittarius arm of the galaxy could be seen, and beyond them the faint band of light that was the Orion arm, one tiny patch of which held all the stars within the Federation.

"How long will this—this exercise in futility take, Kirk?" Crandall snapped, a new level of hostility evident in his voice.

"The original observations were scheduled to take three standard weeks."

"But if there's nothing left to observe—"

"Then perhaps it will take somewhat less time."

"*Perhaps?* Good Lord, man, do you mean to say—"

"I mean only to say," Kirk cut in, "that this disappearance merely deepens the mystery surrounding the nature of these anomalies, and that I can see no reason to cut short our mission until we have learned all that we possibly can."

"Commendable scientific curiosity, I am sure, Kirk, but rather pointless, it seems to me. In any event, I postponed important business to become a part of this mission, and I strenuously object to having it prolonged unreasonably. That is to say, beyond a point at which useful knowledge can be obtained. A point which, I might add, appears to have been reached some time ago."

"You are, of course, free to contact Starfleet Command at any time, Doctor. Lieutenant Uhura will be glad to open a channel whenever you wish."

Crandall's square features hardened as his jaw muscles tensed, and Kirk imagined he could hear the grinding of teeth. Then Crandall slumped slightly, confirming Kirk's suspicions that friendship with the people at Starfleet Command was not the reason Crandall was aboard. He or his political friends had pulled strings somewhere, and Starfleet Command had obliged, as they often did in small matters that did not interfere with Starfleet activities. The string pulling had gotten him aboard the *Enterprise*, in a position to take advantage of any significant discoveries that resulted from the use of his lab's sensors, but that was all it had gotten him. And even that might be lost if he pushed his luck.

"I may do that, Kirk," Crandall said. "If this nonsense continues much longer, I may do just that." But both men knew it was an empty threat.

Kirk remained silent, and finally Crandall turned to leave the bridge. But as he took a step forward toward the turbolift, another shudder gripped the *Enterprise*. Compared to the two previous incidents, it was almost unnoticeable, not even enough to cause Crandall to miss a step.

A moment later, however, Chekov's voice, high-pitched with excitement, sliced through the air. "The screen, sir! Look!"

Kirk spun the command chair instantly to face the viewscreen.

He blinked, and fingers of ice suddenly gripped his spine.

Instead of the sparse stars of the edge of the Sagittarius arm, there were stars by the thousands, by the tens of thousands, a star field immeasurably brighter and more dense than anyone on the bridge had ever seen.

Chapter Two

"FULL STOP, MR. SULU," Kirk snapped. "Maintain present position. Mr. Chekov, determine *precisely* our present position with respect to the point at which we first appeared in this sector."

The helmsman and the navigator responded instantly, their fingers working the controls even as they acknowledged the commands.

"Spock, full sensor scan."

"No vessels in sensor range, Captain. Radiation, though markedly higher, presents no danger."

"Kirk!" Crandall's strident voice overrode everyone else's. "Would someone please tell me what the blazes is going on!"

"We'll tell you as soon as we find out ourselves. Spock, any idea where we are?"

"Not yet, Captain. There is—"

"Kirk! I demand to know—"

"Dr. Crandall, please leave the bridge. Return to your quarters."

"Now see here, Kirk! Who do you think you are? I am, in effect, a representative of the Council itself, and I demand civil answers to my questions!"

"We do not have time for your demands at the moment, Dr. Crandall," Kirk said sharply, punching a button on the command chair arm as he spoke.

"Security detail to the bridge immediately. Escort Dr. Crandall to his quarters."

Crandall's face reddened, and he turned abruptly to

the communications station. "Lieutenant, open a channel to Starfleet Command! At once!"

Uhura looked questioningly at Captain Kirk. "Continue monitoring all frequencies, Lieutenant," he said. "Attempt no communications with Starfleet Command or anyone else at this time."

"Kirk, I'll have your head for this! If you don't—"

The turbolift doors hissed open, disgorging a two-person security detail.

"Escort Dr. Crandall to his quarters," Kirk said, confirming his order. "Make sure he stays there. I'll inform you when he is to be allowed to leave."

Crandall resisted for a moment, but then, blustering a final threat, he allowed himself to be propelled into the turbolift.

"As you were saying, Mr. Spock?" Kirk asked, turning back to the science officer.

"Yes, Captain. There is an area that appears to be the Shapley Center directly ahead, though the computer has not yet positively identified it. If it is indeed the Shapley Center, we have been transported at least five thousand parsecs."

"Five *thousand?*"

"Affirmative, Captain. We are approximately five thousand parsecs closer to this object than we were to the Shapley Center. Of course, if it is not the Shapley Center, then we could well have traveled much farther."

Kirk was silent a moment before turning back to the screen. "Mr. Chekov, have you located our—our point of entry into the sector of space?"

"I believe so, sir."

"Very well. Mr. Sulu, take us to within a half-A.U. and hold there. Warp factor two."

Again the view on the forward screen shifted, but now it was as if the *Enterprise* were turning within a heavy curtain of stars. In every direction, the brightness and density were the same.

"Mr. Spock, prepare to launch a probe directly at our point of entry."

"Prepared, Captain."

"Launch the probe, Mr. Spock."

"It is being transported . . . now, Captain."

"And while we're waiting for the results, Mr. Spock, see if you can find out where we are."

Spock turned again to the data displays. "The computer has been performing a more detailed analysis of the radiation profile of the object that appeared similar to the Shapley Center," he said, pausing to study a set of readouts more closely. "There appear to be a number of basic differences in the spectrum," he added.

"Could the differences be accounted for by the time difference? We are, after all, more than fifteen thousand light-years closer."

"Negative, Captain. Certain of the readings indicate precisely the opposite. The spectrum indicates that the central black hole, for example, is less massive than that of the Shapley Center by a factor of nearly ten, not marginally more massive, as would be the case had we come five thousand parsecs closer. And there are other, independent indications that argue against this object's being the Shapley Center."

"And those are, Mr. Spock?" Kirk prompted when Spock paused to scan a new set of readings.

"The computer has also been scanning for recognizable extragalactic objects since we arrived, Captain. Few external galaxies are visible from within this cluster of stars, but among those few, it has found none that it can positively identify."

"What you're saying, then, Mr. Spock," Kirk said after three or four seconds of silence, "is that, first, we are no longer in the Milky Way galaxy. And second, the computer has not been able to determine what galaxy we *are* in."

"Precisely, Captain."

Though no one did more than glance at Spock and the captain for a fraction of a second, the bridge was suddenly totally silent except for the ever-present hums and beeps of the equipment and the ship itself. There was no panic, no wild questions or howls of disbelief. Instead, after allowing only a moment to inwardly acknowledge Spock's confirmation of what they had already begun to suspect, everyone concentrated all the harder on his or her instruments, knowing that such concentration and the ability to react instantly and effectively could very well be, as it had been so often before, the key to their survival.

"I don't suppose," Kirk said after a good thirty seconds of silence, "that the missing probe is somewhere in this neighborhood, too."

"It has not been detected, Captain."

"Any theories, Mr. Spock?"

"Only the obvious one, Captain. Despite the sensors' failure to detect the characteristic gravitational turbulence, the *Enterprise* has passed through one of the so-called anomalies."

Kirk nodded. "I'd assumed as much. How does this affect your hunch, your unquantifiable possibility?"

"I would say it raises it to the level of a probability, Captain, although it remains unquantifiable." Spock paused, his eyes on the data displays. "The new probe is approaching our point of entry." Another pause, and then: "It has passed through our point of entry and has vanished from our sensors."

"And still no indication of gravitational turbulence?"

"None, Captain."

"What are the odds that if we follow the probe we'll end up back where we started?"

"Unknown, Captain. I would say, however, that whatever the odds may be, they are better than for any other method of return."

"I realize that, Spock. Even if we were no farther away than the Andromeda galaxy, and even if the *Enterprise* could maintain warp eight indefinitely, we would still be several lifetimes away from the Federation."

"Precisely, Captain. As I see it, logic gives us no choice but to make the attempt."

"Agreed. Objections, anyone? Bones? Sulu? Uhura? Chekov?"

No one spoke.

"Very well. Mr. Sulu, do your best to duplicate our flight path in reverse. Warp factor two, I believe it was."

"Correct, sir. Ready to execute on your command."

"Execute."

The starbow resulting from achieving relativistic velocity was always spectacular, but never more so than here in this massive concentration of stars. Even so, it went virtually unnoticed as all eyes waited for the sudden alteration in the star field that would indicate they were back in Treaty territory.

But the change didn't come.

"Time, Mr. Spock?"

"We passed through the entry point two-point-seven seconds ago, Captain."

"Then why—Mr. Chekov, how close were we to retracing our original flight path?"

"Maximum error of two hundred kilometers, Keptin."

"Spock, could the anomaly have been smaller than that? Could we simply have missed it?"

"Anything is possible, Captain. Since the seven for which we have observational data were all greater than five thousand kilometers in diameter, however, it seems unlikely."

"As you say, anything is possible. Mr. Sulu, take us back. Again."

They tried five more times, and each time the failure of the star field to change was greeted by a deeper silence. They even launched a series of probes, but, unlike the first, not a one vanished or even so much as flickered.

Then someone laughed. It was Ensign Rostofski, one of the newest members of the crew. By coincidence a friend of Chekov's family, Rostofski manned the environmental station but seemed to spend much of his off-duty time trying to convince Chekov that he could lose his accent if only he would really try.

"Something amusing, Ensign?" the captain asked quietly.

"Not really, sir. I was just thinking what Dr. Crandall was going to say when he finds out."

Kirk found himself smiling, but then, with a shake of his head, his expression sobered. He turned again to Spock.

"Theories, Mr. Spock? Where did the anomaly—so-called anomaly—go?"

"Unknown, Captain. It could be anywhere. It may have gone out of existence entirely. Without the gravitational turbulence normally associated with them, there is no way of detecting them."

"And our chances of locating it again?"

"Also unknown, Captain. There is no data on which to base such a calculation. I should also point out that, even if we are successful in locating it, there is no guarantee that it would return us to our starting point."

"But it *is* our only chance."

"The only chance of which we are currently aware, Captain."

"I stand corrected." Abruptly Kirk pressed the button that connected him to engineering. "Mr. Scott, to the bridge."

"Aye, Captain, in a minute. One o' the transporter circuits needs a wee bit o'—"

"*Now*, Mr. Scott."

A brief pause, perhaps half a second, and then: "Aye, Captain, I'm on my way."

Kirk stood up and moved to the science station, looking at the flickering displays that, though often meaningless to him, seemed sometimes a physical extension of Spock's mind, so quickly could the Vulcan call up the needed data and interpret it.

"What about Crandall, Jim?" McCoy asked, joining the other two.

Kirk sighed briefly. "Later, Bones. When you have a sedative ready for him."

The turbolift doors hissed open, and Chief Engineer Montgomery Scott emerged onto the bridge, lurching to a halt as his eyes fell on the fog of stars that filled the forward viewscreen. Kirk quickly outlined the situation and then asked, "Is everything in top shape, Scotty? Our little jaunt hasn't knocked any bolts loose this time?"

"None that I know of, Captain. The transporter circuit that was needin' adjustment, that was no' the fault o' what you say happened to us just now."

"Very well, gentlemen, I'm open to suggestions, *any* suggestions. Mr. Spock? A few minutes ago you said something to the effect that the possibility that these so-called anomalies were something other than natural phenomena had been enhanced by our recent encounter. Would you care to elaborate?"

"Of course, Captain, though I feel obliged to point out again that the possibility, though enhanced, is still unquantifiable, as is nearly everything we have thus far encountered in connection with these phenomena."

"Understood, Spock. Go on."

"Very well, Captain. First, if we assume that the phenomena were deliberately created by sentient beings, then we must assume they had a purpose in creating them. Second, the most obvious purpose, considering the one property these phenomena share, would be to serve as a form of transportation."

"Logical enough, Spock," McCoy said, "but I thought you said these things were just plain *il*logical, which was why you thought they were artificial in the first place."

"Correct, Doctor, but allow me to continue. If we assume their purpose to be transportation, then two further assumptions logically follow. First, despite what we have so far observed, there would have to be some form of consistency designed into them. And second, they should be easily approachable, not concealed at the center of a maze of gravitational turbulence that is capable of tearing a starship to pieces."

"Unless," Kirk interjected, "they were *meant* to be hidden. If the Federation had something like this, something we could use to transport Federation ships instantaneously to, say, someplace in the middle of the Klingon Empire, then the one thing we *would* do is hide it and make it as difficult as possible for anyone other than ourselves to approach or leave."

"True, Captain, but that requires the additional assumption that these anomalies were created solely for warlike purposes. I would hope that the creators of devices as sophisticated as these, apparently constructed of pure energy, would be beyond such illogical behavior."

Kirk smiled faintly. "Many humans thought the same thing about warp drive before we met the Romulans and the Klingons. But go ahead, Mr. Spock."

"Thank you, Captain. You will remember that, with one exception, the probes transported by the other anomalies reappeared at distances no greater than five hundred parsecs, the average being ninety-eight-point-three-seven. The *Enterprise,* on the other hand, appears to have been transported at least several million parsecs through an anomaly that apparently possessed no trace of surrounding gravitational turbulence."

"So, Spock?" McCoy said impatiently. "What are you leading up to?"

"I am leading up to a conclusion, Doctor, the conclusion being that those seven anomalies, with their attendant turbulence, may have simply been erratic and malfunctioning versions of the one that brought us here. The gravitational turbulence, in other words, is perhaps not the cause of the anomalies but the result of their faulty operation. Leakage, if you will. If they do indeed operate by distorting space itself—as does the warp drive in a much simpler and more limited way—that distortion would in all probability manifest itself as gravitational disturbances. Remember that according to certain theories all gravitation is the result of distortion of the space-time continuum by the masses of the bodies producing the gravitation."

McCoy blinked. "Spock, much as I hate to say this, I think you've got something." He turned to Kirk. "Like automobiles, Jim. You know, those infernal internal combustion surface vehicles they used back in the twentieth and twenty-first centuries. When they were new and were operating at peak efficiency, they were fast and quiet. The later models didn't even pollute their surroundings all that much. But if they were neglected, they turned noisy and unreliable, and they poured all kinds of garbage into the air, dangerous garbage. There was a time when doctors could get rich just treating the ailments that resulted from them."

"Aye, Captain," Scott added. "I recall readin' about those wee monsters when I was a lad in school. It's hard to believe, but their engines could no' be run in enclosed spaces for fear o' poisonin' the operator."

"Precisely, gentlemen," Spock said. "The analogy is quite apt."

"Interesting, gentlemen," Kirk said, "but I doubt that these historical sidelights help us in our present situation. Unless you're suggesting that the creators of these—these 'gates,' for want of a better term, are still in existence and that we may be able to locate *them* more easily than their missing creation."

"Considering that we have no instruments capable of detecting the gate, as you call it, Captain, and that we have no information that would indicate even a general area in which to search, then a search for those hypothetical creators would indeed seem the most likely avenue to pursue."

"As usual, Spock, your logic is unassailable," Kirk said, then looked at the others in turn. "Well, gentlemen? Any other theories? Suggestions? Any ideas for a more profitable way to spend our time?"

When neither Scott nor McCoy replied, except to shake their heads, Kirk continued. "Very well, gentlemen, that's it, then. Mr. Scott, you and Spock determine which of the nearer stars are most likely to have habitable planets. Mr. Chekov, Mr. Sulu, plot a course that will take us to the nearest half-dozen. And, of course, everyone maintain a continuous lookout for other craft and for any indication of areas of gravitational turbulence. And finally, Scotty, give me five minutes, and then explain our situation to the crew."

"Aye, Captain, but why the delay?"

"To give Dr. McCoy and myself time to break the news personally to our official observer, Dr. Crandall."

The chief engineer grimaced and nodded. "I dinna envy you the task."

When Kirk and McCoy approached Crandall's stateroom, however, it appeared the task might not be as difficult as they had anticipated. According to the two security men at the door, Crandall had calmed down considerably by the time they had finished escorting him to his room, and they hadn't heard a sound from him since. Entering, they saw he was seated at his desk, quietly dictating some notes into his personal recorder. He even smiled when he looked up and saw them.

"Captain Kirk," he said, using the designation of rank for the first time, "I feel I must apologize for my unprofessional behavior on the bridge. You were, I fear, quite correct to eject me as you did. Let me assure you, I fully understand your position."

Standing up now, Crandall offered a beefy hand to Kirk.

With an almost unnoticeable sideward flick of his eyes toward McCoy, Kirk took the hand briefly. "I'm glad you don't bear a grudge, Dr. Crandall."

"Of course not. You were only doing what you thought best. And I have to admit, I did let my emotions run away with me for a moment. But tell me, what is our status? I take it that, since you are away from the bridge, the situation is not as serious as it might first have appeared. And that you have been able to pinpoint our location?"

"In answer to your last question, while we have

hardly pinpointed our location, we do have a better idea than before of just how far we've traveled," Kirk said.

"Good, good, I knew you and your people would come through. Tell me, just how far *have* we gone?"

Kirk hesitated, knowing that Crandall's shell of seeming calm wouldn't last. "We appear," he said, "to be farther from the Federation than we at first thought."

Crandall's smile faded. His brow wrinkled in the beginnings of a frown, and his eyes darted from Kirk to McCoy and back. "And?" he prompted. "Just how far is farther than we thought? A hundred parsecs? Five hundred? What?"

"A minimum of several million, Doctor. The *Enterprise* has been transported several million parsecs."

The color literally drained from Crandall's previously ruddy face. McCoy stepped forward to support him in case he started to fall, but Crandall caught himself and leaned back against the desk.

"Several *million?* Surely that's impossible!"

"I wish it were, Doctor, I truly wish it were. But it obviously isn't, because that's precisely what happened." He nodded at the intercom on the stateroom wall. "Mr. Scott will be giving everyone the details in a few seconds."

"But how—what happened? I thought you said these—these anomalies could only throw us a few hundred parsecs!" He blinked. "And the detectors my labs built—why in God's name weren't you using them? Why did you blunder into—"

"We *were* using them, Doctor. The anomaly that took us here apparently had no attendant turbulence."

"But—"

"It's a long story, Doctor," Kirk cut in. "I suggest you listen to Mr. Scott, and if you have any questions when he's finished, we'll answer them as best we can."

Crandall looked as if he were going to continue protesting, but then the chief engineer's voice, the tension of the situation accentuating its Scottish burr, crackled over the intercom. Still pale, Crandall dropped into the chair behind the stateroom's trapezoidal desk and listened.

When Scott had finished, Crandall was even paler. "He's saying we're *trapped* here! Isn't he? Isn't that what he's saying?"

"We appear to be, at least for the moment," Kirk said, adding, after another glance at McCoy, "but we've been in what appeared to be worse situations than this before, and we've always managed to come out of them all right."

"But there's always a first time, isn't there, Kirk? *Isn't there?*" For a moment, it looked as if Crandall were going to rise and grasp at Kirk's throat, but then he slumped back. He waved a hand in a limply dismissive gesture.

"Go on, get out of here, you incompetent fools!" His voice was as weak as the gesture, but still it was filled with anger. "Just get out and leave me alone!"

McCoy stiffened and started to speak, but Kirk put a restraining hand on his arm. "Very well, Dr. Crandall," he said quietly. "If there's anything you need . . ."

Crandall only snorted derisively and slumped lower in his chair.

Kirk, his hand still on McCoy's arm, turned and stepped into the corridor. As the door hissed shut behind them, he said, "Stick around here a few minutes, Bones, just in case. If he goes off the deep end, I'd sooner one of your sedatives calmed him down than a phaser on stun."

"After the way he talked, I'm not so sure," McCoy snapped. "He had no right—"

"You know better than that, Bones. Look at it from his viewpoint. He's a lot worse off then we are."

McCoy frowned, shaking his head. "Come on, Jim! What's that supposed to mean? We're all in the same boat, literally."

"No, Bones, we're not. Many of *our* friends are

here on the *Enterprise* with us. Virtually the entire four hundred and thirty men and women aboard are, in some ways, an extended family, even the dozen or so new ensigns on their first mission. But Crandall's family and friends, his entire world, is millions of light-years away. A lifetime away, Bones. A large part of ours is right here with us."

McCoy's scowl faded. "All right, Jim. I understand. I'll—"

"Captain Kirk, ta the bridge!" Scott's voice crackled over the intercom.

Kirk slapped the button on the nearest corridor intercom. "On my way, Scotty. Kirk out," he snapped, then turned back to McCoy for an instant. "Remember, Bones, whether we like Crandall or not, he's going to need more help than any of the rest of us."

Then he was loping down the corridor to the turbolift. Seconds later he stepped onto the bridge.

"What is it, Mr. Scott?" he asked even before the doors hissed shut behind him.

Scott, standing and vacating the command chair, pointed at the viewscreen. "We've picked up somethin', Captain, I canna be sure what."

His eyes on the screen, Kirk settled into the command chair. The object on the screen, a hexagonal cylinder, was turning slowly, not about the axis of the cylinder but not quite end over end either.

"Details, Mr. Spock."

"Mass approximately one hundred thousand kilograms. Range approximately fifty thousand kilometers. No life forms indicated on board, and it is not under power."

"A derelict?"

"Perhaps, Captain. There is, however, an operating power source on board, and a primitive sensor field surrounds it, maximum range of ten thousand kilometers."

"Mr. Chekov, can you determine its point of origin?"

"No, sir. It is moving less than one hundred kilometers per second, and its flight path does not intersect any star within two parsecs."

"To travel that distance at that speed, Captain," Spock volunteered, "would have taken twenty thousand standard years. Additionally, there is no indication that the object contains a propulsion system, either impulse or warp drive."

"Could it be a beacon of some sort, Mr. Spock? One that has gone dead for one reason or another? A warning beacon, perhaps?"

"It is possible, Captain."

Kirk nodded thoughtfully. "Any signs of gravitational turbulence in the object's vicinity?"

"Negative, Captain. I take it, however, that you are suggesting a possible connection between this object and the missing gate?"

"Not suggesting as much as hoping, Spock. I was thinking in terms of lighthouses and rocky coasts, actually. Or, more optimistically, navigation markers."

"A possibility, Captain, but a remote one, considering the apparent instability of the gates."

"I know, Spock, but it's worth looking into."

"Of course, Captain."

"Very well. Mr. Sulu, impulse power. Take us in to ten thousand kilometers."

"Impulse power, sir."

As the *Enterprise* moved forward, the object grew on the screen. Soon, blemishes began to appear on its surface, discolorations that might have come from age or radiation or both. Here and there, openings appeared, some jagged, some smooth, as if designed into the object. None was larger than a meter in diameter.

"There are remnants of a second power source, Captain," Spock said as he studied his sensor readings. "Primitive hydrogen fusion, if I am interpreting the residual readings correctly."

"And the one still operating?"

Spock made a small adjustment to a control. "Antimatter, Captain, though of comparatively low power and very low efficiency. And it would appear to be unshielded."

"Unshielded? By design or the result of damage?"

"Impossible to tell, Captain. But it *is* operating, which would indicate that any damage to the antimatter core itself is minimal."

"How close is it safe to approach?"

"With our deflector shields up, Captain, no limit. Otherwise, I would recommend maintaining a minimum separation of one hundred kilometers."

"Ten thousand kilometers, Captain," Sulu reported. "Holding position on impulse power."

"Anything else in sensor range, Mr. Spock?"

"Nothing, Captain."

Kirk studied the screen another moment, and then: "Take us in another thousand kilometers, Mr. Sulu."

"Aye-aye, sir."

"The power usage within the object is increasing, Captain," Spock said, not looking up from his instruments. "I would say that it has detected our presence."

As the science officer spoke, the image on the forward screen began to slow its tumbling motion.

"All stop, Mr. Sulu," Kirk snapped. "Let's see what it's up to before we move any closer."

"Power usage still increasing, Captain," Spock reported. "And the object's sensor beams are strengthening. They are being brought to a focus on the *Enterprise*."

On the screen, the tumbling continued to slow. One end of the hexagonal cylinder was now pointing in the general direction of the *Enterprise*. It could not seem to eliminate a small, circular wobble, however.

"Extreme power buildup, Captain," Spock announced.

"Deflector screens up, Mr. Sulu," Kirk ordered.

"Deflector screens up, sir."

A moment later a concentrated beam of light lanced

out of one of the openings on the end of the cylinder.

"Laser discharge, Captain," Spock said calmly. "It appears to be attacking us."

"So I noticed. Analysis, Mr. Spock."

"Primitive laser weapon, Captain, similar to early Federation equipment, but more powerful and longer range than anything the Federation ever produced. It is much less effective, of course, than phasers of the same power. Also, unless the object can stabilize itself further, the discharge will not touch the *Enterprise*."

"Any other weapons indicated?"

"None operational, Captain, though there appear to be a number of fusion devices in addition to the malfunctioning power source. They could be weapons, but if so, their propulsion systems are inoperative."

"Can the laser be disabled without destroying the object?"

"Since the object has no deflector screens, Captain, I would estimate that a phaser burst of approximately three-point-eight milliseconds would accomplish that objective."

"Mr. Sulu, lock phasers on target."

"Locked on, sir."

Frowning, Kirk hesitated. On the screen, the object suddenly lost what little stability it had displayed and began tumbling end over end, the laser beam flailing even more wildly through space than before.

"Indication of further malfunction, Captain," Spock said, speaking rapidly. "The output of the power source is increasing exponentially. Overload and consequent instantaneous conversion to energy of all antimatter will occur—"

Spock's voice cut off as the forward viewscreen erupted in a flash of light. The *Enterprise*, though safe behind its deflector screens, shuddered before the massive release of raw energy.

"—occurred five-point-nine seconds ago," Spock concluded when the deck had steadied once again.

"Damage report," Kirk snapped. "Engineering."

"Momentary overload to deflector screen circuits, sir, but no apparent permanent damage," came the voice of MacPherson, Scott's chief assistant.

"Tell him I'm on m'way, Captain," the chief engineer called over his shoulder as the turbolift doors hissed open and he stepped in. "Just ta be on the safe side."

Kirk complied as he listened to the other sections report in, slowly relaxing as it became apparent that, aside from a brief shakeup, the explosion had produced no lasting consequences anywhere on the *Enterprise*.

Chapter Three

In his stateroom, Dr. Jason Crandall still sat in the chair where Kirk and McCoy had left him minutes before, but now, instead of slumping in despair, he sat bolt upright, his fingers white-knuckled as he gripped the edge of the desk and waited for the next tremor to rumble through the ship.

What now? his mind screamed in silent fury and terror. What in God's name are they doing to me now?

He started to rise to his feet, but the trembling in his knees stopped him, and he dropped back into the chair, letting despair grip him once again. Whatever was happening, it didn't really matter *what* he did. He was beyond help.

Several lifetimes, that brainless captain had said! Several lifetimes at maximum warp factor to get back to the Federation and earth! And even that was possible only if, by some miracle, they managed to find out where earth *was!* The only bright spot, he thought bitterly, was that, with any luck, he wouldn't last out the decade.

As far as his friends and family—for once in his life, he was glad that he had not married—he was as good as dead right this minute. Dead and buried in a four-hundred-man, warp-drive coffin several lifetimes away from everyone and everything he knew. Everything and everyone that meant anything to him. Not that he had had many intimate friends, but at least he had *known* people, hundreds of them. They had been familiar, often friendly faces, not like these four hundred hostile strangers.

More importantly, he had had a career that was, finally, getting back on track. He had been in charge of Technipower Labs for over a year, and don't think he hadn't had to scramble and bluff and grovel to get that post. After the Tajarhi fiasco, even though it had been entirely the fault of those grasping, never-give-an-inch negotiators on *both* sides, he had begun to fear he would never get another responsible post anywhere in the Federation. But finally, with a slight assist from a skeleton-filled closet or two, he had gotten a halfway decent post. He would have been on his way back up the ladder if it had paid off the way it should have.

If it had paid off . . .

Crandall pulled in a deep breath and shook his head. If he hadn't been so worried that this might be his last chance, if he hadn't been so greedy for one more boost up the ladder, he would still be back on earth, only now beginning to wonder what might have happened to the ship that had been fitted with Technipower's new gravity turbulence sensors. The loss, which his enemies would doubtless blame on the inadequacy of those sensors, would have been bad, but at least he would have had a chance to recover. More work on the sensors, possibly another mission with another ship—a ship with a more capable, more cautious crew—and he might have been on his way up again. Maybe not all the way to the Council, not at sixty-plus, but on his way up nonetheless.

But he had insisted on going along, accompanying the sensors. "Observing." He had called in a few favors, rattled a couple more skeletons, and he had gotten on board the *Enterprise*, knowing that if the mission were a success the publicity would open new doors to him, perhaps even boost him over the heads of those same functionaries he had had to beg favors of in order to get on the *Enterprise* in the first place.

He had insisted on going along, and now it was all

over. His whole life was over, to all intents and purposes.

And to make matters worse, these people—this Kirk and the rest—they *enjoyed* what was happening! He had seen it in their faces, heard it in their voices as the orders and responses darted around the bridge. There had been no fear there, only eagerness and anticipation. To them it was nothing more than a game! Another "adventure!" What did *they* care if they never got back to the Federation? Their lives were here, wherever this blasted ship took them, and the farther it took them, the better they liked it! It had been plain from the moment he had stepped on board that they had little liking or sympathy for Jason Crandall or anyone else outside their own insular ranks. Their looks and their tones, alternately hostile and condescending, had demonstrated that beyond any doubt.

And that obvious dislike had fed upon itself. Crandall's own impatience and anger had grown ever stronger as it became ever more clear that the mission itself was a failure. From the very start, the data had obviously been worthless, but when he had finally pointed it out and tried to get them to cut the mission short, he had been ignored. The military mind was simply not flexible enough to appreciate the situation. They had been ordered to investigate fifteen anomalies, and they would by God investigate fifteen anomalies even though it was obvious after only a few days that it was pointless to continue.

But even that blind obedience was preferable to what was happening now, now that they had their freedom from those orders, freedom from Starfleet Command and the Council. They were like children being let out of school. They were ready to play their dangerous games, heedless of the consequences. The fact that they were playing, in effect, on a totally unknown playing field, where no one knew the rules of the game or even the nature of the other players, didn't seem to phase them. They could all be killed—*he* could be killed—in an instant, and it didn't concern them in the slightest!

Crandall shuddered, remembering the barely suppressed glee he had sensed beneath the chief engineer's seemingly matter-of-fact tone as he had explained their situation over the intercom.

And suddenly he wondered—could the disappearance of the gate be a sham? Could it still be there? Could it be that they—Kirk and the rest of his wild-eyed adventurers on the bridge—simply didn't want to return to the Federation yet? Could they have cooked up this terrifying story to justify themselves in his eyes? And in the eyes of the crew, at least some of whom must have more sense?

Or could the gate itself be a hoax? All he had seen for himself was the viewscreen with its mass of stars, and that could certainly have been faked by anyone on the bridge, particularly that treacherous Vulcan. Beyond that, he had only Kirk's word for what had happened. The fact that the officers backed up their captain meant nothing.

For a moment, hope surged through Crandall, but it faded almost as quickly as it had come. He could not bring himself to believe that even *they* could be so totally irresponsible.

Pulling in a deep breath, he slowly pushed himself to his feet. His legs were again steady, he found, at least steady enough to get him around without falling. He moved deliberately to the door, wondering if he would be allowed back on the bridge yet.

And wondering what good it would do him if he were.

Once it was confirmed that the *Enterprise* had indeed suffered no damage as a result of the cylinder's destruction, detailed observations of the sector of space in which the *Enterprise* found itself quickly got underway. First, the visual impression of the extreme density of the stellar population was confirmed. With stars generally separated by less than one light-year, the entire Federation would have fit into less than fifty cubic parsecs. There was also a certain uniformity that had not been encountered in any previously known sector of space. There were virtually no extremely old or extremely young stars. The majority were also class G, not vastly different from Sol, and all were prime candidates, statistically speaking, for having families of planets.

There were no solidly based theories about how such a cluster, which appeared to extend several hundred parsecs in all directions, could have come about. What generated the most discussion during those first hours, however, was Ensign Chekov's suggestion that there might be a link between the cluster and the gates, or at least between the cluster and the gravitational turbulence associated with many of the gates. Assuming even a moderately dense mass of primordial nebular material, the gravitational turbulence of the gates would be more than enough to trigger the formation of far more stars than would come into existence otherwise.

Chekov's idea, however, raised more questions than it answered. For one thing, the gates would have to have been in existence billions of years ago, when these stars were formed, which meant that if they were indeed artificial as Spock had suggested, their creators were almost certainly long gone and hence would be of little help to the *Enterprise*. For another thing, despite the fact that the *Enterprise* had been deposited here by a gate, there was no evidence now either of that gate or of any of the lesser, "malfunctioning" gates. All of those apparently were back in the Milky Way galaxy, in a sector where star population was, if anything, sparser than average. There was also the rather obvious paradox that if the gravitational turbulence had indeed triggered the formation of the stars, the stars would have formed around the gates, which, if still functioning, would have bled off the infalling matter, thereby *preventing* the formation of the stars the turbulence had triggered in the first place.

Still, the idea was intriguing, and, because of the discussions it generated, it kept a lot of minds occupied that might otherwise have tended to brood about their seemingly hopeless situation. The only person it affected badly was Dr. Crandall, who saw it only as making his situation all the worse. But, then, from the moment Crandall had returned to the bridge, it had been apparent that anything unexpected or unfamiliar affected Crandall badly—and that included virtually everything in this unknown sector of space.

Despite everyone's best efforts to be understanding and sympathetic and even optimistic about finding a way back to Federation space, Crandall's despair and anger only seemed to grow greater. And when he learned that the *Enterprise* was not going to continue to hold its position near where the gate had originally existed but was going to "go exploring," he exploded.

"My God, Kirk!" he shouted, his face paling. "If that gate is going to reappear, it's going to reappear here, not fifty parsecs away! Can't you at least wait a few more days before taking off on this wild goose chase?"

"In the first place," Kirk pointed out with deliberate calm, "there is no evidence suggesting that the gate is going to reappear here as opposed to anywhere else. For all we know, it hasn't disappeared at all. It may have simply moved, or possibly it's flickering on and off, the way some of the ones we were originally investigating apparently did. In the second place, none of the systems we will be visiting in this first foray is more than a standard day away at even moderate warp speeds. And if we don't find anything on this first leg of our 'wild goose chase,' we'll return here to check. As we will continue to do if future legs become necessary. With the density of stars in this sector, we could visit a new system every day for months and still not be more than a standard week away."

But Crandall would not be pacified. "And what happens when you run into another of those—those booby traps?" he almost screamed. "One that's a little more advanced? We could all be vaporized and never even know what hit us!"

And so it had gone. In the end, Crandall had stormed off the bridge, red-faced and trembling. McCoy had followed, offering Crandall first a sedative and then some of the well-aged Scotch he had been saving since his last birthday, but Crandall stiffly and angrily refused everything. He was still in his stateroom the next day when the *Enterprise* dropped to sublight velocity twenty A.U. out from the first star on the list.

It was virtually a twin to Sol, its diameter a few thousand kilometers greater, its surface temperature a few hundred degrees higher. It even had a scattering of sunspots, a phenomenon that had turned out to be relatively rare among suns with habitable planets, though no one had yet advanced an acceptable theory to account for that rarity.

One planet, roughly earth-sized, was well within the zone in which terrestrial life could exist. It was one of seven planets, including the almost inevitable gas giants and a tiny ball of frozen methane at eighteen A. U.

Their first discovery, as they held their position on the fringe of the system, was the hulk of what had once been an observation satellite thousands or tens of thousands of years ago, still orbiting the outermost planet. That, however, was the only indication of life they found. As far as they could tell from that distance, there were no other artificial satellites anywhere in the system, no ships of any kind, and no detectable communications activity in either the electromagnetic or subspace spectra. It appeared to be, despite the remains of the observation satellite, a dead system, and as Kirk ordered the *Enterprise* forward, the feeling began to take hold that they were slowly easing their way across the threshold of a mausoleum. Chief Engineer Scott seemed the most affected despite his protests that he was "no' a superstitious mon," but there was no one on the bridge who didn't share the feeling to some small degree. Even Spock admitted that he expected the worst, though he insisted his expectation was only a logical deduction based on the observations they had already made.

Finally, after a four-hour sublight approach, the *Enterprise* was in standard orbit about the earthlike planet. As expected—or feared—the sensors still showed no evidence of life.

There was, however, ample evidence of death.

What remained of an atmosphere was a veritable sea of radioactivity, and the surface was like the surface of earth's moon or Mercury, pitted by thousands of craters. But these craters were not caused by meteorites or volcanos but by an almost inconceivable bombardment of fusion bombs. Even the oceans had been sterilized of life, boiled away by the heat of destruction and turned into a radioactive soup as they recondensed and settled into the old seabeds and the countless craters.

For several seconds no one on the bridge made a sound. They could only watch as the ghastly images flowed silently across the viewscreen. McCoy's teeth were clenched as he gripped one of the padded rails, and when he finally spoke, his voice was hushed with a kind of terrible awe.

"My God, Jim! What kind of creatures could be capable of something like that? Even the Klingons . . ." His voice trailed away as he shook his head and wiped briefly at his eyes.

"How long ago, Spock?" Kirk asked after another protracted silence.

Spock, whose eyes, like everyone else's, had been riveted on the screen, turned abruptly back to his instruments, his Vulcan training clamping down on the emotion that struggled to emerge from the human half of his heritage.

"Impossible to say precisely, Captain, without detailed information on the number and nature of the weapons used. Assuming the use of devices similar to those on board the object the *Enterprise* encountered earlier, I would estimate approximately eleven thousand standard years has passed since this bombardment took place, with a possible error of plus or minus three thousand."

Spock's numbers and his carefully maintained matter-of-fact tone seemed to restore some measure of objectivity to the others, though McCoy still looked as grim-faced as before.

"Is there any chance the planet's inhabitants could have done this to themselves, Spock?" Kirk asked softly. "Two factions fighting each other for control of the planet?"

"Possible but extremely unlikely, Captain. Both combatants would have to have been totally irrational and suicidal. Less than one percent of the weapons used here would have been sufficient to effectively destroy all life outside the oceans, and anyone capable of launching such weapons would certainly have been aware of that fact. No, Captain, this amount of destruction and this amount of residual radiation are almost certainly the result of an attack by a fleet of spacecraft, an attack that was designed to do precisely what it did—destroy all life on the planet and ensure that the planet itself would be uninhabitable by any life forms for hundreds of thousands of years. Based on an analysis of the elements that are producing most of the radioactivity, it would, in fact, appear that most of the radioactivity is not the direct result of the fusion explosions themselves but the result of the materials in which the weapons were housed. 'Clean' fusion weapons, as I believe your ancestors called them, Captain, can destroy a world but allow life forms to return safely in a relatively short time. These weapons, however, would appear to have been deliberately designed to be as 'dirty' as it is possible to make them."

McCoy shuddered. "What kind of madhouse have we fallen into, Jim?"

"I don't know, Bones. But at least all this happened

a long time ago. There's nothing to indicate that the ones responsible for this are still around."

"And nothing to indicate they aren't, either," McCoy said, his eyes flickering apprehensively at the sheer savagery of the destruction still visible on the viewscreen. "And if they were capable of this thousands of years ago, what kind of weapons do you imagine they've developed by now?"

Chapter Four

On the course the *Enterprise* followed to the next system, two more of the "booby traps" were found, both still partially functional. Once the nature of the objects was determined, both were destroyed by phaser fire, thereby preventing the fusion weapons aboard from detonating and flooding nearby space with the kind of radioactivity the first had left behind when its antimatter fuel had exploded.

In the system itself, two once habitable worlds had been destroyed just as thoroughly as the world in the first system. Whether the worlds in both systems had been destroyed by the same enemy or they had destroyed each other was impossible to say. Spock's sensors could only indicate that the destruction in the second system had occurred somewhere during roughly the same six-thousand-year period they had indicated for the first system.

In the third system, there were no habitable worlds and hence no destruction.

In the fourth, there was one habitable world. It, too, had had life scoured from its surface, but in a different, less permanent way. Here, it appeared that spaceborne lasers had been used. There was no radioactivity, and life survived in the oceans. On the land, some plant life survived as well, and, except for the lack of any animal life larger than insects and except for deserts that had been turned to glass, certain areas looked pleasantly pastoral. The time of the destruction, Spock estimated, was also different—in the twenty-to-thirty-thousand-year range.

In two more systems, no habitable worlds were found. In another, antimatter missiles had apparently been used less than five thousand years ago. In another, there was two-thousand-year-old evidence that massive phasers had been the agent of destruction, along with weapons similar to the photon torpedoes the *Enterprise* carried. In yet another, there was the residue of a deadly, corrosive chemical gas that had blanketed an entire planet, still present after at least thirty-five thousand years. And in still another, a world destroyed by the same hellish radioactive weapons that had obliterated the first two was still hideously barren after more than forty thousand years. Between systems, more than a dozen of the spacegoing booby traps were found and destroyed.

On only one planet in all the systems they visited on that first leg of exploration was there anything that didn't fit the pattern of total destruction.

The planet itself, dead for at least thirty-five thousand years, was no different from a half-dozen others. All plant and animal life was gone from the land, devoured by enough antimatter missiles to do the job a hundred times over. Deep beneath the surface, however, apparently beyond even the reach of the radiation that still poisoned space for a thousand kilometers around, Spock's sensors detected an operating antimatter power source. More than five kilometers below the surface, small amounts of power were being produced and used, and at the same point there were peculiar and extremely low-level life readings.

"Fascinating, Captain," Spock said after nearly two minutes of steady concentration on the readouts. "I have never encountered anything quite like it."

"Artificial life, perhaps?" Kirk suggested.

"Negative, Captain, at least no type of artificial life I am familiar with."

"Don't forget, this is another part of the universe. Who knows what could have been created here?"

"Granted, Captain. But this reading is not only different but . . . diffuse. In some ways it appears to be a single being, and yet it is not." Spock paused, looking again at the readouts.

"I apologize, Captain," he continued after a moment, "that I must express myself so imprecisely. It is a most disturbing feeling to suspect a pattern exists and yet to be unable to define that pattern or even to describe logically why I suspect its existence."

"It's called intuition," McCoy said, but without the grin that would normally have accompanied the remark. Here, in a universe of seemingly endless death, smiles had been rare. "It's from your mother's side of the family, that's all."

"Perhaps you are right, Doctor," Spock said, without the argument or the arched eyebrow that, like McCoy's missing mischievous grin, would normally have been a part of their byplay.

"An organic computer, then," Kirk said. "Remember, the Federation experimented with them for a time before Duotronics came along."

"I have considered that possibility, Captain. I have also considered the possibility that the readings are the result of distortion caused by the intervening mass of rock or even the radiation. Neither theory, however, has proven satisfactory."

"At least," McCoy said, "whatever it is isn't shooting at us the way those booby traps did."

"And no sensor probes have been detected," Kirk added. "And Uhura's found no indication of subspace activity of any kind. My own guess is that, whatever it is, it was put out of commission when the surface of the planet was destroyed, and that was at least thirty-five thousand years ago. In any event, it is obviously not the builder of the gate, and I can see no way of learning more without beaming someone down—through five kilometers of solid rock and a thousand kilometers of radiation—to look."

Spock stared at the readouts another few seconds and then straightened. "You are correct, Captain.

Such a risk would be illogical simply to satisfy one's curiosity."

After two standard weeks and twenty-seven planetary systems without finding anything more advanced than insects anywhere outside the oceans, even McCoy was becoming inured to the seemingly endless destruction. His eyes began, like everyone's, to glaze over with each new scene of devastation.

Finally, as the twenty-seventh system fell astern, Kirk ordered a new course laid in, and they returned to their starting point. There was, however, no indication that the gate had reappeared, and after half a day, despite Dr. Crandall's strenuous objections, they resumed their explorations. Now, however, instead of spiraling slowly outward, the *Enterprise* struck out radially, putting as much distance as possible between itself and their starting point. And instead of stopping at every system that might hold a habitable world, they leapfrogged over ten for every one they investigated. For the first fourteen days, nothing changed. Destruction was everywhere, and everyone was beginning to wonder if every habitable world in this entire cluster had been destroyed.

But then, on the fifteenth day, more than thirty parsecs out, as the *Enterprise* dropped to sublight velocity to take detailed readings on yet another planetary system, the routine they had fallen into was abruptly shattered.

Spock, studying his instruments as always, was the first to spot the new intruder.

"Captain," he announced, "sensors indicate approaching craft."

Kirk, who had been concentrating on the magnified image of the planet they had dropped out of warp drive to inspect, looked around sharply. "Another booby trap?"

"I do not think so, Captain. It is moving under its own power, and there are indications it is capable of warp speed."

"Bearing, Mr. Chekov?"

"Three-seventy-five, mark twenty-three, sir."

"Mr. Sulu, get that on the screen, maximum magnification."

"Aye-aye, sir." As the helmsman spoke, the planet vanished abruptly from the screen, replaced by yet another view of the impossibly dense star field. After an instant of hesitation, the view expanded, the countless stars spreading outward and shooting off the edges of the screen. Finally, near the center, something nonluminous appeared in the star field, and soon its seven-sided shape was fuzzily evident.

"Details, Mr. Spock."

"Mass approximately thirty million kilograms. Heavy shielding indicated. Range one-hundred-seventeen-point-six-million kilometers, moving at point-two-three-five-c on a heading that will, at its closest point, bring the craft within thirteen-point-two-million kilometers of our present location. Preliminary indications are that the craft is technologically comparable to early Federation cruisers of the Cochrane or Verne class. There are only five life forms aboard, however."

"Any sign that they're aware of our presence?"

"None, Captain. No sensor beams detected as yet. The probability is that we are well beyond the range of its sensory apparatus."

"You mentioned shielding. What about weapons?"

"Unknown, Captain, but based on the type of shields detected, lasers are the most likely. Their shields would present no resistance to phaser fire."

"Estimated time of closest approach?"

"Twenty-seven-point-nine minutes, Captain."

"Lieutenant Uhura, any indication of subspace radio activity?"

"None, sir."

"Is it possible they don't have subspace radio capability, Mr. Spock?"

"Possible, Captain, but unlikely since they appear to have warp drive. It is more likely that they are simply not broadcasting. From the amount and type of shielding they carry, they would appear to be intentionally trying to avoid letting their presence be known. To another craft of the same technological level, without sensors similar to ours, they would be virtually undetectable beyond direct visual range."

"Then they could be listening?"

"Of course, Captain."

"Is it possible that this ship could be related to the destruction we've seen?"

"Impossible to say, Captain, but if by 'related' you imply responsibility, I would think it unlikely for a number of reasons."

Kirk nodded, sighing. "I know. Most of these worlds were destroyed thousands or tens of thousands of years ago, so no ship we come across now could possibly have had any part in whatever happened that long ago. And one would expect whoever was responsible for that destruction to have come up with an even more sophisticated and destructive technology in the interim, while this ship appears more primitive."

"Precisely, Captain."

"Then who are they? Mr. Chekov, does their flight path, fore or aft, intersect any nearby star system?"

"No, sir. Except for the one we are both in right now."

Kirk paused, studying the seven-sided dot on the screen as if trying to force it to yield its secrets by simple concentration. Finally he said, "Lieutenant Uhura, see if you can get any response."

"Right away, sir." Her lithe fingers stabbed at the controls as she spoke.

"Sensor beams, Captain," Spock announced. "However, though we can detect the beams themselves, it is unlikely that the alien craft is able to gain any useful information from them. We are still well beyond their effective range, probably indistinguishable from background noise."

"Subspace radio transmission, sir," Uhura said, "but nothing intelligible. And it's already stopped."

"Let the computer have it, Lieutenant. Maybe it can make something out of it."

"Analysis in progress," she said, "but it doesn't look hopeful." She paused, listening. "There *is* a pattern, though, Captain. It could be an identification code of some kind. A challenge to us, perhaps."

"Apparently they heard us, at least," Kirk mused. "And they obviously have subspace radio and sensor capability. Let's get a little closer, Mr. Sulu. Lay in an intercept course and proceed on impulse power, deflector shields up."

"Laid in, sir, and deflectors up."

"Lieutenant Uhura, continue broadcasting and monitoring all subspace frequencies."

"Yes, sir."

"Any change, Mr. Spock?"

"None, Captain. Their course and speed remain unchanged, and their sensor beams continue to operate. No further subspace emissions."

On the screen, the alien ship was no longer simply a dot, and the relatively primitive nature of the ship was becoming ever more apparent. A single, massive warp-drive engine mounted behind a much smaller, blunt-nosed pyramid that apparently contained the living quarters reminded Kirk of the probes the *Enterprise* had been using to investigate the anomalies. The craft was purely utilitarian, and it was little wonder that there were only five crew members aboard.

"What would you estimate the range of their sensors to be, Mr. Spock?"

"Based on their intensity, they should be at least marginally effective at our present range."

"In all likelihood, then, they know not only that we exist but where we are," Kirk said thoughtfully.

"Affirmative, Captain."

"But except for the sensor beams and that one subspace emission, they're ignoring us." Kirk paused, frowning at the craft as it continued to expand on the viewscreen. "Or, more likely, pretending to ignore us. All stop, Mr. Sulu. Let them come to us."

"All stop, sir."

"And Lieutenant Uhura, cease broadcasting but maintain surveillance of all frequencies."

"Yes, sir."

Shields up, the *Enterprise* waited.

As the alien, stolidly maintaining its original course, closed to within five million kilometers, Spock said, "Definitely laser weaponry, Captain. It is detectable through their shields at this range. Sixty-three seconds to closest approach, now estimated to be three-hundred-twenty-seven-point-six-thousand kilometers."

"Our own deflector screens can handle anything they can put out, I assume."

"Of course, Captain."

They continued to wait and listen, but the approaching ship remained totally silent. At two million kilometers, Kirk ordered Uhura to resume transmitting. Still there was no response.

At just over five hundred thousand kilometers, the alien emitted a single concentrated burst of nondirectional subspace radio energy. A split second later, it changed course abruptly and began accelerating.

"Collision course, Captain," Spock said. "At present acceleration, impact in seven-point-three seconds. Lasers preparing to fire."

"Evasive maneuvers, Mr. Sulu."

Almost instantly, the *Enterprise* leaped ahead on impulse power, but not before the alien craft's lasers fired at what, in space, was the equivalent of point-blank range. A moment later, the alien's drive proved itself far closer to being truly inertialess than any comparable early Federation starship's had ever been. In a matter of seconds, the craft came to a virtual halt, reversed its course almost as quickly as the *Enterprise* itself could have done, and put itself once again on a collision course. Sulu and the navigation computer responded, and the alien ship shot by a hundred kilometers below, its lasers still drenching the *Enterprise*'s shields and surrounding space in concentrated radiation.

"They apparently do not like us, Captain," Chekov commented.

"Apparently," Kirk agreed. "If this is the way everyone in this neighborhood reacts to strangers, it's no wonder all these worlds were destroyed."

"They are persistent, too, sir. The ship is returning again."

Again the alien craft was on a collision course, and again it was firing its lasers steadily, putting out prodigious amounts of energy. Though they were no more advanced than early Federation weapons, they far surpassed them in sheer brute force.

Again the *Enterprise*, under Sulu's sure hand, avoided the alien, and the *Enterprise*'s deflector screens absorbed the coruscating laser energy without damage.

"How long can they keep this up, Spock?" Kirk asked as the alien executed yet another U-turn and began yet another blazing run at the *Enterprise*.

"Not more than another five-point-four minutes, I would estimate, Captain. No laser device can continue to produce that level of power for long without beginning to seriously malfunction. In addition, the repeated rapid course changes appear to be straining not only the craft's primary power source but the structure of the craft itself."

"Very well. When their weapons become inoperative, perhaps we'll be able to talk."

As Kirk spoke, Sulu once again took the *Enterprise* safely out of the path of the charging alien craft. This time, however, the alien did not immediately turn and resume its attack. Instead, it paused and emitted another concentrated burst of subspace radio energy.

"Anything intelligible this time, Lieutenant Uhura?"

"Nothing, Captain. But these last two transmissions were much more complex than the first. They were obviously nothing as simple as an identification code or a challenge. The computer indicates that both transmissions contained massive amounts of information, compressed into periods of less than forty-three milli-seconds."

"They're telling their friends about us?" Kirk wondered aloud.

"It is a distinct possibility, Captain," Spock said.

"Perhaps *they* will be less belligerent."

"They well *have* to be, sir," Chekov said, shaking his head in annoyed disbelief as he watched his instruments. "This one is coming back *again*!"

"But this will be its last run, Captain," Spock said. "It appears to be purposely inducing an overload in its primary power source. Unless something is done, all its matter and antimatter fuel will be simultaneously converted to energy in eighteen-point-three seconds, which time will coincide with its closest approach to the *Enterprise*. If that approach is as close as previous approaches, our deflector shields will not be able to withstand the energy release."

Chapter Five

"WARP SPEED, MR. SULU, *now!*" Kirk snapped, even before Spock had finished speaking.

Acknowledging the command only by his actions, Sulu stabbed at the controls, and the *Enterprise* surged ahead, warp drive engaged within seconds.

In another second, the relativistic starbow in the viewscreen was replaced by the computer-generated star field and the now slightly off-center alien craft.

"Destruction of alien craft no longer imminent, Captain," Spock said. "The overload sequence has apparently been aborted!"

"A bluff?" Kirk wondered aloud, relieved but not yet relaxing. "Or perhaps they were only simulating an overload. Possible, Mr. Spock?"

"Possible but unlikely, Captain. The power drain was real and of massive proportions. Obviously, however, it was under their control at all times, and they were able to cut it off within seconds of the *Enterprise*'s departure."

"So, the danger of an explosion was real, but the alien's actions could still have been a bluff."

"Again, possible but unlikely. For the alien to undertake such an action, it would have to assume that we were continually monitoring the craft's internal workings and were aware of the impending explosion. The technological level of their own equipment would not allow such monitoring."

"Therefore," Kirk finished when Spock paused,

"they weren't bluffing. They intended to commit suicide in hopes of taking us with them."

"Almost certainly, Captain."

"And yet, when the *Enterprise* warped out of range, they were able to remove the overload and stabilize their engines in a matter of seconds."

"In three-point-four seconds, Captain."

"Such proficiency would seem to indicate that they have done that sort of thing before."

"Very likely, Captain."

"Which would indicate any number of possibilities. For example, just because their own technology doesn't allow them to monitor the internal workings of other spacecraft doesn't mean that they aren't accustomed to meeting ships like ours that *can* monitor such things. Meeting and attacking." Kirk grimaced. "Any progress in analyzing those subspace bursts, Lieutenant Uhura?"

"The computer has been working on it," she said, studying one of the small screens in front of her. "Most of it is still unintelligible, but part of it appears to be a crude image of the *Enterprise*. There are several accompanying symbols that might specify a scale for the image. Perhaps Mr. Spock can make more sense out of them."

"So they *were* telling their friends about us." Kirk looked back at the image on the screen, once again vanishingly small among the stars. "Are we out of range of their sensors, Mr. Spock?"

"Affirmative, Captain."

"All stop, Mr. Sulu. Let's watch and see what happens." He paused, glancing around the bridge. "Unless someone has a better idea. Now that we appear to have a breather, I'm open to suggestions, gentlemen."

"The course you suggest seems eminently logical, Captain," Spock said when no one else volunteered anything. Then, his full attention back on his instruments, he announced, "The alien craft is in motion, accelerating away from us. It will—it has just achieved warp speed and is continuing to accelerate."

"Don't lose them," Kirk snapped. "Mr. Sulu, keep us within sensor range—our sensor range, not theirs."

"Aye-aye, sir."

"They are at warp two-point-five and holding, Captain. That appears to be their maximum speed."

"Antimatter drive, but without dilithium crystals to focus the power?"

"Apparently, Captain."

"And their heading—I don't suppose they're aiming for any particular star?"

"None within a dozen parsecs. Nor does their present course bear any discernible relationship to the course they were initially following."

Frowning, Kirk settled back in the command chair. Where *were* the aliens going? Did they think the *Enterprise* had simply run away, or did they suspect they were being followed? And if they did suspect it, were they, like a bird defending its nest, trying to lure the intruder away from their home world? Was that why its course was not aimed at any of the thousands of relatively nearby stars but at the empty space that separated them?

Or, he wondered, could they be hoping to lead the *Enterprise* into a trap? Now that it was clear they could not destroy the Federation ship on their own, not even with their kamikaze maneuver, did they hope that whoever had been on the receiving end of those subspace radio bursts *could* do the job?

Dr. Jason Crandall lay fully dressed on his bed, futilely trying to decide which was worse—the terrifying nightmare from which he had just awakened or the bleak reality that had replaced it.

The nightmare, he thought grimly, had at least come to an end, just as the dozen before it had done. Its repeated scenes of his own grisly death on one outlandishly alien world after another had left him bathed in icy perspiration, but they *had* ended. What passed for reality, on the other hand, showed no signs of ending. He was imprisoned on a ship of hostile strangers a lifetime away from everything and everyone he was familiar with, and that very real imprisonment, he was now convinced, could have no end but his own equally real death.

He had come to accept that fact more than a dozen standard days ago, shortly after the *Enterprise* had finally and briefly returned to its starting point in this alien sector of space. Instead of staying and using the remaining supply of probes in an attempt to locate the gate that had brought them here, Kirk had almost immediately ordered a resumption of his pointless search for the remnants of some civilization which, if it had ever existed at all, had almost certainly been destroyed thousands if not millions of years ago.

Until then, Crandall had often fostered the forlorn hope that the gate was not truly missing, that its disappearance had all been a fiction generated by Kirk to give him an excuse to play the explorer for a few days or weeks more. Even though that hope had faded further with each new scene of devastation that appeared on the viewscreens, he had managed to keep it alive throughout those first days.

But then, with one mindless order, Kirk had shattered that hope. After sending the *Enterprise* on a half-dozen uneventful runs through the spot where the gate had once been, he had ordered the search resumed, this time not limiting it to the nearby stars but moving straight out through the cluster at a warp factor that he doubted the ship could safely maintain for any length of time. At that point there had no longer been any doubt in Crandall's mind that his predicament was real. Unless the mad captain's pipe dream of finding the so-called gate civilization came true, the whole lot of them would be destroyed out here in this interstellar no-man's land.

And then, less than five standard hours ago, Kirk

had taken yet another giant step toward that destruction. The *Enterprise* had made its first contact with a spacefaring race in this sector. Not with another of those decaying relics of past destruction they called booby traps but with an actual ship, under the control of living, sentient beings.

Predictably, the encounter had been a disaster, even based on the drastically censored version Crandall and the crew had been given. And, to make matters worse, Kirk was now intent on playing some insane game of interstellar cat and mouse. Despite all common sense, he was trailing the retreating alien, sublimely overconfident that the *Enterprise* could handle whatever he was blindly leading it into.

A knock on the door of the living quarters section of Crandall's stateroom snapped him upright on the bed, his booted feet hitting the carpeted floor with a thud. Pulling in a deep breath, he sat quietly for a long moment, composing himself. Now that he had come to accept the depressing fact that the *Enterprise* was going to be his home for the rest of his life, he had no intention of letting his emotions once again get out of hand, as they had in his earlier, uncontrolled outbursts. Those had done quite enough damage to his image, making him seem not only impatiently autocratic but, worse, childishly fearful, even weak. From now on, his personal feelings would remain just that—personal. Whatever emotions he displayed would be, as they had been throughout his career in public life, limited to those that would further his own ends, no more and no less.

Standing up, he smoothed his green tunic and hurriedly wiped the remaining beads of perspiration from his forehead as he strode past the room divider between his sleeping quarters and his equally sparsely finished living quarters.

"Enter," he said, and a moment later the door hissed open.

A young ensign, blond with uneasy gray eyes,

stepped hesitantly into the stateroom, casting a nervous glance over her shoulder as the door closed behind her.

Crandall suppressed a frown as he searched his memory for the ensign's name. Normally, among civilians and their varied dress and hair styles, he would have no trouble making the mental associations that would allow him to put a name to any one of hundreds of people he was introduced to, but here on the *Enterprise*, where uniforms and regulations cut individuality to the bone, he felt lucky to keep the officers and their duties separate in his mind, let alone the names and functions of the hundreds of others who swarmed the ship's corridors. He could only remember that this particular ensign had been one of a group of a dozen or so who had been pointed out to him as being fresh out of Starfleet Academy, the *Enterprise* their first spacegoing assignment.

"Yes, Ensign, what can I do for you?" he asked.

"I'm sorry to bother you, Dr. Crandall," she said, obviously having trouble forcing the words out, "but I felt that I had to speak to you."

Crandall softened his own expression a fraction, suddenly sensing that in this young woman he might have found his first ally. She was obviously upset, but equally obviously she was not upset with him but with something about the *Enterprise*.

"That's perfectly all right, Ensign. Won't you have a seat?" Motioning her to the lounge chair in the corner of the stateroom, he sat casually on the edge of the trapezoidal desk in one corner of the room. "For a start, how about telling me your name?"

"I'm sorry," she said, blushing as she sat down. "My name is Davis, sir."

"No need for the 'sir,' Miss Davis. I'm just a civilian, not an officer."

"I know, sir, but as a representative of the Council—"

"Only unofficially, as I'm sure you are aware, Ensign," he said, letting just a trace of his annoyance with that state of affairs color his voice.

"But tell me, Miss Davis, what is it you wish to speak to me about?" he continued, arranging his features into a rueful smile. "Much as I'd like to, I'm afraid getting you—or myself—shore leave is a bit beyond my current capabilities."

A nervous, answering smile flickered across her softly rounded features. "I realize that, of course, sir. And I don't want you to think that I'm being disloyal to the captain in any way by coming to speak to you."

"Of course not!" he said, giving her a reassuring smile. "In any case," he added in a confidential tone, "one's ultimate loyalty is to the Federation itself, not to any one individual. So please, feel free to be completely open and honest with me. Whatever you say will be just between us—unless you specifically tell me otherwise."

For just a moment, as he had spoken of loyalty to the Federation as opposed to loyalty to Kirk, a new kind of tension had flickered across her expressive features, and he wondered if he had overplayed his hand and lost her.

"Please, go ahead," he said softly. "Why not begin by telling me about yourself? How is it that you're on the *Enterprise*, for instance? I seem to recall being told that this is your first assignment out of Starfleet Academy."

With those questions, he could see her visibly relax, and he allowed himself a mental sigh of relief. Then she was pulling in a deep breath and raising her eyes to meet his.

"That's right, sir. I graduated just three months ago. And I don't know how I happened to be assigned to the *Enterprise*. The luck of the draw, I imagine. Even so, it was quite an honor."

"I'm sure it was. The *Enterprise* is, after all, a rather highly regarded vessel."

She nodded, a shy smile flickering around her lips

and eyes as memories drove some of her current tensions away. "All my classmates were green with envy. There wasn't one who didn't want the chance of serving with Captain Kirk."

Suppressing his impulse to laugh derisively, Crandall nodded his encouragement instead. "But you weren't counting on anything like this," he suggested.

For a moment, she was totally silent, the faint smile vanishing as she was reminded of the reasons that had brought her to Crandall. "No, I wasn't," she said, and suddenly her voice was tight with emotion. "This was supposed to be strictly a scientific mission! We were supposed to be back on earth in only a few weeks! My fiancé graduated last year, and he's on the *Krieger,* and we were both scheduled for duty on the *Republic* next year. His family knows Captain Halston, and—"

As abruptly as the emotions had broken free, she clamped down on them, pressing her lips together into a tense line, blinking back a tear as she averted his eyes in embarrassment. "I'm sorry," she said.

"No need to be," Crandall said, debating briefly whether or not he should put a comforting hand on her shoulder. "Graduating from the Academy doesn't mean you have to stop being human."

"Thank you, sir."

"You have nothing to thank me for, Miss Davis. Believe me, I know how you feel. I don't have a fiancée waiting for me at home, but I do have friends and family."

Slowly, she looked up at him, and he could see in her eyes that, no matter what her training or her uniform said, he had gained her trust. She was—and with careful handling would remain—his ally.

Favoring her with another smile, this one a mixture of reassurance and sympathy, he stood up from where he had been half seated on the corner of the trapezoidal desk and lowered himself into the other lounge chair. After a moment, he hitched it forward and turned it a fraction so he was facing her more directly.

Leaning forward but still not reaching out to touch

her, he said, in his best just-between-friends tone, "You said you felt you had to speak with me, Miss Davis. I hope you haven't changed your mind."

"No, it's just that—"

"Whatever it is, you can tell me. As I said, it will go no farther than these walls unless you want it to."

"As I understand it," she said hesitantly, "you're an expert on the gravitational anomalies the *Enterprise* was investigating—the anomalies that—that got us where we are now."

"I know a little about them, yes. I was in charge of the laboratory that developed the detectors the *Enterprise* was using." He didn't add that his function had been purely administrative and that, until the announcement that the *Enterprise* would use the detectors on this special mission, he had barely known of the existence of either the anomalies or the detectors.

"I—I understand that you don't agree with the captain's assessment of our situation," she said, "and, well, I would just like to know what *you* think our chances are. Based on your knowledge of the anomalies, do you think we can ever get back to the Federation?"

"I rather doubt it," he said cautiously, letting his eyes flicker upward in the general direction of the bridge as he added, "at least not under the present command structure."

And then, when she didn't bridle at his implied criticism of Kirk, he went on, his voice firmer. "As you said, I have my disagreements with Captain Kirk. In the first place, I strongly suspect that we are wasting precious time chasing after this mythical gate civilization that he hopes still exists. What's even more disturbing to me, however, is the fact that, if I'm to believe what the captain announced over the intercom a few hours ago, he's begun playing some kind of cat-and-mouse game with the alien ship that attacked us. To tell the truth—and here I'm trusting *you* not to let *my* words go any farther—I think the captain's course of action is not only putting us in unnecessary danger of another, more serious attack but is virtually destroying what little chance we do have of getting home."

As he spoke, he watched her eyes, ready to backtrack at the first sign that her Academy-instilled obedience to rank was staging a comeback, but none came.

"Unfortunately," he went on, "I am in no position to do anything about it. As the captain has pointed out, I am on board strictly as an observer, despite my being, in effect, a representative of the Federation itself."

"But there must be *something* you can do," she said, some of the restrained emotion escaping once again into her words. "Captain Kirk would certainly listen to anything you have to say. With your knowledge of the anomalies . . ."

Her voice trailed off as she saw him shake his head grimly. "In the first place," he said, "I fear he does not share your estimate of my knowledge. In the second, starship captains are not known for their receptiveness to unsolicited advice from unwelcome civilians. And in his eyes—and in the eyes of his officers, I'm sure—that is precisely what I am." He gave a minuscule shrug. "Not that I can fault them for that, of course. Or the rest of the crew for seeing me in the same light."

"I'm sure not everyone feels that way," she protested. "I certainly don't."

"I thank you for your confidence," he said, allowing just a touch of sarcasm into his tone but following his words almost immediately with his best apologetic look. "In any event, there's little either of us can do about the situation except watch and listen."

"Watch and listen? I don't understand."

He was silent a long moment, as if debating whether or not to take her into his confidence. Finally, he leaned toward her again. "Has it ever occurred to you," he said conspiratorially, "that the briefing we've all been given concerning our contact with the alien ship is not the complete story?"

She shook her head. "I'm sorry, but I still don't understand."

"What I'm saying is, while I'm sure the captain wouldn't lie, I can't help but fear that there are a few things that he's simply not telling us." He held up his hand to forestall the protest he saw building in her face.

"Believe me," he went on, "I've often dealt with people in positions of power, both military and nonmilitary, and they virtually *never* tell the public—or their subordinates—the whole truth."

Pausing, he gave her a self-deprecating smile. "And I include myself in that category, Miss Davis. I have to admit that I have not always been one-hundred percent open. Truthfully, no one in power—no one, for that matter, in the public eye at all— can *afford* to be totally open. Now, I'm not saying I ever did anything that I didn't honestly believe was in the best interests of the Federation in the long run, and I'm *certainly* not suggesting that Captain Kirk would ever do anything he didn't firmly believe was in the best interests of his ship and crew. There have been starship captains who might put their own interests above that of their people, but Captain Kirk, I'm sure, is not one of them. His reputation for integrity and competence is among the best in Starfleet, as I'm sure you're aware. No, all I'm saying is that, probably for what he sees as the best of motives, he's not letting us know everything that is happening, either with the alien craft or with the anomalies themselves. The problem is that, since he is probably not as knowledgeable as he could be concerning the anomalies, he just might be keeping to himself the one piece of information that, in the hands of someone more knowledgeable, could be the key to our return to the Federation."

As he spoke, he continued to watch the play of emotions across her guileless face, and it came to him once again that, unless he fumbled badly, Ensign Davis was firmly in his camp. And with that recurring thought, he realized that, sometime in the last few minutes, some of the bleakness of his imprisonment had begun to lift. He still could see little hope of ever returning to the Federation; the gate had in all probability simply vanished, never to return, or perhaps it only operated in the one direction.

But now he was not totally alone. In Ensign Davis he had an ally, a useful ally in what he had in that moment begun to think of as a campaign. His *Enterprise* campaign. For a moment, nostalgic memories of those long-ago campaigns that had launched him on his public career filled his thoughts. Then strategies began to leap into his mind, almost unbidden, and he wondered suddenly why he had been so slow to take that final mental step.

But at last he had taken it. With the realization that he had established a firm toehold in the enemy ranks, he had taken it. And now, using the kind of maneuvering he knew best, he could build on that toehold. His life, he realized with an inner smile, once more had a purpose.

Chapter Six

ALMOST PRECISELY THIRTY-SIX standard hours after the first contact with the alien ship, Kirk was snatched from a dreamless sleep by the excited voice of Lieutenant Jameson, the third-watch science officer.

"Captain Kirk, to the bridge," Jameson's staccato voice crackled over the intercom. "Five more alien craft detected, apparently rendezvousing with the first."

Within minutes, Kirk, brushing his still-rumpled hair back from his forehead with a quick motion of his fingers, emerged onto the bridge only to find Mr. Spock already at the science station, absorbed in the readouts and looking as if he had been there throughout the watch. Lieutenant Jameson, standing back out of the way of his superior, turned briefly toward the turbolift as Kirk entered. Despite a firmly neutral expression on Jameson's face, Kirk could see in the young officer's quick glance and in the fractional stiffness of his motions that he was not pleased to have been displaced, even by Spock. This, however, was neither the time nor the place to call him on an attitude problem.

"Situation, Mr. Spock," Kirk said, sliding into the command chair vacated seconds before by Lieutenant Tanaka, who moved smoothly to a point beyond the circular handrail, never taking his eyes from the forward screen.

"As Mr. Jameson first stated, Captain, five craft,

traveling in formation, appear to be rendezvousing with the craft we have been tracking."

"Rendezvousing? Not attacking?"

"It would seem not. They are all within range of each other now, and no hostilities have been initiated by either side."

"Reinforcements? These are the ships those subspace radio bursts were intended for?"

"In all likelihood, Captain. From the limited sensor data available, all five craft appear to be identical to the first. However, based on the formation in which the five craft were traveling, it would appear that one of those craft was being purposely shielded by the others. The craft we have been following has joined that protective formation."

"A flagship of some kind?"

"Unlikely. As I said, Captain, all craft appear to be identical. It is only the shielded position in the formation that distinguishes the one craft from the others."

"Interesting. Keep track of that craft, Mr. Spock, even if the formation changes. Lieutenant Granger," Kirk went on, turning toward Lieutenant Uhura's third-watch counterpart, "any subspace radio activity?"

"None," Granger's bass voice returned. "There hasn't been a peep out of *anyone* since those bursts."

"And no possibility of tight-beam transmissions?"

"Not from *that* ship, sir, not without our knowing it."

"Rendezvous complete, Captain," Spock announced. "All have dropped to sublight and are clustered within kilometers of each other."

"Could they be communicating using something we can't pick up at this distance?"

"Affirmative, Captain. Direct visual communication is only one of many possibilities our sensors could not detect."

Whatever the six ships were discussing, if anything, it didn't take long. After less than five minutes clustered in normal space, their velocities so precisely matched they could have been linked by invisible rods, the six split apart and resumed warp speed.

"Where are they headed, Mr. Spock? And is the same ship still in the center of the formation?"

"Affirmative, Captain. They are now, in effect, retracing the path of the first craft."

Kirk grimaced. "Now that they have a posse together, they're coming back to look for us."

"Apparently, Captain."

"If the situation arises, how would our screens hold up against the lot of them?"

"Adequately, Captain, assuming all have the same capability as the first, but we could not resist a great many more."

"Rather imprecise, Mr. Spock. How many is a great many?"

"In this case, assuming the *Enterprise* maintains peak efficiency, I would estimate we could withstand the combined force of those six and another four-point-seven ships before long-term overloading became a significant danger."

"That's all it would take? Eleven ships like that?"

"Affirmative, Captain. You must remember that, though their weapons technology is at the level of the very early Federation ships, the destructive energy they can deliver is greater by a factor of more than fifteen. Virtually all their power is devoted to their drive and their weapons, whereas only a small fraction of the power in the early Federation ships was available for weaponry use. With crews of over a hundred on Federation ships, a much greater percentage of available power was utilized in maintaining the necessary environment. These ships do not appear even to maintain an artificial gravity except by constant rotation."

"Thank you for the history refresher, Mr. Spock," Kirk said with a faint smile as he rotated the command chair once again to face the viewscreen.

"Mr. Woida," Kirk said to the massive, muscular third-watch helmsman, "continue to track them—but keep us safely outside their sensor range."

"Yes, Captain," Woida responded in a voice surprisingly soft for a man of his size. "And if they split up?"

"Unless you receive orders to the contrary, stay with the ship in the center of the formation, the one apparently being protected."

Nodding his acknowledgment, Woida hunched more closely over his controls, his bulk almost completely hiding them from Kirk's view.

"Captain Kirk?" The voice came from behind him, superimposed on the hiss of the closing door of the turbolift.

"Yes, Dr. Crandall?" Kirk said without turning from the viewscreen.

"What's this about new ships? I heard you summoned to the bridge."

Kirk gestured at the screen. "Five more ships," he said. "They met and apparently conferred with the first a few minutes ago. Now they're retracing the path of the ship that attacked us."

"I see. And your plan of action?"

"For the moment, Doctor, the same as before. Wait and watch."

"For how long?"

"At this point, no decision has been made."

"And if they detect the presence of the *Enterprise*?"

"They won't, Doctor, unless we want them to."

"How can you be—" Crandall began, but he was cut off in midsentence.

"Another ship, Captain," Spock announced, giving its coordinates. "This one is not identical to the others."

"More advanced?"

"It appears to be the product of a roughly equivalent technology. It is traveling at warp two." Spock paused, calling up new readouts. "Antimatter engines and similar armaments. Six life forms on board, not five."

"Get the new ship on the screen, Mr. Woida, maximum magnification."

"Yes, sir."

In a swirl of light, the pinpoint images of the six vanished, replaced by a barely larger image of the seventh.

"Lieutenant Granger, any indication of subspace radio activity?"

"None, sir. This one's buttoned up just as tight as the other six."

"Like the others," Spock added, "its sensors are active, but that is all. The range of its sensors would appear to be slightly less than that of the six."

"Is it rendezvousing with them?"

"It would not appear so. However, its present course will take it within sensor range of the six in no more than two-point-five minutes."

Drumming his fingers lightly on the arm of the command chair, Kirk settled back to wait. Crandall, standing behind the handrail to one side of the turbolift, watched as well, volunteering no comments or further questions.

"If ye need me," Scott's distinctive burr came over the intercom from engineering, "I'm at the controls."

"Nice to know, Mr. Scott. Just keep things in their usual first-class shape."

"Aye, Captain, full power available to all systems—and a wee bit more if ye need it."

A moment later, the turbolift hissed open again, and a scowling Dr. Leonard McCoy emerged. Looking more rumpled than usual, he came to a stop at the handrail on the opposite side of the platform opening from Dr. Crandall, his eyes darting from Kirk to Spock and back before settling on the viewscreen.

"Is that the one that attacked us?" McCoy asked after a few seconds.

"No, Bones," Kirk said, still watching the screen.

"It and the other five are off the screen. This one just showed up. It *could* be from a different faction altogether."

"Let's hope so. And let's hope this one will give us a chance to talk before it starts shooting."

"I wouldn't count on it," Kirk said. "According to Mr. Spock, this one is at least as heavily armed as the others, and just as heavily shielded."

"The six are aware of the newcomer, Captain," Spock announced.

Kirk's fingers ceased their drumming as he sat up straighter. "What are they doing?"

"The first to detect it has just now made a subspace transmission apparently identical to the one transmitted to us by the first ship."

"So it probably *is* some kind of identification code or recognition signal. Is the other ship responding?"

"Negative, Captain. It is apparently unaware of the transmission."

"And of the other ships?"

"It would seem so." Spock paused, studying his instruments with seeming impassivity. "The same ship has now sent out a burst of subspace energy similar to the one transmitted by our attacker, except that it is shorter by ten milliseconds. And the six are changing course, converging on the newcomer, who is now apparently aware of at least one of them. It, too, has transmitted what appears to be an identification code. Its makeup, however, is quite different, as is the frequency on which it was transmitted."

"Any response from the six?"

"None, Captain. And now the newcomer has emitted a burst of subspace energy as well, this one of seventy-nine milliseconds duration."

"Get us closer, Mr. Woida," Kirk said abruptly, "as close as you can without getting within their sensor range."

"Yes, sir," the helmsman responded instantly, his square fingers darting across the panels before him.

The newcomer was still centered in the viewscreen,

and as Kirk watched, one of the six appeared in the upper right quadrant, then another in the lower left.

"All lasers on five of the six are readying to fire, Captain," Spock said. "Except for the ship that has been at the center of the formation, they appear to be about to launch an attack. The one ship appears to be purposely staying out of range."

"So they *are* from different factions," Kirk said, as if thinking aloud.

"Obviously," McCoy said, moving up next to the command chair. "Aren't you going to *do* something about it, Jim?"

"Something like intervene on the newcomer's side? By firing on the other six?"

"If that's the only way to help, yes!"

Kirk, his eyes still on the screen, shook his head. "Getting involved in a local war our first day on the block doesn't strike me as all that prudent, Bones. Besides, since we haven't been able to talk to either side yet, we don't even know which side, if either, we should be on."

McCoy's scowl grew deeper. "We know which side attacked us without warning, Jim!" he said, waving a hand in exasperation. "What the devil more evidence do you need?"

"There's nothing to say the other ship wouldn't have done the same."

"The newcomer's lasers are now also preparing to fire," Spock announced.

On the screen, four of the six were now in view, closing in on the newcomer.

A moment later, space was crisscrossed with beams of fire, the same brute-force fire that had washed over the shields of the *Enterprise* thirty-six hours before.

This time the results were far different. Within seconds, the shields on three of the ships, including the newcomer, had flared upward through the visible spectrum and far into the ultraviolet, then collapsed precipitously. Once the shields were down, the ships were disabled, almost destroyed, in even less time than it had taken to dispose of the shields. Their outer hulls scorched and half melted, their propulsion units dead, they floated helplessly. The remaining four, however, did not close in for the kill, nor did they make any attempt to rescue anyone on their own companion ships. Instead, the three that had launched the attack retreated, reestablishing as much of a protective formation as they could around the fourth.

"Survivors, Mr. Spock?" Kirk snapped.

"Four of the six life forms in the newcomer, Captain, but only for another forty-nine seconds. An automatic self-destruct sequence similar to the one observed in the first ship is beginning in all three disabled vessels."

Kirk's fingers tightened on the arms of the command chair. "Mr. Woida, get us in there, maximum warp! Transporter room, prepare to lock onto survivors! Security, full detail to the transporter room! Be ready for anything when and if the survivors are beamed aboard!"

Abruptly, the star pattern shifted as the *Enterprise* reached warp eight in record time. The newcomer's disabled ship swelled explosively on the screen.

Even before Kirk had completed his orders, McCoy was darting from the bridge. "After what they've been through, they'll need medical help, not a blasted security detail!" he muttered angrily, his voice loud enough for everyone on the bridge to hear.

"Transporter range coming up, Captain," Spock said. "First antimatter detonation in twenty-six seconds."

"Sublight, Mr. Woida, and shields down for transporter lock-on!"

"Shields down," Woida responded instantly, and at the same time the motion of the dense star field on the screen slowed almost to a stop.

"Transporters locking on," a voice said from the transporter room seconds later.

Then, for an agonizing ten seconds, there was total

silence on the bridge except for Spock's countdown to the seemingly inevitable explosions.

At eight seconds, a triumphant "Got 'em!" came from the transporter room.

"Maximum warp and shields up! Transporter room, don't bring them in yet. Keep them in transit until further orders."

As the disabled ships fell astern, a small nova appeared precisely on schedule, and then, seconds later, two more blossomed into brief, searing life, their deadly energies dissipating harmlessly in the space occupied seconds before by the *Enterprise*.

"Mr. Woida, back to warp factor six. Take us to extreme sensor range and hold at that distance. Track the remaining four ships as before. Mr. Spock, is the ship that originally attacked us among the survivors?"

"Negative, Captain," Spock supplied. "It was the first to be hit."

"Very well." Abruptly, Kirk stood up. "Mr. Tanaka, you have the con. If they split up, track the one they seem to be protecting. Keep me informed."

"Yes, sir." His eyes on the screen, Tanaka slid into the chair as Kirk stepped down.

"Mr. Spock," Kirk said, "let's get down to the transporter room. I'd like to see what we've got."

Uncharacteristically, Spock did not respond instantly. Instead, he remained bent over his readouts for several seconds, calling up new information. Finally, with a wordless nod to Lieutenant Jameson, the third-watch science officer, he picked up his tricorder, slipped its strap across his shoulder, and hurried to join Kirk at the turbolift.

"I would advise extreme caution in dealing with the survivors being beamed aboard, Captain," the science officer said as the turbolift door closed behind them.

"You have some new information, Spock?"

"My review of certain seemingly anomalous sensor readings confirmed initial indications that the crew compartments on all three ships survived the battle intact. All deaths came after the battle had concluded."

Kirk frowned as the door opened and the two strode into the corridor toward the transporter room. "You're positive?"

"Yes, Jim, I'm sure," he said, his voice as controlled as ever but with a trace less formality.

"And it was the same on all three ships?"

"Precisely. The only difference is that in the lone ship, four continued to survive."

"And your instruments couldn't tell you *how* the other twelve died?"

"Only that they died with remarkable suddenness. Their life readings vanished within milliseconds. Even violent death is not normally so swift."

Then they were at the transporter room. Scotty had made his way up from the engineering deck and was manning the controls. A security detail led by Lieutenant Ingrit Tomson stood facing the transporter platform, their phasers in hand. McCoy, a pair of nurses, and several orderlies with stretchers stood behind them, the doctor obviously unhappy that he and the other medical personnel were not in the front row.

"Jim," he half growled, "after what happened to their ship, these people aren't going to be any threat to anyone! And these blasted security people won't—"

"Spock, tell Dr. McCoy and everyone else here what you told me," Kirk said, moving to stand beside Scotty at the transporter controls as Spock repeated his findings.

When Spock had finished, Kirk said, "So you see, gentlemen, these are not ordinary survivors, to say the very least. We don't know what we're bringing aboard. And it would be prudent to keep in mind not only how the disabled ships deliberately exploded their entire antimatter fuel supply but how the ship that originally attacked us acted once it became apparent that it couldn't destroy us with its standard weapons. Whoever and whatever these people are, destruction—including self-destruction—seems to be a way of life with *all* of them."

McCoy, though maintaining his skeptical scowl, motioned for the nurses and orderlies to move back, away from the security detail.

"All right, Mr. Scott," Kirk said, "let's bring one of them in. Security, phasers on stun, and don't hesitate to use them."

"Number one on the way, Captain," Scott said, sliding the materialization control slowly downward. "He'll be comin' in on transporter number six, at the back."

All eyes but Spock's swiveled toward the indicated transporter unit, and a moment later the expected shimmering silhouette began to form. Spock, though the arrival registered on his peripheral vision, kept his attention focused on his tricorder.

"Whatever it is, it's flat on its back, probably unconscious," McCoy said as the shimmering took definite shape, showing a generally humanoid form lying sprawled across the transporter unit and well beyond.

"Keep back anyway, Doctor," Kirk said, "just in case."

Slowly, the shimmering faded and was replaced by the very solid body of the first of the aliens. As McCoy had said, it was unconscious. It was also humanoid, probably male, very stocky and muscular, hairless, and as pale as something that had lived its entire life in darkness. Barely five feet from boot to crown, it was dressed in a drab, utilitarian coverall with short sleeves and half a dozen bulky pockets. There was no sign of anything resembling a weapon. Blood as red as any human's oozed from a cut on the hairless scalp.

McCoy started forward, but Tomson blocked him. "Reems, Creighton, check for weapons," she snapped, and two of the security detail darted forward, one holstering his weapon and performing the search while the other stood close over the alien, her phaser pointed directly at the sprawled form.

"This is insane, Jim!" McCoy protested. "He obviously needs medical attention!"

"No weapons, sir," the searcher reported tersely, standing and retrieving his phaser from its holster.

"All right, Bones, you can have him. But Security stays with him, too. Lieutenant Tomson, send one guard with Dr. McCoy. And don't hesitate to stun the alien at the first sign of any sudden move. Understood?"

"Understood, sir," she said, nodding at the man who had conducted the search. "Stay with him, Mr. Reems. You heard the captain."

"Yes, sir."

Shaking his head in renewed exasperation, McCoy hurried forward, motioning one of the nurses, an olive-skinned brunette named Garcia, to follow. As he ran the medical tricorder over the alien's body, his scowl faded slightly. "Hard to tell without knowing what's normal for these people, but his injuries *appear* to be minor. And with red blood and only one heart, he's probably more human than some of *us*."

Standing up, McCoy motioned for two of the orderlies to get the alien on a stretcher. One of the two glanced questioningly toward Kirk as he helped shift the body, and when Kirk nodded, the orderly fastened the stretcher's security straps firmly across chest and legs. McCoy only shook his head again, saying nothing but making his impatience plain.

With the alien fully restrained, the two orderlies lifted the stretcher easily, crossed the transporter platform and walked down the steps. Nurse Garcia stayed close to the stretcher on one side while Ensign Reems, the security man, stayed slightly to the rear on the other side. The rest of the security detail and McCoy's people parted to give them a clear path to the door to the corridor. Spock, his attention still on the tricorder, kept the instrument centered on the alien.

"Well, Jim, what about the next one?" McCoy prompted irritably.

"As soon as—" Kirk began, but he was cut off by an abrupt, wheezing sound from the stretcher.

The two orderlies came to a sudden stop, and Reems took a single step to one side, keeping his phaser trained directly on the alien. Nurse Garcia put a hand lightly on the alien's arm and looked down at him, hoping the touch and her expression would appear more reassuring than threatening.

For several seconds, the only sound was that of the alien breathing, now only a faint rasping, not the loud wheeze of the initial intake of breath. He was the focus of all eyes in the transporter room. Even Spock glanced up briefly from his tricorder.

Then the alien's eyes opened, suddenly, as if the lids were shutters of a pair of cameras. For the first fraction of a second, the eyes, an almost fluorescent green, stared straight up, unseeing, their huge pupils shrinking rapidly, but then, as they focussed on Garcia's dark features and glossy black hair, they widened in what, in a human, would have been sheer terror.

For another instant, the eyes darted in all directions, flickering across everyone in the room. The slitlike mouth opened a fraction of an inch, just enough to reveal almost human-looking teeth, and then it and the eyes clamped tightly shut, and the entire body stiffened so abruptly it shook the stretcher.

Instinctively, Garcia reached out again, and this time her hand came to rest on the alien's chest. "It's all right," she said softly, but the alien's body seemed sent into convulsions by her action. The stretcher was almost wrenched from the orderlies' hands.

Pulling back, Garcia turned to cast a helpless look at Dr. McCoy. In the same instant, the alien's convulsive motions stopped, and he became not just motionless but stiff, as if every muscle in his body was tensed and fighting every other muscle. Any tighter, and bone and tendon would begin to snap. The only sound, though, was the grinding of the alien's teeth and a brief sigh of relief from one of the orderlies as they recovered their grip on the stretcher and moved through the door to the corridor.

"I *told* you—" McCoy began, but the rest of his protest was cut off by an urgently barked order from Spock.

"Drop the stretcher! Everyone move back, *immediately!*"

Chapter Seven

STARTLED BY THE INTENSITY in the Vulcan's normally impassive voice, the orderlies responded instantly, though their training forced them to take a split second to lower the stretcher to the corridor floor rather than dropping it.

A moment later, as they and Ensign Reems were scrambling back into the transporter room, the corridor was filled with a blinding, almost silent flash and a wave of heat that scorched the walls.

Garcia, whose obvious concern for the alien had caused her to react more slowly than the orderlies, was still in the door, turning to follow them, when the flash came. Soundlessly, she completed the turn, but her right hand and arm, which had been extended into the corridor, were caught in the brief inferno.

As the glare faded and a hubbub of voices erupted around her, she stood motionless just inside the transporter room door. But then, as her effort to move the arm brought the momentarily deadened nerves back to screaming life, she gasped. Suddenly she was bathed in the cold sweat of shock, and the room began a dizzying whirl that ended only when she crumpled, unconscious, to the floor.

Dr. McCoy, seeing the arm discoloring and blistering even as he watched, spun on a second pair of orderlies. "Get her down to surgery, *now!*"

When the orderlies hesitated even a fraction of a second as they glanced toward the scorched corridor through which they would have to pass, McCoy snatched the stretcher from them and slammed it to the floor next to Garcia. Sliding his hands under her, he smoothly, swiftly slid her onto it. By that time, the orderlies had recovered, and they quickly snatched up the stretcher and raced into the corridor, past the virtually vaporized remains of the alien. With a wordless glance toward Kirk, McCoy followed at a run.

"Obviously you saw it coming, Mr. Spock," Kirk said as he glanced at Spock's tricorder, "but do you have any suggestions for keeping it from happening again if we bring the others in?"

"Only to keep them unconscious, Captain, so they are unable to activate the devices. Then we can attempt to locate and disarm those devices."

"You know what happened, then?"

"I know only that there was a short pulse of electromagnetic energy, followed by a power buildup within a device buried somewhere in the being's body. In some ways, it was similar to the power buildup that precedes the firing of their ships' lasers."

"At least they're consistent," Kirk said, shaking his head grimly.

Minutes later, the next alien was brought in from the transporter matrix. He was as unconscious as the first, but even so, he was immediately subjected to a precautionary phaser burst that sent him even deeper into oblivion. Like the first, he was stocky and hairless and, except for the large-pupiled green eyes, could have passed for an odd-looking human.

"Monitor his vitals at all times," Kirk cautioned as the alien was placed on another stretcher. "And trust what the tricorder says, not how the alien looks or acts. If your readings give the slightest indication that he's waking up, stun him again. Now get him down to the medical section fast, and find out how to keep him from vaporizing himself—and us!"

The three-dimensional, computer-generated image on the diagnostic screen showed that the alien was indeed as close to human as the earlier tricorder scannings had indicated. The heart was oddly bell-shaped, and the rib cage extended over much of the solidly muscled abdomen, but there were no really fundamental anatomical differences. The blood, iron-based, was similar to human blood but not similar enough to allow transfusions. Body temperature was a cool ninety-one degrees, giving his skin an oddly snakelike feel which seemed to match his total hairlessness and slitlike mouth.

The major difference was not anatomical but, as expected, artificial. Buried deep in the chest cavity, directly beneath the heart, was a small but powerful omnidirectional laserlike device. Embedded in the center of the device was an almost invisible kernel that Spock's science tricorder identified as a radio receiver which, when activated, would trigger the surrounding device. Even with the knowledge the instruments gave of the alien's anatomy and metabolism, however, it would be virtually impossible to surgically remove the device, even without having to worry about how to keep from setting it off. Disabling it remotely without inadvertently triggering it seemed equally difficult.

In the end, however, Dr. Rajanih, in charge of the ship's dental unit, discovered what everyone else had overlooked. What had appeared at first to be one of a dozen similar fillings in the alien's teeth turned out instead to be a seed-sized transmitter operated in much the same way that long-ago Terran spies had operated the cyanide capsules that a few of the more fanatical had had installed in their teeth. Simply grinding the teeth in a particular way would break the seal over the transmitter, and the alien's saliva, even more acidic than a human's, would act as an electrolyte, instantly activating the minuscule battery that powered the transmitter, until then totally inert and undetectable. Within less than a second after the saliva touched the almost microscopic battery plates, the transmitter would receive a short spurt of power, enabling it to send out a short-range microwave pulse that triggered the receiver embedded beneath the alien's heart.

Once the transmitter had been removed from the tooth and transported to another part of the ship, well shielded from the receiver, the nature of the pulse it transmitted was analyzed. With that knowledge, then, the receiver itself could be safely disabled so the device couldn't be triggered intentionally by more distant but more powerful transmitters or accidentally by any of the countless forms of energy that permeated virtually every cubic centimeter of the *Enterprise* and every other functional starship.

Once the living but still unconscious alien had been successfully disarmed, Kirk, on his way back to the transporter room, paused to glance into surgery. McCoy, he saw, was putting the finishing touches on Garcia's hand and arm.

"Will she be all right, Bones?" he asked as McCoy, pulling in a deep, relieved breath, extracted his hands from the surgical machinery, removed the vision helmet and stepped back.

"It looks good so far," he said. Pausing, he looked back at the operating table and the machine—largely an enclosed cluster of micro-manipulators and optics—that was only now being removed from the arm. "You know, Jim, I make a big deal now and then out of being just a country doctor who doesn't trust every new gadget that comes down the pike. But every now and then, I have to admit that I'm damned glad I've got a few of them."

"They're no better than the person who operates them, Bones," Kirk said quietly. "That was good work, as usual."

A faint, crooked smile worked its way onto McCoy's still-haggard features. "Thanks, Jim. And thanks for not saying I told you so. You and the green-blooded goblin both."

"There are times when such things are neither appropriate nor logical, Bones, and this was one of those times. Meanwhile, if you're interested, we've discovered how to defang our friends."

"Those walking disintegrators, you mean?" McCoy's eyebrows twitched upward inquiringly, and some of the tiredness seemed to fade from his face.

"Exactly. We brought a second one back, and now that we've defused him, we're going to haul in the other two." As they made their way back to the transporter room, Kirk filled McCoy in on the last hour.

The doctor only shook his head. "What kind of people would *do* something like that?" he asked incredulously when Kirk finished.

"People who are desperate or fanatical or both," Kirk said. Then he added quietly, "Humans have been doing it for millennia in one form or another. Don't forget where the term 'kamikaze' originated."

McCoy sighed. "I know, Jim. Every now and then I try to forget that that kind of insanity was a part of our history, but it always comes back. And it's always just as hard to understand."

"Hard to accept, perhaps, Bones, but not always that hard to understand," Kirk said. And then he continued before McCoy could protest, "Now let's see if we can find out what drove *these* people to such measures. Now that we know how to keep them alive long enough to ask them some questions, maybe we've even got a chance of getting some answers."

It was fifteen hours and a fitful sleep later when Kirk, Spock, McCoy, Nurse Chapel, Rajanih, and Dr. Crandall, along with Tomson, Reems, and Creighton from security, stood in the largest diagnostic room of the medical section waiting for the first of the three surviving aliens to awaken. Cushioned straps held him firmly to the similarly cushioned table, the upper half of which had been tilted upward so that the alien was half upright, facing his captors. A universal translator, linked directly to the main computer, would pick up every sound the alien made as well as monitor and map his neuronic activity. Under these conditions, with the translator augmented by the full capacity of the computer, communication would be possible in a matter of minutes.

Finally, after nearly ten minutes of silence except for the nervous shifting of Crandall's feet, the instruments monitoring the alien's condition indicated he was fully awake.

Yet he did not move.

"Playing possum, do you think, Bones?" Kirk asked softly.

His answer came not from McCoy but from the alien. At the sound of Kirk's voice, the alien stiffened, but his eyes did not open. Instead, after sucking in a single rasping breath, he clamped his teeth together, grinding them forcefully.

When the expected sudden death did not come, he ground his teeth together even more violently, until the grating sound was audible to everyone in the room.

"When he finally decides to open his eyes, Dr. Rajanih, show him what you took from his tooth," Kirk said, still purposely keeping his voice as calm and unthreatening as he could.

For nearly half a minute in all, the grinding continued, the alien's face becoming more contorted with each second, his entire body stiffening as every muscle tensed. There was, however, none of the convulsive jerking that the first alien had exhibited.

Suddenly, as if some mental switch had finally been turned off, the grinding stopped, and the alien seemed to collapse, every muscle going limp.

Then, slowly, the eyes still closed, one arm moved, coming to an abrupt stop as it pressed against the cushioned restraining strap. Then the other arm moved similarly, and finally the legs, but the motions remained slow and fluid and deliberate. Even so, after a few seconds it became apparent from the faint creaking sounds made by the straps that he was exerting a startling amount of pressure.

"What about the light level, Bones?" Kirk asked, frowning abruptly as he turned to McCoy. "We should have thought of it before, but their large pupils and extreme paleness probably mean they're accustomed to lower levels of light than we are."

"You don't worry about lighting when you're trying to keep your patient from exploding in your face!" McCoy flared, but a moment later he subsided.

"You're right, Jim," he said, a touch of apology in his voice. "Nurse Chapel, bring it down fifty percent. And we should probably lower the temperature, too. Remember that their body temperature is almost eight degrees below ours."

"Good idea," Kirk said. "Tell environment to lower the temperature—how much, Bones? Eight degrees?"

McCoy shook his head. "Five or six is enough for a start."

With the light level reduced, Chapel spoke into the nurse's station intercom, passing on the instructions.

The temperature dropped, though not as quickly as the light level had. Dr. Crandall, who was wearing a short-sleeved blue tunic, folded his arms, chafing his hands along his upper arms.

Finally, the alien's limbs relaxed once again, his arms falling back against the surface of the table. For more than a minute, then, the only motion was that of his chest as it moved in a rapid, shallow breathing pattern.

Then, at last, the eyes opened, but just a slit. The motion would have been missed entirely had everyone not been watching so closely. Underneath the lids, the eyes moved surreptitiously from side to side. Other than that, the alien was now totally motionless.

"The implant, Dr. Rajanih," Kirk prompted.

Rajanih, who had been watching the alien raptly, cast a quick, apologetic glance toward Kirk as he raised the small transparent container that held the device. Shaking it gently, he moved closer to the alien and held it directly in front of his slitted eyes.

For another long moment, the alien was totally motionless, including his eyes. Even his breathing once again halted, and his heartbeat, after a momentary spurt, slowed as well.

McCoy, startled by the suddenly reduced heart rate, started to approach the alien but stopped after only a couple of steps. "If we missed something else," he said, shaking his head, "some kind of organic backup system that allows him to simply stop his heart, it's too late to do anything about it now."

"I would say he simply has excellent mental discipline," Rajanih said. "Many races have similar abilities."

Spock nodded his agreement. "If he is determined to die and is able to induce death through mental control of normally automatic functions such as heartbeat, there is little we can do."

"Except keep him unconscious while we try to figure out what we *can* do," Kirk said, nodding to the security team. "Be ready if I give the word."

But even as Kirk spoke, the heart rate leveled off. A moment later, the alien's eyes opened, not as widely as those of the first alien, but in what looked like a partial squint, as if the light were still slightly too bright for comfort. They were fastened on the implant in Rajanih's hand, and as the alien looked at it, his almost nonexistent lips parted slightly, and his jaw and cheek moved in a very humanlike pattern that indicated he was probing the formerly deadly tooth with his tongue.

Apparently feeling the smooth solidity that had replaced the transmitter and its comparatively uneven and fragile seal, the alien abandoned the probing and began looking at his watchers more directly, his eyes meeting and briefly holding first Rajanih's, then Kirk's, then those of each of the others who stood watching him. The alien's eyes held not so much a challenge as an acknowledgment of his situation, yet by no means a surrender. There was nothing submissive in those eyes.

"Lower the light another twenty percent, Bones," Kirk said quietly, and McCoy complied.

As the light lowered, the alien's lids raised until, when another five percent of the light was removed, his eyes were fully open.

They were also fastened on Kirk, as if the alien had deduced that he was the one in charge simply from the fact that when he had spoken, someone else had immediately responded.

"Now if we can just get him to talk, at least enough to give the computer a start on figuring out his language," McCoy said.

"Based on his behavior so far," Kirk said, "that doesn't seem all that likely. And even if we do get his language sorted out, I suspect we will get little more than his equivalent of name, rank, and serial number, if that much."

And they didn't. After nearly half an hour of trying, during which everyone, even Dr. Crandall, took turns trying to elicit some speech from the alien, he remained silent. He was obviously listening very closely, but, equally obviously, he had no intention of making a single sound.

Nor did they do any better when, over the next two hours, they allowed the other two aliens, held in separate facilities, to awaken. Both went through variations on the same routine as they awakened, both attempting to activate the missing transmitter and both feigning unconsciousness as soon as they realized death was not forthcoming. One of them, according to the monitors, actually did lose consciousness for a brief period, growing even paler as he slumped against the padded straps, while the other, the tallest of the three by inches, broke into uncontrollable convulsions even more violent than those of the first one beamed aboard. Briefly, a series of sounds, more like keening wails than screams or shouts, poured from the taller one's barely opened mouth, but even the most complete computer analysis of the sounds couldn't extract any meaning or even any patterns, and once the outburst was over he remained utterly, rigidly silent.

Finally, after a second twenty-minute session with the first of the three aliens, Kirk called a halt to the increasingly frustrating operation and turned to Dr. McCoy. "Now that they're stable—they are stable, aren't they, Bones?"

"They seem to be, yes, but I can't guarantee they don't still have a few surprises for us."

"Understood. That will have to be good enough." Kirk turned to Lieutenant Tomson of security. "Lieutenant, release the straps on this one. Let's see what he does."

While Creighton and Reems held their phasers at the ready, Tomson released the straps, the alien's eyes following her every motion. For a few seconds after the straps retracted invisibly into the surface of the table, the alien remained motionless. Then, moving tentatively, he sat up straighter and turned and slid off the table, holding onto its edge as his booted feet settled on the floor. Releasing the table, he swayed unsteadily, as if he couldn't quite keep his balance. All the while, though, his eyes moved about the group, pausing on the pair of phasers in the guards' hands, obviously assessing them as weapons.

"Escort him to one of our detention cells," Kirk said. "Then take the other two and put them in the same cell. Perhaps, with none of us around, they'll talk to each other."

"Yes, sir," Tomson replied. "Creighton," she said, motioning the ensign forward. He reached out and took the alien's arm, firmly but not harshly.

The alien didn't resist. His eyes went briefly to the hand on his arm, and, when Creighton urged him forward, he moved.

Until they drew abreast of Captain Kirk.

Without warning, without even a premonitory flicker of his eyes, the alien tore loose from

Creighton's grip and threw himself at Kirk, who barely had time to half raise his arms before the alien had slammed into his shoulder, spinning him around. A fraction of a second later, the alien's short but powerful arm was reaching up and around Kirk's neck from behind, bringing the forearm up under Kirk's chin with a force that in another second would snap his neck.

Chapter Eight

IT WAS ONLY the phasers of the two security guards that saved Kirk, both beams catching the alien squarely. One, however, also caught Kirk in its periphery, sending him reeling to the edge of unconsciousness himself. An instant later, Tomson was pulling the now limp form of the alien from Kirk while McCoy and Spock both gripped Kirk's arms to support him until he could steady himself.

"Jim! Are you all right?" McCoy's gravelly voice was tense in Kirk's ear.

After a second, Kirk nodded. "A little shaky from the phaser, but that's all. Which is, as they say, vastly preferable to the alternative," he went on, still a little unsteady on his feet as he turned to the two security guards. "Thank you, Lieutenant Tomson, Ensign Reems, for your prompt action.

Kirk looked at the alien then, its stocky body now slumped to the floor. "Get this one to the detention cell," he said, pausing a second to blink away yet another brief wave of dizziness from the phaser. "Then put one of the others—just one, the taller one, not both—in with him. We'll watch and listen and hope something develops. Use your largest cell, and see what can be done about making it look less like a cell before they wake up again."

Tomson nodded, and, with Creighton and Reems, picked the alien up and carried him out.

"One thing for sure," McCoy said as the door slid

shut behind the security guards and the alien, "they aren't stupid. That one's been listening even if he can't understand the language, and he's already figured out who the boss is."

Kirk nodded ruefully. "So he'd know who to try to kill first."

"You have to start somewhere," Crandall offered, "and it *was* a form of communication."

At first, Kirk took the words to be Crandall's first modest attempt at humor in all the weeks since he had boarded the *Enterprise*, but a look at the man's deadly earnest expression quickly persuaded him otherwise.

By the time the two aliens were installed in their barless detention cell, it resembled a small stateroom more than a cell. Kirk doubted that the comparatively pleasant surroundings would impress the aliens to any noticeable extent, but, as he had told the chief of security who had supervised the hasty redecoration of the cell, it couldn't hurt.

The taller alien was the first to awaken from his phaser-induced unconsciousness, and he began once again to tremble even before he opened his eyes. But then, when his eyes twitched open and he saw his companion stretched out on a second narrow cot on the opposite side of the disguised cell, the trembling stopped abruptly, and he lay rigidly still for several seconds, as if trying to gain full control of himself.

Briefly, then, he poked at his deactivated tooth, first with his tongue and then, more forcefully, with his finger. Even as he checked his own tooth, however, he moved to the other cot and just as quickly checked his companion's tooth. When he saw that its implant, too, had been removed, he slumped momentarily but then straightened himself, moved stiffly back to his own cot, and sat down to wait.

After another minute, as if acting on an afterthought, he stood and tried the door and made his way slowly around the tiny room, closely inspecting the walls, then peering up at the translucent ceiling through which the room's only light was provided. Finally, apparently satisfied there was nothing else he could do, he sat down once again to wait.

Five minutes later, the other alien awakened. Like the first, he checked his tooth almost immediately.

And that was the last thing either of them did for more than twelve hours. When food, which McCoy's metabolic analysis of the aliens had enabled the computerized galley to synthesize, was brought in, they both ignored it.

Watching them on a screen in the wardroom, Kirk did not seem surprised. "If they can't kill themselves any other way, they'll starve themselves to death," he said with a sigh to Dr. McCoy, who was watching with him. "They'd probably try to strangle each other except they know we'd stop them. What about intravenous? Can you whip up something that will keep them going in spite of themselves?"

McCoy nodded. "Probably, but I don't think it's going to get us anywhere. These are very stubborn people, Jim, even more stubborn than your average starship commander."

"Have some prepared anyway," Kirk said. Then he added, with a quick grin, "And thanks for the encouragement. If you'd said they were more stubborn than your average ship's doctor, I might've given up hope altogether."

For a long time, then, Kirk sat alone watching the two, almost as silent and motionless as the aliens themselves. He had hoped that, left alone with each other, they would talk enough for the combined capabilities of the universal translator and the computer to come up with a first pass at their language, enough for at least the beginnings of communication, but that obviously was not going to happen. Even the translators, with their ability to analyze a subject's neuronic activity, required *some* spoken words to work with, some sounds to match with the neuronic patterns. These beings were apparently not only fanatically determined to kill themselves while doing the most possible damage to their supposed enemy in the process. They were also fanatically stoic and patient once they had recovered from the initial shock of learning they couldn't kill themselves. They were simply determined to have no meaningful contact with the enemy. They were, he realized more forcefully with each passing minute, the ultimate embodiment of the "name, rank, and serial number" philosophy. As long as they thought the *Enterprise* was the enemy—

Abruptly, he stood up. "Lieutenant Tomson," he said, speaking into the wardroom intercom, "Kirk here. Bring three guards and meet me ASAP at the aliens' cells. We're going to give them a tour of the *Enterprise*."

Restrained only by padded wrist manacles that fastened the three together and by the prominently displayed phasers of the security team, the aliens were escorted first to the engineering deck. From the moment the three emerged suspiciously from their cells, Kirk kept up a running commentary on everything they passed through or by. During the first moments of the tour, as the seemingly endless corridors they were led through began to give them some small appreciation of the true vastness of the *Enterprise*, they allowed some emotion to show on their faces, but by the time they reached the turbolift, their faces were once again the expressionless blanks they had maintained for the past dozen hours in their cells.

As they were urged from the turbolift on the main engineering deck, the group was met by Chief Engineer Scott, who, after an initial skeptical glance at Kirk, took the three on basically the same tour that his assistant had taken Crandall on during his first days on board. Predictably, they remained stone-faced throughout, barely deigning even to turn their eyes in the direction of the control consoles, the repair shops, or even the impulse power units, even though Kirk was positive that all three were meticulously recording each and every detail somewhere inside their hairless skulls.

Only once did they lose some small measure of their composure, and that was when, in the remote-scanning monitor room, they were suddenly confronted with the brilliantly vivid image of the dilithium-focused, antimatter heart of the *Enterprise*. Even then, no sound came from their almost lipless mouths. Only their eyes widened, and the tallest of the three twitched backward involuntarily from the inferno on the huge screen. Within another second, however, the impassivity was restored to their features, and it was as if the mind-boggling release of power they were observing was nothing more than an oversized candle flame.

An hour later, with no further cracks having appeared even momentarily in their facade of indifference, the three were escorted onto the bridge. As it had everywhere the aliens were taken, the overall lighting had been reduced to a level McCoy had estimated would be tolerable to them.

Even though the three appeared as impassive as ever, two of them half stumbled when the security detail urged them down the steps and closer to the main viewscreen, where the computer-generated images of the stars were every bit as real and probably twice as vivid as anything the aliens had ever seen, even at sublight. The four alien craft, still being tracked, were nonluminous dots, one in each quadrant of the screen.

"Mr. Spock," Kirk said, "is our little show-and-tell ready to roll?"

"Of course, Captain."

"Very well. Let's get the show on the road."

With only the slightest arch of his eyebrow at Kirk's choice of words, Spock turned back to the science station. "Computer," he said, "begin."

Immediately, the real-time image on the viewscreen was replaced by another, this one also computer-generated but totally different from the star field it replaced.

The new image was a view of the interior of the bridge itself, including all bridge personnel and the aliens themselves, standing exactly where they were actually standing, moving as they moved.

After a few seconds, the viewpoint from which the image was seen began to shift, rising from a point above the viewscreen toward the upper bulkhead. But it didn't stop there. Slowly, it continued to rise until it had passed through the bulkhead, itself appearing as if part of a blueprint transparency, leaving the interior of the bridge still visible beyond it. The structural members and the miles of cables running between the multiple layers of the bulkhead directly above the bridge were visible and yet did not obscure the bridge itself and the people inside.

And still the viewpoint continued to rise, until finally the entire hundred-and-thirty-meter saucer that was the primary hull was included on the screen, the transparent "cutaway" area above the bridge now only a tiny circle in the center, the people inside little more than dots.

Then, as the viewpoint continued to rise even higher above the *Enterprise*, the transparent cutaway section opaqued, becoming just another segment of the gleaming metal of the hull. After another full minute, the entire ship, including primary and secondary hulls and the massive warp-drive units, was on the screen. For yet another minute, the viewpoint lingered there, giving the aliens sufficient time to fully appreciate the size of the vessel, and for a moment Kirk wondered if the computer were going to superimpose an image of one of the relatively tiny alien vessels for comparison.

But Spock and the computer had come up with nothing that simple.

Again, the viewpoint began to move, this time swooping gracefully down toward a spot on the primary hull immediately above the bridge. Instead of continuing through the bulkhead and into the bridge, however, it slowed and stopped and oriented itself to look forward, directly over the hull, the upper skin of which remained massively visible across the bottom of the screen.

That was when what Kirk remembered as real images began to appear, selected excerpts from the computer's records of what had happened to the *Enterprise* since it had first appeared in this sector of space. One after another, the scenes were seamlessly woven together and superimposed above the ever-present image of the hull. The only episode of interest that was omitted was the brief and frustrating investigation of the planet that had, far below its radiation-soaked surface, given readings indicating both a functional antimatter power source and a form of life that not even Spock had been able to classify.

The aliens remained impassive, even at the repeated scenes of planetwide destruction, but when the image of the first ship appeared, they stiffened. And when the ship attacked, its lasers slicing through the intervening space, they could not keep from flinching, nor could they keep their faces totally expressionless as the laser beams flared harmlessly but spectacularly against the *Enterprise*'s shields, leaving the ship itself untouched.

And so it went, until the re-creation of those few deadly seconds when the three ships had been destroyed. Then, as the two ships in the attacking group were shown struck and disabled, the three aliens for the first time turned their eyes briefly toward each other. They were, Kirk was sure, grimly congratulating each other on having taken two of the enemy with them.

Then, as the illusory *Enterprise* on the screen shot forward at warp eight, the aliens turned abruptly back to the screen, unable any longer to maintain their pretended indifference. Watching closely now, they saw the *Enterprise* drop out of warp drive even more quickly than their own ships were capable of doing.

As the *Enterprise* came almost to a standstill only

kilometers from the alien ship, a ghostly beam, obviously not a laser, stabbed out from the *Enterprise,* touching and penetrating the alien vessel. At the same time, the viewpoint of the image darted along the beam, halting a bare hundred meters outside the scorched and fused surface of the alien vessel. In another second, the massive thickness of the vessel's hull faded, just as that of the *Enterprise* had done at the start of the display. Here, though, there were no blueprintlike details, only an indistinct grayness, in the center of which appeared the tiny crew compartment, the only internal structure for which the sensors had determined a true size and shape in the seconds the *Enterprise* had been within detailed scanning range. Inside one of the crew compartments, indistinct images of four aliens appeared, floating unconscious in their now gravitationless environment. In another compartment, its walls scorched, were the sparse remains of the other two.

For several seconds, then, the ghostly beam—apparently the computer's imagined representation of the transporter beams—rested on both compartments. Finally, the beam shrank and focused on the four aliens who remained alive, its illusory substance splitting into four beams, each solidifying around one of the surviving aliens and, a moment later, magically lifting them out of the ship to hang in empty space, seemingly protected only by the beams themselves.

As quickly as it had in reality, the *Enterprise* shot away, rainbowing into warp drive in seconds, taking the aliens with it. Behind it, the three ships blossomed once again into miniature novas.

Finally, with the *Enterprise* tracking the four surviving ships, the computer's representations of the rescued aliens were shown being drawn in toward the *Enterprise,* making the imaginary transporter beams look even more like visible manifestations of tractor beams than they had before.

From that point on, the screen showed the aliens the computer's record of precisely what had happened to them once they were on board—how their comrade had destroyed himself and nearly destroyed Nurse Garcia's arm, how the remaining three had been returned one at a time and kept unconscious while they were examined, and, finally, how the transmitters had been removed from their teeth. The show ended when the first of the three was allowed to awaken.

"Very impressive," Kirk said when the last image vanished and was replaced by a real-time view of the super-dense star field around them, including the four dots that were the remaining alien ships.

Looking at the aliens once again, Kirk was surprised to see that something bearing a suspicious resemblance to a tear was emerging from the eyes of the one on the end. *More and more human,* he thought. *And less and less the total automatons they appear to be forcing themselves to be.*

A moment later, as if to confirm Kirk's speculation, the alien who seemed to be crying suddenly spun about to face the other two as well as he could with the manacles still attaching his right hand to the left of the one next to him.

And he spoke, the first intentional sounds uttered by any of the three since they had been beamed on board.

The voice was harsh and keening but with a singsong quality that reminded Kirk of the tonal inflections of some Terran Oriental tongues. The alien in the middle, the tallest of the three and the one who had come closest to losing control when he had first been awakened, barked a single syllable and brought his right hand up in an obvious gesture for silence, though it was robbed of some of its effectiveness by the manacle that linked the hand to that of his comrade on his right.

In any event, the first alien did not stop talking, and after a few seconds he began gesturing with his free hand, waving it in the direction of the viewscreen and then in all directions, as if trying to include the entire *Enterprise* in his gesture. In response, the middle alien, perhaps the senior of the three, perhaps trying to make up for what he considered his own earlier lapse of control, repeated the single syllable he had uttered before, adding a brief string of harsh, staccato sounds.

The third alien then spoke up for the first time, pointing toward Dr. McCoy, who stood not far from Spock near the science station.

Not wanting anything to interrupt the sudden flow of words, Kirk gestured to the security team, motioning for them to lower their phasers and stand back. As they complied, the first alien caught the motion and gestured wildly in the direction of the security team, then erupted with a new torrent of words.

The one in the center, however, would still have nothing to do with it. With a final harsh repeat of the one syllable he had already used, he clamped his mouth shut and turned his face away.

"Sir," Tomson said quietly, almost in Kirk's ear, "Mr. Spock would like a word."

Looking around quickly, Kirk saw Spock motioning subtly to him. Glancing briefly at the aliens, Kirk stepped back and made his way past the command chair and up the steps to the science station.

"Yes, Mr. Spock?"

"I believe the computer will be able to provide us with a rudimentary translation capability very shortly," Spock said, keeping his voice low in order not to risk interrupting the aliens' sudden talkativeness. "Ordinarily a totally unknown language would require a much more extensive data base than we are receiving verbally, but it appears that much of the needed data has already been acquired by means of the subspace burst this ship initiated. In addition, because those bursts appear to have been primarily descriptions of two of the other ships, and because images of those ships were included in the information in the bursts, the computer has been able to establish additional relationships and cross-references."

"Excellent. But how soon is shortly?"

"You should be able to exchange very basic information already, Captain."

Kirk turned back to the aliens. The tallest one was still rigidly silent, and the other two had apparently given up arguing with him. And one of them, the one whose tears Kirk had noticed only minutes before, was now looking directly at Kirk. But it was also the same one, Kirk realized with a touch of uneasiness, who had tried to break his neck earlier, when he had decided Kirk was the one in charge and therefore the one to kill.

Chapter Nine

KIRK KNEW IT could be sheer folly to assign Terran human emotions to expressions appearing on the faces of totally unknown non-Terran humanoids, no matter how closely those expressions appeared to match corresponding human expressions. Even so, the expressions existed and had to be taken into consideration. And the seeming similarities so far noted—the tears, the momentary panic upon first awakening in totally alien surroundings, the stoic passivity broken briefly when confronted by objects or images they couldn't quite control their reactions to—did appear to outweigh the differences.

And now the face of the one looking directly at Kirk held neither the rigid passivity of the long hours in the cell nor any indication of the hatred that had briefly twisted his features during the attack. The eyes, more deeply recessed than most humans', were still moist from the apparent tears of a minute before. The jaw, rounded but solid, no longer appeared thrust belligerently forward but, because of the slightly lowered head, seemed almost to recede. The entire body, while not slumping in defeat, stood more loosely, its posture somehow softer, conveying both defiance and something else, perhaps a form of apology.

"We are not your enemies," Kirk spoke slowly into the translator, deliberately holding it up in full view and looking directly at the aliens.

For a moment, there was silence as the computer

made the billions of decisions necessary to attempt a translation at this uncertain point. Finally, a string of sounds emerged, faithful imitations of the aliens' voices, at least to Kirk's ear.

The reaction was instantaneous.

The tallest alien, the one who had refused most recently to talk to the other two, released a truncated version of the same keening wail he had made when first awakened. For a moment it looked as if he were about to fall, and the other two had to support him, one on each arm. He recovered quickly, however, and harshly repeated the single syllable that was the only intentional sound he had so far uttered.

After another pause, the computer, simulating a generic human male voice, translated. "Be silent."

Ignoring McCoy's muttered "*I* could have told you *that,* Jim," Kirk spoke again into the translator.

"You do not need to be silent or try to keep any secrets from us. We are *not* your enemies."

Obediently but still slowly, the computer translated, and for a moment it looked as if the tallest alien were trying to locate the precise source of the voice and hurl himself at it.

Ignoring the tallest alien's protests, the one who had tried to strangle Kirk responded. More quickly this time, the computer supplied a translation, highlighting every third word or so with a faint tone, indicating that those words were, in effect, still only educated guesses.

"What you have shown us does prove that you are not our enemy," the alien began, but then the other broke in harshly.

"It does not matter that he is not *the* enemy," the computer translated. "The fact that our speech is known to *anyone* could lead to our destruction!"

"Who is this enemy you speak of?" Kirk asked when the computer fell silent. "Were those his ships that first attacked our own ship and then yours?"

"Did you think they were our friends?" the tallest one sneered, apparently having given up his attempt to maintain silence. "They are no one's friend! They have already destroyed a thousand worlds and will continue as long as worlds exist to destroy."

Half turning toward Spock, Kirk briefly lowered the translator. "Bring back the images of the planets we've visited so far," he said quietly.

Spock, nodding almost imperceptibly, leaned closer into the science station. Speaking barely above a whisper, he addressed the computer, then looked toward the viewscreen as the images began.

As the first of the fused planetary surfaces appeared on the screen, Kirk spoke again into the translator. "Are these some of the worlds your enemy has destroyed?"

The aliens watched in silence as a dozen incinerated worlds flowed across the screen. Then the tallest one spoke. "These are the ones you displayed for us before. I do not know that they are the worlds I personally have seen, but they bear the unmistakable mark of the Destroyers."

For a moment, Kirk thought of trying to explain that, not only had these worlds been destroyed tens of thousands of years ago, but much of the destruction was simply beyond the capability of the ships of either of the warring groups. That, however, could easily lead their guests to conclude that more advanced ships—such as the *Enterprise*—were responsible.

"How many such worlds are there?" he asked instead.

"No one can know," the alien replied. "We know of none in this part of space that have *not* been visited by the Destroyers."

"Then your world is not nearby?"

The question brought total silence from all three aliens, not just the tallest one.

"I apologize," Kirk said quickly. "I realize that you do not dare reveal any information about the location of your world for fear that it might enable your enemy to find you."

"That is correct," the shortest one said, and then

added in what could have been an apologetic manner. "We believe you when you say you are not our enemy, but belief is not enough in a matter as vital as this."

"I understand," Kirk said. "The location of your world is not important to us. But can you tell us what you call yourself?"

"We are the Hoshan," the computer translated the reply, indicating by an accompanying tone that the word "Hoshan" was, as Kirk had expected, the computer's humanized version of the actual sounds made by the alien. It would do the same in the other direction when it had to translate "human" or "vulcan" or any proper name into the Hoshan language.

"And yourselves? Your own personal names?"

When the Hoshan glanced quickly at each other, saying nothing, Kirk went on, "My name is James Kirk. As you guessed earlier, I am in command of this vessel. And this," he added, gesturing toward Spock, "is Mr. Spock, my second in command." Slowly, he continued around the bridge, giving the names of everyone there.

Finally, the tallest of the Hoshan spoke. "Are we to be released, James Kirk?" he asked, holding up his still manacled wrists.

Kirk glanced at the security team and their drawn phasers. Then he nodded. "Very well," he said. "Lieutenant Tomson?"

Hesitating only a fraction of a second, the security chief tapped the release code into her control unit. When the manacles fell from the Hoshans' wrists, she quickly retrieved them.

"Now," Kirk said, "will you tell us your names?"

"I am Tarasek," the tallest one said, the computer seeming to insert vowels in what otherwise would have been altogether unpronounceable. "I was in command of the vessel that was lost."

"I am Radzyk," the second said, adding nothing.

The third, the one who had tried to strangle Kirk, met his eyes squarely. "I am Bolduc," he said. "I regret that our earlier actions have caused you and your crew member injury, and I thank you for your kind treatment."

"We understand your reasons. In any event, I was not harmed, and Nurse Garcia, whose arm was damaged when your comrade died, will recover."

Pausing, Kirk looked toward the forward viewscreen, where the four enemy ships maintained their steady pace, still retracing the path of the first ship the *Enterprise* had encountered. "Now, what can you tell us of this enemy you have spoken of?"

"There is little we know to tell," Bolduc said. "We have seen only his ships and what he has done with them. As you can imagine, none of his race has allowed itself to be captured alive, nor have we been able to obtain even a body for study. Our knowledge is limited to knowledge of his actions, which we know all too well. He has slaughtered many thousands of our people and would slaughter us all if given the chance."

"But *why?* Why does he want to kill you? How did this war between you begin?"

"You have twice shown us what the Destroyers have done to countless planets," Tarasek broke in, "and still you can ask such a question?"

Except, Kirk thought again, this particular enemy *hadn't* done any of what they had seen so far. He still did not want to get into that particular bucket of worms, however.

"I only meant," he said, "how did you first come in contact with the Destroyers?"

"They attacked us, of course," Tarasek said, "just as they attacked you."

"There was no attempt at communication? By either of you?"

"As you yourselves have seen, the Destroyers communicate only with their weapons!"

"But your people did try?"

"I cannot speak for the first two ships that were attacked. At that time we knew nothing of the Destroyers or the worlds they had obliterated, so those first ships undoubtedly did make an attempt. If they had the time. We know only that they ceased to exist. Their subspace beacons, which linked them to the nearest colony world, simply stopped transmitting."

"How did you discover they had been attacked, then?"

"If you require a living Hoshan to bear witness for you, there is none! Our ships of that time were built for exploration, not for war! They could not stand up to the Destroyers' weapons. Those first two were almost certainly totally destroyed, vaporized. If they had not been—if any of the crew had survived, or any of their charts—we would not be here today. Our colonies and our home world would have been found and destroyed generations ago."

"And then?" Kirk prompted when Tarasek fell into a brooding silence.

"And then," he continued, his voice suddenly sounding more tired than angry, although the computer's bland translation was unaffected by this change, "a third ship was attacked. This one, however, was in subspace communication with a colony world more than a parsec away. Before it was destroyed, it was able to transmit an image of its attacker and a description of everything that happened until the moment of destruction. Those images and that description are a central part of every Hoshan's earliest education."

"What did you do once you knew these Destroyers existed?"

"At first, not knowing the extent of their power, we did little but avoid the sector of space where the attacks had occurred. But then one of our colony worlds was destroyed. Hundreds of thousands of Hoshan were killed. Shortly after, we began to find those other worlds that had been destroyed in the past. At that point, we realized we had little choice in the matter. We knew we were no match for the Destroyers and their planet-killing weapons. Our only chance for survival lay in remaining hidden from them while we developed our own weapons, our own defenses. We had to retreat from space altogether, evacuating our colonies and destroying anything we could not take back with us. For decades, then, we worked only on our defenses. We constructed fleets of warships to match theirs, and we turned our planetary system into a fortress. Now, finally, after generations of sacrifice, we have grown strong enough to return to space, to begin seeking *them* out."

Though the computer's translation was neutral in tone, the intensity of feeling was more than evident in the Hoshan's own voice.

"But even after all this time, you still don't know *why* they attacked you in the first place?" Kirk asked quietly. "Why they destroyed your worlds and your ships?"

"Ask *them,* if you dare."

"If we get the chance, we will," Kirk said, noting that the translations had become virtually instantaneous, with the tone indicating uncertainty accompanying less than one word in ten.

"You still have them there before you," Tarasek said, gesturing at the viewscreen, where the real-time image of the star field and the four alien ships were still on display. "Can you not steal them from their ships as you stole us from ours?"

"It would be considerably more difficult. When we took you from your ship, you had no functional weapons and no shields."

"That is true, but the Destroyers' weapons do not appear to have any effect on your vessel. *If* we are to believe everything that you have shown us."

"When our shields are up, that is true. They must be briefly lowered, however, if we are to take you or anyone else from your ships in that manner."

"So, you are *not* invincible?"

"Far from it," Kirk said, hoping that he was not making a mistake in continuing to be so open.

"And there are other ships like yours?"

"Many, but they are not here, in this region of space."

"Where, then? I could not help but notice that none

of the scenes you so effectively displayed for us gave any indication of where *your* home world is located."

"Believe me," Kirk said with a rueful shake of his head, "there is little I would like better than to be able to show you precisely where our home world is. Unfortunately, we do not *know* where it is."

"You do not know where your own home world is? Your ship has transported you so very far?"

"Unfortunately, it was not our ship that transported us."

"What, then? What scientific magic do you control in addition to this ship of yours?"

"Whatever it was that brought us here, we did not control it. It was as much magic to us as it would be to you."

"And what might this magic be?"

Turning his eyes toward the science station, Kirk said, "Mr. Spock, show our friends here how we arrived."

"As you wish, Captain."

A few brief instructions to the computer, and the sparse stars of the Sagittarius arm of the Milky Way galaxy appeared on the screen. In the distance was the denser band of the Orion arm.

"This is our home galaxy," Kirk said, feeling the words tug at his throat. "Our home planets—we are not all from the same one—are somewhere in that band of stars across the screen."

A luminous circle appeared at a point in the Orion arm, and Spock's voice said, "The Federation is there, gentlemen."

"Thank you, Mr. Spock."

"Then you *do* know where your world is," Tarasek said.

"In one sense, we do," Kirk said. "However, we don't know where *we* are right now. Just watch the screen, and you will see how we came here."

All eyes, Hoshan and crew alike, were glued to the screen until, without warning, with only the briefest tremor of distortion, the scattered stars of the Milky

Way galaxy were replaced by the glowing curtain of stars that had surrounded the *Enterprise* since that moment of transition.

For several seconds there was only silence. Finally, Tarasek said, "It happened that quickly?"

"It happened that quickly. I believe our computer analysis showed the actual transition period to have been approximately ninety-eight microseconds." Kirk smiled. "Correct, Mr. Spock?"

"Precisely, Captain. During that period, we were, for lack of a better term, in limbo. The sensors detected literally nothing, neither matter nor energy, not even that of the *Enterprise* itself."

"Thank you, Mr. Spock. Now show them what happened to the one probe we sent back through the gate before it vanished."

The computer, responding directly to Captain Kirk's voice, complied.

Tarasek's eyes narrowed. "You are saying that you simply vanished from somewhere in your own galaxy and appeared here?"

"That is what I am saying," Kirk confirmed.

"And this gate that you came through—why can you not simply return through it?"

"It has vanished. For all we know, it could still be nearby, but we haven't been able to find it."

"But it could still be here, lurking anywhere, and even you could not detect its presence?"

"Not unless we sent a probe through it. Or simply ran into it ourselves."

"And more such gates could exist? Gates that could make *our* ships disappear as easily as they do yours?"

"I have no reason to doubt it." Kirk paused, looking from one to the other. "*Have* some of your ships disappeared in this way? Without having a chance to transmit the customary description of their attackers?"

"Description? What description?" Tarasek bridled.

"Shortly before the battle, we observed and recorded highly compressed subspace broadcasts made both by you and by one of the Destroyer ships. Also, prior to attacking us, the first Destroyer ship that we encountered made a similar broadcast, containing an image of our own ship. We have assumed this is standard procedure for any ship about to go into battle."

When none of the Hoshan spoke, Kirk went on. "In fact, your own broadcast was very helpful to our ship's computer in learning to speak your language. However, you need not be concerned. Neither signal gave us the slightest hint as to the location of your home worlds."

Still there was silence, but then Bolduc, the Hoshan who had first begun to speak willingly, said, "You are right. We always transmit as much information as possible before going into battle, though we were not aware that the Destroyers did so as well. You are also right when you suggest that some of our own ships have disappeared without warning. We have assumed until now that their transmitters malfunctioned or that the Destroyers had been able somehow to take them unawares. These gates of yours, however, would be a less worrisome explanation."

"They aren't *our* gates," Kirk emphasized. "We discovered them only recently and were trying to learn more about them when we were suddenly transported here, who knows how many millions of parsecs from home."

"You would have us believe that you are alone here?" Tarasek asked. "With no possibility of returning to your homes?"

"Our only hope is to find the gate that brought us here. At the moment, the odds do not look good, but we haven't given up hope."

"And us? What do you want of *us?*" Tarasek continued, seeming more skeptical by the moment. "Why have you shown us all these things? Why do you openly confess your problems and weaknesses to us?"

"Because we hoped that, if we demonstrated our

trust in you, you might come to trust us, at least a little."

The Hoshan made a rasping sound deep in his throat as his eyes swept across the security detail's drawn phasers. "It is easy to trust those who are your prisoners and have no opportunity to betray you. If you truly wish us to trust you," he added, his eyes locking with Kirk's, "use your great ship to help us wipe out the Destroyers!"

Chapter Ten

DR. CRANDALL HAD barely seated himself at the conference table with Kirk and the three *Enterprise* senior officers when a scowling Dr. McCoy said, "It seems clear enough to me, Jim. There's no doubt that the Hoshan need our help."

"And you think we should give it to them, Bones?" Kirk asked, settling into the chair at the head of the table.

"You're darned right I do!"

"Reasons?"

"How many reasons do you need, Jim? They attacked us the second they realized we existed. They did the same with the Hoshan. They've been doing it with the Hoshan for at least a hundred years!"

"If we believe everything the Hoshan tell us."

"And you don't?"

"As a matter of fact, I do," Kirk said. "But the important part is what they didn't tell us. Or weren't able to tell us. The reasons the Destroyers attacked them."

McCoy shook his head in exasperation as he slumped back in his chair. "Sheer cussedness is reason enough for me. These Destroyers are the local version of the Klingons. They like to fight, and they like to kill."

"You could be right, Doctor," Spock said, "but that hypothesis does not take into account many of the obliterated worlds we saw. The so-called Destroyers do not have phaser technology, and yet several of the worlds were destroyed by phaser fire. Are you suggesting their race possessed the technology thousands of years ago but lost it in the meantime?"

"Just because the six ships we've seen so far didn't have phasers doesn't mean they don't exist! Besides, it doesn't matter who destroyed those other worlds. That happened ages ago. This is happening now, and we've seen how these people operate! The Hoshan call them Destroyers, and that's exactly what they are!"

"However, Doctor," Spock countered, "we have not seen the people themselves, nor have we been able to speak with them and ask the reasons for their behavior. Under such circumstances, I find it difficult to logically determine the truth of the situation."

"There are times, Spock," McCoy snapped, "when you don't *need* logic to know what the truth is!"

"Possible, Doctor, but I very much doubt that this is such a time."

"Scotty," Kirk said, interrupting another angry retort by McCoy, "any opinions?"

"Aye, Captain, more than plenty, but no' a one that comes with a guarantee. If it were no' for Mr. Spock's sensor readings, I would ha' my doubts that anything living was even on board those ships. Even Klingons do not automatically destroy themselves and their ships the instant they are defeated, and certainly not when there is every chance that they could still be rescued by their comrades."

"Mr. Spock?" Kirk turned to the science officer. "Any possibility of error in the life form readings? Could the Destroyer ships be totally automated? Programmed to destroy?"

"Possible but highly unlikely. The readings indicated conscious, humanoid life forms. And do not forget that the Hoshan performed in a markedly similar fashion."

"True," Kirk said, "but the Hoshan ship was alone, with no chance of rescue that the crew knew of. And they had a reason for the suicide and the destruction of their ships. If they were captured alive or their ship taken intact, the location of their home world would be in jeopardy. Under similar circumstances, facing an enemy that could wipe out earth, I can imagine doing the same to the *Enterprise*. These so-called Destroyers, if we are to believe the Hoshan, have never had any such reason for similar fears. And with four of their fellows looking on, those two certainly had no such reasons. If they themselves had not ended their own lives and their ships had not automatically destroyed themselves, there was no reason they could not have been rescued by the remaining four ships."

"Who can say what their fears are, Captain?" Spock said. "Without speaking with them, none of us here can do that, nor can the Hoshan. And all too often among races which, like your own, are not ruled by logic, fears need to be neither rational nor logical in order to be real. It was one of your human philosophers, I believe, who spoke of the possibility that fear itself was sometimes the only thing that one might have to fear."

"A politician, not a philosopher," Kirk said, "but your point is well taken, Mr. Spock. Dr. Crandall? Any thoughts from the civilian viewpoint?"

"I'm afraid not, Captain Kirk. Contacting new civilizations, even under normal conditions, is not my area of expertise. I'm more than happy to leave it in your capable hands."

Kirk suppressed a grimace, wondering if he had been right to invite Crandall, ostensibly as a representative of the Council, to participate in the meeting. After those first few days of imperious demands and constant criticism, Crandall had done a complete about-face, apparently totally conquering the fear that had driven him at first. Ever since, he had been the soul of cooperation, at least on the surface. Everything he did, every word he spoke, seemed aimed at wiping out the memory of those early outbursts, of establishing himself as reasonable and cooperative and understanding. Kirk, however, was not at all sure he didn't prefer the earlier version. At least you knew where he stood. With this new, oily-smooth, anything-to-help facade, there wasn't even a glimmer of certainty.

And the man was everywhere. Dropping in on the bridge. Roaming the corridors and chatting with the crew, sometimes even shaking hands as if he were on a planetside campaign trail. It wouldn't surprise Kirk to find him cozying up to the Hoshan, now that the language problem had been licked.

"All right, then," Kirk said, turning back to the others, "except for Dr. McCoy, we agree that we need to know more before taking sides. The question is, how do we go about it? Scotty, what about the Hoshan suggestion? *Could* we use the transporters to snatch someone from a Destroyer ship? Could we do it fast enough to keep from getting blasted before we can get our deflectors back up?"

"You could disable the ship first," McCoy said.

"And have them blow *themselves* up instead of us? From our limited experience so far, they seem to be even quicker on the self-destruct trigger than the Hoshan." Kirk smiled faintly and then added, "It's too bad we can't set the ship's phasers to stun, as we can the hand phasers. That might take care of our problem. But how about it, Scotty? If we approach one of the ships the same way we approached the disabled Hoshan ship, would we be able to lock the transporters onto the crew fast enough?"

"It depends on how quickly they react. We can try. If it does no' work—and if we can get the deflectors back up in time—we can try to think of something else."

"Very well, gentlemen," Kirk said, standing, "unless one of us comes up with something better before the next watch, that's it."

Lost in thought, Dr. Jason Crandall walked slowly down the corridor toward his stateroom. The situation was changing far too rapidly for his liking. His plans, his campaign, required time, a great deal of undisturbed time. He could not afford the turmoil and the distractions that the Hoshan and their problems presented. Without the necessary time, it would be virtually impossible for him to build the kind of trust among the crew that would be required if he were to have any hope of success when he eventually evoked the name of the Federation Council and challenged Kirk openly and directly.

And challenging Kirk was not, he had decided in the last few days, as impossible a task as he had first feared. After his first chat with Ensign Davis, he had talked to dozens more of the crew, even a few of the officers, cautiously sounding them out, looking for areas of vulnerability, areas in which he could influence them. Somewhat to his surprise, he had found that Kirk's obvious popularity, even charisma, did not always translate into blind faith in his every decision. Virtually everyone on board knew of the dozens of hair's-breadth escapes the *Enterprise* had undergone since he had taken command. Most had participated in several, and, despite their admiration and respect for the captain, there was often an undertone of doubt in their voices, even of uneasiness, that the *Enterprise* should have been allowed to fall into so many hazardous situations in the first place. There were even some who made sour comments about Kirk's reputation—of which even Crandall himself had been aware—as a lady's man, but since no one could point to an instance where it had affected his performance as captain, Crandall dismissed them primarily as the result of envy. Even so, the names of those who had made the comments were filed in Crandall's growing bank of information.

But then, just as Crandall felt he was beginning to make real progress, not only with the crew in general but with some of the officers, most notably with Lieutenant Jameson, the third-watch science officer, the Hoshan had been brought aboard. At first, after Nurse Garcia's injuries and the Hoshan's adamant refusal to speak, even among themselves, Crandall had thought the whole incident could be turned to his advantage. After all, Kirk *had* risked the ship in a foolhardy maneuver to snatch the Hoshan aboard, and a well-liked member of the medical department had been seriously injured. Also, if it had taken just a few seconds longer to lock the transporters onto the Hoshan, or if the overload in the Hoshan ship's anti-matter power generators had been induced at only a fractionally faster rate than Spock had calculated, it wouldn't have been just the Garcia woman who would have been injured. The entire *Enterprise* and everyone aboard would have been vaporized. And for what? To save the lives of four comparatively barbaric aliens who wanted nothing more than an instant death that allowed them to take as many non-Hoshan as possible with them.

But then McCoy had patched Garcia up, and Kirk had gotten the aliens talking, leaving Crandall with nothing more than a litany of what-if's.

Or so he had thought until the meeting today. After listening to McCoy's angry objections, he had begun to wonder if his plan to build a power base among the regular crew was the most effective alternative. He would have to study the other officers further, particularly the noncommittal Mr. Scott, who seemed more devoted to the *Enterprise* itself than to any human aboard it. It was obvious, however, that no love was lost between Kirk and his chief medical officer. McCoy's remarks, made on the record and before not only the other officers but Crandall himself, a civilian observer, were the sort that, in Crandall's mind, verged on open mutiny. He should have paid closer attention to the rift before, he told himself irritably. It had been there for him to see, if only he had paid attention, when the aliens were first being brought aboard. McCoy had openly defied Kirk then, too, in full hearing not only of other officers but of several members of the crew.

And nothing had been done about it either time,

which might say something about the captain, something that Crandall could find useful. A captain who was slow to clamp down on an officer who defied him might also be slow to clamp down on others who defied him. At first, remembering the way Kirk had had him forcibly removed from the bridge, Crandall had assumed that the captain was quick and calm in his decisions. But now he wondered if that first time could have been an anomaly, a panic reaction to the circumstances of the moment. Unable to cope with the distraction that Crandall had presented, Kirk had had the distraction removed. Even the "rescue" of the Hoshan could be seen in that light—a spur-of-the-moment action that had, despite a disastrous beginning, turned out to his advantage in the long run.

And both incidents would, Crandall thought, fit his newly emerging image of Captain Kirk, an image that was almost diametrically opposed to what he had first believed. Kirk no longer seemed the carefree adventurer Crandall had first imagined him to be. Instead, he now appeared to Crandall to be as frightened as anyone else on board, himself included, and his command decisions had been bad—even disastrous—not because of any desire to play explorer but because Kirk was, under his artificially calm exterior, panicked out of his mind, grasping at whatever straws came within his reach. The first straw had been the gate itself, and when that had vanished, he had grasped at the even flimsier straw of the imaginary race that had "built" the gates.

But then, when the Hoshan and their enemies had appeared, he had once again switched direction, though what he hoped to gain from his current course of action Crandall couldn't imagine. Now that he had managed to establish communications with the Hoshan, his course should have been obvious. He should have promised to help the Hoshan, not from the altruistic motives that the ship's doctor professed but from a simpler, more practical motive. If they helped the Hoshan, then the Hoshan would be in their debt, and virtually everyone on the *Enterprise* could, if they played their cards right, end up on the receiving end of more gratitude than they could use up in a lifetime.

Kirk's fence-sitting act, however, could rob them of that chance forever.

On the other hand, Crandall thought, perhaps Kirk's inability to make a decision to help the Hoshan was just the opportunity he himself could make the most of. If he could somehow turn the tables on Kirk, forcing him to do the sensible thing—or if he could at least be seen by the Hoshan as having forced Kirk to come to his senses . . .

Yes, he thought with an almost invisible smile as he reached his stateroom, it did bear thinking about. However, despite his dislike for acting on the spur of the moment, he would also have to be constantly on the lookout for opportunity and be constantly ready to act, quickly and decisively. Considering the rate at which events were moving, he could well have only one chance, and he dared not pass it up.

"Locked on, sir!" the voice crackled from the bridge intercom.

"Seven-point-four seconds, Captain," Spock announced.

Kirk frowned. "You're positive, Mr. Spock?"

"Of course, Captain."

"Of course," Kirk repeated, the frown altering into a rueful smile. "I gather that we may have reached the point of diminishing returns that you and Dr. McCoy warned me of."

"Precisely."

"Reached and passed it!" McCoy's gravelly voice snapped from behind the command chair where he stood. "The last ten simulations haven't varied as much as half a second."

"Point taken, Bones. And Ensign McPhee did beat Scotty's best time by—what was it, Spock?"

"One-point-two seconds, Captain."

"We're as ready as we're ever going to be, Jim," McCoy said. "So unless you come to your senses and change your mind—"

"Keptin!" Chekov's voice broke in. "Another ship, bearing one-twenty-seven, mark sixteen!"

"Get it on the screen, Mr. Sulu," Kirk snapped. "Maximum magnification!"

"Already done, sir," the helmsman acknowledged.

"Mr. Spock, Hoshan or Destroyer?" The tiny dot on the screen was indistinguishable from the four it had replaced.

"It matches neither profile perfectly, Captain. There are seven life forms on board, and it is traveling at warp one-point-eight."

"Security," Kirk said, stabbing at the buttons on the arm of the command chair, "bring the Hoshan to the bridge, immediately!"

"If it maintains its present course and speed," Spock said, correlating Chekov's readings with a dozen from his own instruments, "the new ship will be within sensor range of the Destroyer ships in approximately ten-point-six minutes, Captain."

"Weapons, Mr. Spock?"

"Similar to both Hoshan and Destroyer ships, Captain. The antimatter core, however, appears to be capable of greater output than either."

"Dilithium crystals?"

"Negative, Captain, simply a larger engine. The level of technology is no more advanced in this ship than in any other we have encountered here."

"Lieutenant Uhura, any subspace radio activity?"

"None, Captain. This one is maintaining as low a profile as the others."

"Spock, you can't refine the life form readings enough to distinguish between Hoshan and Destroyer?"

"Negative. Readings show all ships are occupied by humanoid life forms—that is all."

The turbolift door hissed open, and the three

Hoshan lurched onto the bridge, followed closely by Lieutenant Tomson and two other security guards.

"Get us closer, Mr. Sulu, maximum warp factor. I want a decent picture on that viewscreen."

"Done, Captain."

The power channeled to the drive engines seemed to pulse through the bridge as the image on the viewscreen shifted dizzyingly and swept toward the dot at its center. Within seconds, the dot expanded into a featureless hexagon. Like the others, it appeared to be a massive warp-drive unit fastened to a heavily shielded crew compartment.

"One of yours, Tarasek?" Kirk asked, glancing toward the Hoshan. "Or one of theirs? Bolduc? Radzyk?"

"Eight minutes to sensor range, Captain," Spock said.

"Quick, Tarasek!" Kirk snapped. "One of yours? If so, it will be detected by the four Destroyer ships in less than eight minutes."

"Yes, it is Hoshan!" Bolduc said.

"Will you help us now, James Kirk?" Tarasek asked sharply.

"How? By attacking the four Destroyer ships?"

"Of course! Even without your help, at least three will be destroyed! The Hoshan ship you see there is more powerful than our own, and *we* eliminated *two* Destroyers ourselves before our own destruction!"

"He's right, Jim," McCoy said. "If we don't do anything, there's going to be another slaughter out there. The Hoshan ship may be able to take two or three of the Destroyer ships with it, but *it* will be destroyed, too! You *have* to help them!"

"For what it's worth, Captain, I agree," Sulu said, an unusual intensity in his voice. "I've heard all the arguments for holding back until we've been able to talk to both sides, but I've *seen* what the Destroyers have done."

"And I, sir!" Chekov said quickly.

"This is *not* a democracy, gentlemen. Mr. Sulu, put us—"

"Captain Kirk!" A new voice, harsh and commanding, overrode Kirk's voice and the sounds of the ship, and it was only when everyone turned, startled, toward the back of the bridge that it became clear that it had come from Dr. Crandall, who now stood next to the security detail and held one of their phasers, its force setting almost at maximum, its muzzle aimed directly at Kirk.

Chapter Eleven

FOR WHAT SEEMED like forever, there was total silence except for the distinctive electronic sounds of the *Enterprise* itself, and Dr. Jason Crandall had to pull in a deep breath to try to calm himself. Had he, in this impulsive move, picked the right moment? Or had he miscalculated?

For days, he had watched for an opportunity, half hoping one would not present itself, but now it had. For more than an hour, he had wandered unobtrusively about the bridge, watching impatiently as simulation after simulation had been run, first with Chief Engineer Scott at the distant transporter controls, then with various of his assistants. As far as Crandall was concerned, the point of diminishing returns Kirk had alluded to had been reached before the simulations had ever been started. Kirk, unable to make the obvious decision—to help the Hoshan—had been manufacturing one delaying tactic after another for more than three days, with these ridiculous simulations being only the latest. Even those crew members who had come closest to openly criticizing the captain for his "recklessness" in allowing the *Enterprise* to be drawn too easily into dangerous situations in the past were becoming impatient now that they had all heard the story of the Hoshan. Like Dr. McCoy, they felt there was nothing to be gained by waiting, certainly nothing to be gained by risking the entire *Enterprise* in an effort to snatch one or more of the Destroyers from the heart of a fully functional Destroyer ship.

Crandall had been on the verge of leaving the bridge, perhaps to talk once again with the Hoshan, when the new ship had appeared, and now, with all eyes turned toward him, he almost wished he *had* left.

But he hadn't. Instead, he had stayed, and he had heard McCoy once again urge an attack on the Destroyers. And then, when the helmsman had for the first time come down openly on McCoy's side, he had decided. It was now or never. He had already spoken with enough of the crew to know that he and McCoy were far from alone in their feelings about the Destroyers. He had even spoken with the Hoshan themselves, who, while craftily refraining from making any outright commitments while still on the *Enterprise*, had made it clear that they would see to it that his efforts on their behalf would be fully recognized and rewarded once they were back on Hoshan worlds.

And so he had acted, snatching a phaser from Ensign Creighton, who, though alert for Hoshan moves, had never suspected that Crandall presented a threat. Hastily Crandall had thumbed the force setting well above the stun range Creighton had been using.

"Dr. Crandall!" Kirk began, but Crandall waved him to silence with a quick jerk of the phaser.

"As a representative of the Federation Council, Captain Kirk," Crandall said, enunciating his words slowly and carefully, "I hereby relieve you and Mr. Spock of command of the *Enterprise*. Dr. McCoy, as next most senior officer present, you are to assume command. And if you are to take advantage of the situation, I would suggest you order Mr. Sulu to prepare immediately to fire on the Destroyer ships. And tell security to escort the captain and his first officer to their quarters!"

"Now just a blasted minute—" McCoy began, but a quick shake of the head from Kirk and a glance at the phaser's force setting silenced him.

Crandall acknowledged Kirk's intervention. "A wise man knows when to accept the inevitable, Captain."

"All right," McCoy said hesitantly after a moment of blinking silence, "let's do things sensibly for a change. Mr. Sulu, you heard Dr. Crandall. Prepare to fire. Lieutenant Tomson," he added, looking toward the security chief, "be prepared to escort the captain and Mr. Spock to their quarters as Dr. Crandall suggested."

As he spoke, McCoy put his hand on Kirk's wrist in what Crandall saw as an apologetic gesture. Kirk stood up slowly from the command chair. "I hope you know what you're doing, Bones," he said, slumping as he stepped down and moved toward Crandall and the security detail. "Mr. Spock?"

With only a slight arching of his eyebrows, Spock turned from the science station and followed Kirk, his hands raised roughly to shoulder level in the face of the leveled phaser. Crandall stepped back out of his way, his grip tightening on the weapon.

"Everything is under control, Dr. Crandall," McCoy said, still standing to one side of the command chair. "However, there's something you should see, there, on the viewscreen."

"What?" Crandall frowned. "I see only the Hoshan ship."

"There," McCoy said, "in the corner of the screen. Mr. Sulu, bring that object to the center of the screen, maximum magnification."

With a darting glance toward McCoy, Sulu turned sharply back to the viewscreen, his fingers playing rapidly across the controls. An instant later, the image on the screen shifted, the Hoshan ship sliding off the upper left corner.

"I *still* don't see anything!" Crandall snapped impatiently.

"Look more closely," McCoy said.

"There," Sulu said, raising his finger to point at a spot near the center of the screen. "Right there."

Squinting, Crandall took a step forward. "There's nothing—" he began, but suddenly he was silent, slumping to the deck as Spock's fingers closed precisely on the junction of his neck and shoulder. Kirk caught the phaser, unfired, as it tumbled from Crandall's limp fingers.

"Good work, Bones, Mr. Sulu," Kirk said. "Spock is apparently not the only member of the crew with a touch of telepathy."

"Just common sense, Jim. Once you gave us a chance to see the way he had his phaser set, we knew we couldn't allow it to be fired. Even if it missed us all, it could've wiped out half the controls. And there was only one way to overpower him quickly and quietly enough—to distract him and let Spock's magic fingers take over."

Spock, glancing briefly sideways at McCoy at the word "magic," was already back at the science station. "Three-point-four minutes to sensor range, Captain."

"Right," Kirk said, striding toward the command chair. "Security, take Dr. Crandall back to his quarters. Leave the Hoshan here, but keep watch on them."

Already the Hoshan ship was again centered in the viewscreen. "Mr. Sulu, lay in a course that takes us directly across the path of the Hoshan ship, behind it but within its sensor range. Get us within sensor range as quickly as possible, but once there, don't exceed warp two. And keep our deflectors up."

"Aye-aye, Captain."

"Two-point-nine minutes, Captain," Spock announced as the *Enterprise* surged forward.

"Decoy duty, Jim?" McCoy asked, shaking his head.

"That's the general idea, Bones."

"You may lose the Destroyers."

"Once we get the Hoshan out of their way, we can come back to them. Unless they change their course while we're gone."

"Two-point-three minutes, Captain."

Kirk glanced briefly toward his science officer, then

turned to the communications station. "Lieutenant Uhura, tight-beam directional transmission. Send a randomly modulated subspace carrier directly at the Hoshan ship. Scan up and down the spectrum until you get their attention."

"Aye-aye, sir."

"Two minutes, Captain."

For another thirty seconds, the only sound was Uhura's fingers as they danced across her control panels. Then, abruptly, the image of the Hoshan ship flipped on its axis, turning nearly a hundred and eighty degrees.

"Maximum power drain on Hoshan antimatter generator, Captain."

"Not heading for overload, I hope."

"Negative, Captain. It is simply supplying the power needed to allow them to make the same kind of U-turn that was made by the Destroyer ship that we first encountered. And its weapons are preparing to fire."

"So," Kirk said, turning to look at the Hoshan, "the Destroyers are not the only ones who attack on sight."

"We have never said otherwise," Tarasek said. "You know our reasons."

"Whoever is on this ship, do they speak the same language as you?" Kirk asked. "Would they be able to understand us?"

"They will understand, but they will not listen."

"Tarasek, you were the commander of your vessel. If you were to speak to them, they would certainly listen." Kirk paused, his eyes narrowing as he watched the alien's face. "Particularly," he went on deliberately, "if you transmitted the proper identification code."

"Code? What code is this you speak of?"

"Whatever code Hoshan ships use to recognize other Hoshan ships. We have a record of what your ship transmitted when you first became aware of the presence of the Destroyer ships. We don't, however, know what the required response is, since the Destroyers obviously didn't make it." Kirk paused, watching Tarasek digest the information.

"You are right," the Hoshan finally admitted. "Such recognition codes exist. When an unknown ship is detected, a challenge is issued, and if the proper response is not received, it is assumed that the ship is a Destroyer."

"And you can show us how to produce the proper response?"

"We cannot. Both challenges and responses are controlled by the ship's computers, and both change from hour to hour. No crew members possess this knowledge."

Kirk grimaced. "You don't take any chances, do you?"

"Would you, under such conditions?"

"Perhaps not. But you're saying that, without the proper interaction between the computer on this ship and the one on that Hoshan ship out there, communication is impossible?"

"Not impossible, only pointless. They will receive whatever you broadcast, but they will not listen. They will not believe."

"Not even if they hear your voice? You couldn't convince them we are not Destroyers but friends? Even though we do not return fire?"

"What would you have me say to convince them, James Kirk?"

"You could tell them the truth, that you have found an ally in your war against the Destroyers."

"But you have refused to be our ally."

Kirk grimaced in exasperation. "We have only refused to shoot the Destroyers down before we find a way of communicating with them!"

"Thirty seconds until we are within range of the Hoshan ship's weapons, Captain," Spock said. "It has increased its speed to warp two-point-three."

"Thank you for the reminder, Mr. Spock. Mr. Sulu,

take us directly away from the Destroyer ships, and keep us just outside the range of the Hoshan weapons."

"Aye-aye, sir."

"So," Kirk said, turning back to the Hoshan, "according to you, meaningful communication with your people is impossible."

"Unless you demonstrate your friendship toward the Hoshan, I am sure it is."

"And the only way to demonstrate that friendship is to wipe out a few Destroyer ships?" The computer did not pick up Kirk's sarcasm as it translated for the Hoshan.

"I know of no other way," Tarasek admitted.

"And even that would prove it only to *you*, the three of you on board the *Enterprise*. How could we go about proving it to anyone else? Would we have to make sure a suitable number of Hoshan ships had a ringside seat for the destruction?" Kirk broke off, shaking his head angrily. "Security, escort our guests back to their quarters."

Standing up as the turbolift door hissed shut behind the Hoshan and their guards, Kirk stepped forward and glanced over Sulu's shoulder at the controls, then at the viewscreen and the Hoshan ship in its center.

"Maintaining specified separation, sir," Sulu volunteered as Kirk turned away.

"I didn't doubt it, Mr. Sulu. But I think we've carried this on long enough. Our initial objective of keeping that particular ship from running into the Destroyers has been accomplished. Mr. Spock, are the Destroyer ships still within sensor range?"

"Affirmative. Course and speed remain unchanged."

"Very well. Mr. Sulu, ahead warp factor six until we are safely out of Hoshan sensor range, then double back and resume our tracking of the Destroyers."

"Aye-aye, Captain."

As the Hoshan ship began to shrink on the screen,

Kirk turned to McCoy, still standing near the handrail not far from the elevator. "Bones," he said, "I think we had better have a talk with Dr. Crandall."

It was a thoroughly chastened, almost trembling Dr. Crandall that Kirk and McCoy found in his quarters.

"I—I don't know what came over me," he said, even before the door had closed behind them. "I didn't intend—"

"We all know exactly what you intended, Doctor," Kirk said evenly. "What we don't know is how you thought you could get away with it. Would you care to explain?"

"That's right," McCoy grated, frowning as much in puzzlement as anger. "What the blazes ever gave you the idea that I'd go along with *mutiny?*"

It was at that moment, as he heard the mixture of anger and outright incredulity in McCoy's tone, that Crandall realized how completely he had miscalculated, not just the timing of his move but everything. The arguments between Kirk and McCoy, the differences of opinions had meant nothing. In a sense, he had been right in his first, instinctive assessment of the officers and crew. No matter what their complaints or fears, they were all bound together in some peculiar form of extended family, with the captain as patriarch, and there was no way he could ever gain admittance to it, let alone any degree of control over it.

Reluctantly, but knowing he had no choice anymore, he began to talk.

To his utter surprise, when he finished, he was neither transferred to a detention cell nor even restricted to his stateroom. The engineering deck was made off limits, and he was barred from the bridge until further notice, but other than that his freedom was unimpaired. McCoy seemed annoyed at the captain's seeming leniency, but Kirk said only, "Now that he knows how things stand, I don't think he'll cause any more problems." And then, looking at Crandall,

"You're a practical man, am I right, Dr. Crandall?"

Crandall only nodded, his relief, even gratitude, mixed with a tightness in his stomach that he did not realize until later was the beginning of a new crop of anger.

Six hours later, with the four Destroyer ships showing no sign of breaking formation or changing direction, Captain Kirk turned sharply from the viewscreen.

"Lieutenant Uhura, it's time we tried *something*. Tight-beam transmission aimed directly at the three guard ships. Transmit the same signal, the identification code, that the ships themselves transmitted during rendezvous. We'll see what happens."

What happened was that the three guard ships immediately closed up their formation, tightening the shell of protection around the fourth ship.

"Like the Hoshan, Captain," Spock commented, "they apparently change the password frequently, and an out-of-date password is more suspect than no password at all."

"So, Mr. Spock, do *you* have any suggestions?"

"A diversion, sir," Sulu said when Spock remained silent, "as was discussed before. We still have quite a number of unused probes. We could send a half-dozen of those along one side, and while the guard ships are disposing of them, we could come in from the other direction."

"Simple, Captain," Spock said, "but possibly effective."

And it was.

By the time the probes, traveling at low sublight velocities on their impulse engines, were within sensor range of the guard ships, the *Enterprise* had, in effect, circumnavigated the Destroyer ships and was waiting for them to attack the probes.

"Probes within sensor range, Captain," Spock finally announced. "Guard ships moving to intercept."

"Ready, McPhee?" Kirk asked.

"Ready, sir," a faintly accented voice came from the transporter room.

"Security?"

"Ready, sir," Lieutenant Tomson's voice came, also from the transporter room.

"Very well," Kirk said. "Now's as good a time as any. Mr. Sulu, prepare to take us to within transporter range, warp eight. Mr. McPhee, prepare to lock onto at least one of the life forms on the Destroyer ship as quickly as possible. Lieutenant Tomson, phasers ready, heavy stun." He paused, glancing around the bridge. "You all remember the simulations," he said after a moment. "Let's see what we can do for real. As soon as—"

"Guard ships about to fire on probes, Captain."

"Go, Mr. Sulu, now!"

Chapter Twelve

IN THE FOLLOWING moments, Ensign McPhee set a new record for transporter lock-on. Even so, the first blast from the Destroyer ship caught the deflector screens before they had a chance to build back up to full power, and a brief, bone-rattling moment of overload shuddered through the entire ship. Within seconds, however, Scott had the situation under control, and the deflectors were fully in place when the second blast came. By the time the guard ships turned their attention from the obliterated probes and joined in the attack, the *Enterprise* was out of range.

Moments later, the central Destroyer ship emitted another concentrated subspace pulse, and Kirk wondered briefly if it were going to destroy itself. Instead, the three guard ships closed more tightly than ever about it, then dropped to sublight and clustered together the way they had when they had first rendezvoused with the other Destroyer ship.

"Probably trying to decide what happened to whoever it was we snatched out from under their noses," Kirk said with a faint smile as he turned toward the image of the transporter room currently on the auxiliary screen above the science station. "Now let's see what a Destroyer looks like. Mr. McPhee, bring him in."

Lieutenant Tomson and her two subordinates—the only people in the transporter room except for Ensign McPhee—triggered their phasers even before the shimmering materialization was complete. The Destroyer, as tall and thin as the Hoshan were short and muscular, fell to the deck the moment the transporter field released him.

Taken instantly to an isolation ward in the medical section, the Destroyer was found to have a suicide device similar to that of the Hoshan but more automated. Luckily, the primary triggering mechanism was an external signal, probably generated by a transmitter in the Destroyer ship. A secondary trigger was located in a ring worn on one of the Destroyer's long, slender fingers. The device itself, containing a powerful explosive rather than the laserlike device in the Hoshan implants, was worn as a collar rather than implanted within the body. Even so, it took virtually every analytical device the medical and science departments possessed to remove it without exploding it.

The Destroyer himself, taller than Spock, appeared to have sprung from avian stock, his hair looking very much like thousands upon thousands of tiny feathers. His bones, though not hollow like those of flighted birds, were comparatively light, and the entire impression he presented was one of delicacy. Even the "uniform" he had worn and which had been replaced on his body after removal of the collar was light in both weight and color, pale blue, and loosely fitting with no pockets, only a single pouchlike container attached at the waist.

The Hoshan were allowed a brief look from behind a transparent barrier before the Destroyer regained consciousness. Only Tarasek spoke. "Now you will see what they are like," he said, deliberately turning his back on the unconscious Destroyer.

Unlike the Hoshan, the Destroyer was allowed to awaken alone in a stateroom with a vision screen as well as a direct link to the computer's translation circuits. Also unlike the Hoshan, the Destroyer opened his eyes the moment the monitoring devices indicated he had regained consciousness.

Immediately, he sat up, his eyes taking in everything

in the room in a single, almost owl-like turn of his head. His heartbeat, according to the monitor, spurted drastically at first but then dropped back to what appeared to be normal and stayed there. His fingers, long and slender with narrow, diamond-shaped nails that could, generations ago, have been claws, went to his throat, feeling for the missing collar.

And he began to talk, rapid-fire and nonstop, his voice a startlingly clear, trilling sound, at least as birdlike as his appearance.

"At least he's being more cooperative than the Hoshan," Kirk remarked.

"*If* what he's doing is really talking," McCoy snapped. "He could be just chirping to himself, like a big canary."

"No, Doctor," Spock said, cocking his head sideways, a gesture itself almost birdlike, as he listened to the computer's voice through his earpiece, "It is definitely a language, a very complex language. And at this rate, the computer will be able to begin rudimentary translations very shortly."

And it did. Within minutes, the computer began to overlay the Destroyer's trills with words, at first sporadically, then more steadily. The first complete sentence was, "If I have offended in any way, I ask that I be forgiven."

"It's time we met face to face," Kirk said abruptly, moving toward the hall that led to the Destroyer's stateroom as he spoke. "Lieutenant Tomson, stay in the background, but have your phaser ready, on light stun. Mr. Spock, is the computer's new show-and-tell ready to go?"

"Ready whenever you give the word, Captain."

The instant the door to the stateroom opened, the Destroyer fell silent. His eyes, yellow and vertically slitted like a cat's, darted from one to the other of the four men as they entered. On Spock's tricorder, the Destroyer's pulse rate shot up sharply, and he emitted a complex series of trilling sounds.

"What are you?" the computer translated, almost

instantaneously, through the universal translator clipped to Kirk's belt. "Are you to be my punishment?"

"We mean you no harm," Kirk said. "We—"

"Are you, then, to be my reward?"

Kirk frowned at the translator. "Spock, are you sure—"

A snort of laughter from McCoy cut him off. "Don't you get it, Jim? He thinks he's dead! He just wants to know if this is heaven or hell."

"Of course I am dead," the Destroyer said, his trilling sounds growing more shrill, even though the computer's translation remained neutral. "The ship I was on was attacked and destroyed."

"No," Kirk said, "you aren't dead. And your ship was neither attacked nor destroyed. Mr. Spock, let's have those pictures."

"Sequence one," Spock said quietly, and the stateroom viewscreen came to instant life.

"Watch," Kirk said. "This is what happened. You are simply aboard a different ship."

"Then you—"

Abruptly, the Destroyer's slender fingers darted once more to his neck, grasping futilely for the missing collar.

"There is nothing to be afraid of," Kirk said. "We mean you no harm. Just watch the screen. We will show you what happened."

For another several seconds, the Destroyer's fingers fluttered helplessly about his neck while his eyes went from face to face. On Spock's tricorder, his heart rate was higher than it had been even during the initial spurt after awakening.

But then, as abruptly as the agitation had begun, it stopped. The birdlike alien was suddenly still, his fingers motionless at his neck. As if by an effort of sheer will, the pulse rate slowed.

"I will look," he said, the trills of his words now lower-pitched, slower. "I will see what you have to show me."

For the next two minutes, then, the computer presented a simulation similar to a small part of what it had earlier shown the Hoshan, this one showing the *Enterprise* as it swooped in close to the Destroyer ship and snatched their guest from its crew compartment.

When it was over, there was only silence. The Destroyer's yellow eyes looked from the screen to the four men several times. Finally he spoke.

"Then you are not our enemy? You are not the World Killers?"

"We are not," Kirk said.

"Then who?"

As simply as possible, omitting all mention of the Hoshan, Kirk explained what he could. Then, before the alien could ask more, he nodded to Spock and pointed to the screen, where an image of a Hoshan ship appeared. "Is this the enemy you speak of?"

"Yes!" Another brief spurt of the alien's pulse rate testified to the truth of the answer.

"These are the ones you call World Killers?"

The alien hesitated, as if trying to bring his emotions back under control. "That is what I have been told. Are you now telling me differently?"

"Why do you call them World Killers?" Kirk asked, ignoring the alien's question.

"Look at any world in this sector of space, and you will know!"

Nodding to Spock, Kirk once more gestured at the screen. "Worlds such as these?" he asked as the first of a dozen images appeared.

After the first, the alien closed his eyes, refusing to look at more. "If I am truly still alive, who are you?" he trilled, the pitch so high it was almost inaudible. "What do you want?"

"It would be nice," McCoy put in, "if all you people would stop shooting at us on sight!"

"Show him, Spock," Kirk said.

A moment later, an image of the stars of the Sagittarius arm of the Milky Way galaxy appeared on the screen, and Kirk talked the alien through an abbreviated version of what the Hoshan had been shown. When he finished, the screen returned to its real-time display of the local star field and the dots that were the four Destroyer ships.

"Now," Kirk said, "tell us who *you* are. Tell us how this war with the ones you call World Killers started."

For a long time there was silence. Briefly the alien's fingers again fluttered to his neck and then dropped to his side. "It started," he said finally, "when we were attacked."

Slowly and haltingly, then, the story came out, and it was remarkably similar to the one told by the Hoshan, except that for these people, who called themselves the Zeator, it had started nearly four hundred years ago, not one hundred. Like the Hoshan, they had been peacefully expanding into space, but when they found the first of the Slaughtered Worlds, as they called them, they became cautious, adding weapons to what had previously been purely exploratory ships and taking precautions to keep the coordinates of their home world safe from discovery. The weapons, however, apparently proved ineffective, for ships began to disappear.

Like the Hoshan, the Zeator retreated from space long enough to build up their weapons technology and establish a defense around their home world. After nearly fifty years, in ships similar to the ones they still used, they began to move cautiously back into space, toward the Slaughtered Worlds. Once again, their ships were attacked, but now they were able to fight back. At one point, they were certain they had located their enemy's home world and destroyed it, but after nearly a century of uneasy watchfulness, the attacks had begun again.

"Now we have only one hope," the Zeator finished, "to find and destroy their true home world before they can find and destroy ours. In these last few weeks, as I have been shown the Slaughtered Worlds first-hand, there have been times when I would have welcomed *either* conclusion to our centuries of fear. And when two of our escort vessels were destroyed, I only wished that I could have taken their place."

"Who are you that they were protecting you?"

Once again there was silence, and the Zeator seemed to shrink in stature. Even the featherlike hair on his head and hands seemed to flatten against his skin.

"I am called Atragon," he said at last, "and I fear that I am a fool. Until I boarded the ship that you took me from, I had never been off the surface of our home world. Prior to that, I had known only what I had seen in our history books. For years I had taught others from those books, but I did not believe what they said, not truly, not completely. I had not seen the destruction for myself, any more than any of the planetbound had seen it, so I did not truly believe it. The words were just words, not facts, not living people. Naively, I could not believe that any race of beings intelligent enough to travel through space could be as savage as those books told us our enemies were. I could not believe that even if the World Killers had done everything we were told they had done, they had not had a reason. I even thought that the war might only be a hoax, something used by the military to bleed the planetbound of their money and resources.

"Unfortunately, other members of my family had much influence, and I used that influence to make others see things as I did. I was even elected to an influential office, and it was then that the authorities—the military authorities—decided that the only way I could be convinced of the truth was to be shown it first-hand. As I said, I was a fool, and I gladly accepted their offer, certain I would prove them wrong. That is why I was on that ship, being shown the Slaughtered Worlds first-hand. And because I was on that ship, it did not enter the battle when it should have. To protect me, those ships were lost."

"And the collar you were wearing? The collar filled with explosives?"

"Even I could not be allowed to endanger the home

world. Everyone else on the ships, everyone in the military, has similar devices surgically implanted, but mine was to have been removed when—if I returned safely home."

"And now? With the collar gone?"

"With or without the collar, I will never be able to return."

"We could return you."

"To the ship you took me from? You would deposit me there as you took me?"

"Possibly."

"If you were immune to our weapons, perhaps, but if I have understood your story properly, you are not. And my people will not be as easily fooled as they were before. And even if you were to succeed, I doubt that I would long survive."

"Why? Certainly your own people wouldn't kill you."

"I do not know, but I suspect they would. No one has ever been taken from a ship in the manner you took me, so no rules exist for my treatment if I am returned. However, I cannot believe that I could ever be allowed to return to our home world. Nor would I wish to, no matter how strongly you profess to be our friends. You have shown me too much to allow me to trust you."

"Too much? I don't understand."

"You have shown me how you are able to track our ships without your own being detected. You could follow whatever ship I was on. You could find our home world, and that is unthinkable."

"We can follow your ships whether you are on them or not."

"Of course. But none now will ever return to our home world. Only rarely do ships return under any circumstances, but now that your ship, obviously superior to ours, has been observed, none will return, ever. None in this sector of space dares risk it, and I suspect that none anywhere will risk it, at least not for many years."

"If we are able to convince you we are not your enemy, you could direct us to your home world and we could take you there directly. We could talk to your leaders."

"There is no way I can be sufficiently convinced, not when the fate of my world hangs on my decision to trust you. But my decision is of no importance. I could tell you nothing of our home world's location, no matter what my decision. For I do not *know* its location. I am a planetbound, and I was told nothing of such matters."

The alien paused, his narrow shoulders moving in what could have been a shrug, or perhaps a shudder. "The rest of my life, I fear, must be spent elsewhere than with my own people. Whoever you are, once you took me from them, I became as dead to them as if the collar had done what it was intended to do. As dead as all those on our ships are to our home world."

Which was, Kirk thought grimly, not all that different from what the Hoshan had said. Communication might be possible with the Zeator, but they would listen no more than would the Hoshan.

Unless something could be done.

"I think," he said, glancing at Spock and McCoy, "it's time for the Destroyer to meet the World Killers."

Chapter Thirteen

To no one's surprise, the meeting between the Hoshan and the Zeator accomplished little.

"He lies, of course!" Tarasek said.

"Atragon?" Kirk said, turning to the Zeator on the opposite side of the conference table. "Do the Hoshan lie as well?"

For a long moment there was only silence. "I do not know," he said finally, his trilling voice dull, virtually lifeless. "It is possible that he tells the truth. If so, we deserve the fate we have been given."

Of the Hoshan, only Bolduc openly admitted there might be some truth to Atragon's words. "When for generations you have known only enemies and when the life of your entire race is at stake," he said, "you do not take chances. Mistakes will be made under such conditions."

"Shoot first and ask questions later," McCoy said, his voice oddly flat. "The only trouble is, when the shooters are as efficient as you two, there's never anyone left to answer the questions. Or even to ask them."

At McCoy's words, a thoughtful frown creased Kirk's forehead. "Bones," he said, standing up abruptly, "thank you. I think your collection of archaic sayings may have saved the day. At least it's given me an idea how to start."

"I dinna like it, Captain." Chief Engineer Montgomery Scott's eyes had a look of betrayal in them as he stood protectively in front of the line of main control panels on the engineering deck.

"I don't blame you, Scotty. I'm not very happy with it myself, but I don't have any other ideas at the moment."

"Could ye no' just *talk* to them?"

"We'll try, of course, but you've seen how they react to us—to *anyone* besides themselves. Even now that we have their languages in the computer, all we can do is talk *at* them. And all they're going to do is shoot at us from the moment they see us."

"And ye want to *let* them!"

"According to Mr. Spock, the deflectors will take anything either the Hoshan or the Zeator can dish out. If you have any doubts, Scotty—"

"I dinna have doubts, Captain!" Scott said, an offended note entering his voice as he waved his hand in a gesture that included not only the control panels behind him but the antimatter engines and everything else that was under his care. "I ha' no doubts about these bairns! They can take care of themselves, but to allow—"

"If there were another way, I'd take it, Scotty."

Scott fell silent, pulling in a breath. "Aye, Captain," he said finally, "I know ye would. We'll be ready."

"Thank you, Mr. Scott," Kirk said, his hand briefly and uncustomarily gripping the chief engineer's shoulder. "I never doubted it for a second."

For several minutes, Kirk and the entire first-watch bridge crew had been watching the approaching Hoshan ship. Both the Hoshan and the Zeator were watching on monitor screens in their guarded staterooms, as was Dr. Crandall. Only the aliens' rooms, however, were hooked up so they could talk directly to the bridge and could be channeled, by the touch of a button, into Lieutenant Uhura's broadcasts.

"In effect, Mr. Sulu," Kirk had said, "we're going to park in the middle of the road. Just be prepared to take us into the ditch, fast, at the first indication that they're intentionally overloading their main antimatter power unit. Or that any weakness is developing in the deflectors, of course."

"Aye-aye, Captain," Sulu replied, a certain grim satisfaction in his tone and expression.

"Lieutenant Uhura, ready to transmit our recorded message at them until further orders."

"Message loaded and ready, sir."

"The *Enterprise* will be within the Hoshan vessel's sensor range in one-point-three minutes, Captain," Spock announced.

"Lieutenant Uhura, start the message."

The Hoshan reaction was virtually instantaneous. Obviously not taking the time to listen to the words of the message, the ship—the same one the *Enterprise* had decoyed away from the Zeator fleet earlier—altered its course fractionally to home in on the transmission. Seconds later, it transmitted what was apparently today's computer-generated request for today's recognition code. Almost simultaneously, a compressed thirty-seven-millisecond subspace burst was sent out.

"As predicted, weapons preparing to fire, Captain," Spock announced.

But none was fired. Nearly a minute went by, and nothing happened.

"Tarasek," Kirk said, "does this mean they are listening to the message?"

"It is possible," the computer said, translating the Hoshan's words virtually simultaneously.

"Speak to them directly, Tarasek," Kirk said. "Lieutenant Uhura, open Tarasek's channel."

"Done, sir," she said, tapping a single button on the control panel.

"I am Tarasek." The computer translated the broadcast words of the Hoshan. "I was in command of Defender ship *Tromak,* which was recently lost in battle with six Destroyer vessels. I and two of my crew, Radzyk and Bolduc, have been taken aboard a ship called by its masters the *Enterprise*. It is the same ship that you saw and pursued two days ago. Its owners say they wish to be friends to the Hoshan, but—"

"Hoshan ship accelerating to warp two-point-three, sir," Chekov broke in. "It is on a collision course with us!"

"Lieutenant Uhura, give me the channel!" Kirk snapped.

"Aye-aye, sir." With a touch of Uhura's finger, the Hoshan's voice was cut off.

"This is the commander of the *Enterprise,"* Kirk said, speaking rapidly into the translator. "You have heard our message. We are not your enemies. You have no reason to fear us or attack us. We will not fire on your ship. If we wished to harm you, we could have destroyed your ship when you first attacked us two days ago. We could destroy it now if we wished. We have been observing you for the past hour and could have destroyed your ship at any time during *that* period as well, but we have not. I repeat, we have no wish to harm you. We only wish to talk and to transfer Commander Tarasek and the remainder of his crew to your ship."

"Within laser range in thirteen seconds, Captain," Spock said. "No sign of overloading in antimatter generator as yet."

"To demonstrate our peaceful intentions—and our patience—we will allow you to fire at the *Enterprise* if you wish to do so," Kirk said, speaking even more quickly. "We will not return the fire."

Even as Kirk finished speaking, the deflector shields flared violently, cutting off the direct visual image of the approaching Hoshan ship.

"Deflectors holding as predicted, Captain," Spock said, continuing to study the science station instruments. "Still no sign of intentional antimatter overload."

"The ship is no longer on a collision course, sir!" Chekov said, a note of triumph in his voice. "It will now miss us by more than fifteen kilometers."

"And how long can they keep that up, Mr. Spock?"

Kirk asked, gesturing at the viewscreen image of the flaring deflector shields.

"Approximately seven minutes at the present level, Captain."

At two minutes, the Hoshan ship shot past the *Enterprise,* still firing.

At two minutes and forty seconds, it made a second, even closer pass.

At three minutes and ten seconds, it made a third.

At three minutes and thirty seconds, it came to a dead stop little more than three kilometers distant, still firing. The deflector shields toward the Hoshan ship were a wall of scintillating radiation, stretching into the ultraviolet and beyond.

"All Hoshan power drive being diverted to lasers, Captain," Spock said a moment later. "The additional power will reduce the effective life of the lasers by approximately forty-five seconds. Still no sign of antimatter overload."

"Open the channel to the Hoshan ship, Lieutenant Uhura," Kirk said, and when it was done he repeated what Spock had said, except for the remark about the antimatter. "When your lasers cease functioning in another two minutes," he finished, "perhaps we can start talking. Lieutenant, leave the channel open."

The first laser failed in less than one minute, the final one a minute and a half after that. Five seconds after the final failure, yet another burst of compressed subspace radiation was emitted, this one forty-eight milliseconds in length.

"Antimatter overload sequence beginning, Captain."

"Destroying yourself by exploding your antimatter generators will not harm us," Kirk said quickly. "We can monitor the process and be out of danger before the explosion occurs. The ones you call the Destroyers already tried it with us, and it didn't work for them, either."

"Still increasing, Captain. Twenty-six seconds to terminal overload."

"Ready for maximum warp, Mr. Sulu, at my command."

"Ready, Captain."

"You saw how easily we outran you the first time we met," Kirk said. "We can do the same again. We can outrun the danger from your exploding antimatter generators. You will kill *only yourselves, no one else!*"

"Fourteen seconds, Captain."

"Mr. Sulu, max—"

"Overload stabilizing, Captain," Spock cut in.

"Stay ready, Mr. Sulu. Spock, what's happening?"

"It is similar to what the Zeator ship did, Captain. They have stablized the overload. However, they have not yet reversed the sequence."

"In effect, they're holding—at what? Ten seconds?"

"Twelve, Captain."

"And presumably they could restart the clock whenever they want?"

"It is likely, Captain."

"Tarasek? Any thoughts?"

"That they stopped at all is surprising. If it were my ship, I would have allowed it to continue!"

"Of course you would!" the computer translated for Bolduc, in whose voice Kirk detected what he had come to recognize as sarcasm. The Hoshan had made several oblique remarks before but had always backed down when pressed for further information. Nor had he ever before sounded so vehement, and Kirk couldn't help but wonder if the Hoshan were simply unable to hold back any longer or if the fact that the words were being broadcast to another Hoshan ship might have something to do with the sudden outburst. "I have seen your performance under fire before, Commander!" Bolduc finished sharply.

"That is enough, Bolduc!" Tarasek snapped.

"Is it, now? When the *Tromak* was struck by the Destroyer ships, I was knocked unconscious, but not before I saw you try to reach the override control! If you had been able—"

"Silence!"

"Tarasek!" With startling suddenness, a new voice burst from the speakers on the bridge, and everyone's eyes snapped to the Hoshan ship on the main viewscreen. "Are Bolduc's words true?"

"They are." The computer translated Radzyk's thin, distinctive voice.

"He lies!"

"I do not believe so, Tarasek," the new voice said. "Their words have the ring of truth about them."

"But you yourself have just now overridden the—"

"Present circumstances are quite different, Tarasek! Whether or not I believe the words of this alien commander who has captured you, I must believe my eyes and my instruments. I have seen those things of which he speaks, and I have seen my weapons rendered useless by his ship's defenses. I think it is time we learned more."

Abruptly, there was silence, and when the voice came again, it was obvious that it was no longer addressing Tarasek. "I will speak with you, Commander of the *Enterprise*. I will not, for now, reverse the overload sequence you say you are able to monitor, but neither will I continue it. We will speak."

A collective sigh of relief swept the bridge. Even Spock seemed to relax a tiny fraction.

"That is all we ask at the moment, Commander," Kirk said. "That's all we ask."

For more than an hour, they talked—Hrozak, the commander of the Hoshan vessel, Bolduc and Radzyk, and Kirk and the others on the bridge, even, briefly, the Zeator—with Kirk slowly allowing himself to feel a grudging admiration for the alien commander. He could easily see himself in Hrozak's position had he been born a Hoshan rather than a human a billion parsecs or a billion years away. Protection of his home world was everything to Hrozak, as protection of the Federation—of earth—was to Kirk. But Hrozak paid a dearer price than most Federation Starfleet captains. Even under so-called normal circumstances, Hrozak's chances of ever again setting foot on his home world were slim. With the *Enterprise* in the picture, those chances had been essentially reduced to zero.

"We cannot take the chance," Hrozak said, much as the Zeator had said earlier. "No matter what my personal judgment is, we cannot take the chance."

"And if we had joined you against the Zeator?" Kirk asked. "The Destroyers, as you call them? If we had put on a show of attacking them and destroying their ships? Would you have trusted us enough then?"

"Perhaps, in time, but I cannot know what others would say. We would have only your word that the ships you destroyed were genuine, not simply dummies constructed to be destroyed for our benefit. Or even that the ships were truly destroyed. I strongly suspect that our sensors can be fooled as easily as our eyes by the devices you possess."

"But why would we *want* to trick you?" Kirk asked for what seemed the hundredth time.

"If I knew that, then I would know everything," Hrozak said. "As it is, I can only assume the worst, that you have allied yourself with our enemies—or that you *are* our enemies, despite the appearance and apparent abilities of your ship."

Kirk sighed faintly, unable to think of any argument not already made, any demonstration that he himself would, in Hrozak's place, consider proof positive. "If you would like—" he began, but Spock's voice cut him off.

"Antimatter overload becoming more unstable, Captain."

"How much time—"

"Unknown, Captain, but the overload is growing at a much slower rate than before. The rate, however, is itself uneven."

"Commander Kirk," Hrozak's sharply spoken words were translated, "I have not resumed the sequence!"

"I suspect he has not, Captain," Spock said. "Nonetheless, the overload is once again growing."

He paused momentarily, his eyes taking in a new reading even as it appeared. "The rate of increase appears to have stabilized. Barring further changes, terminal overload will occur in twelve-point-eight minutes. At the previous rate, it would occur in less than twelve seconds."

"A malfunction, Mr. Spock?"

"It would seem so."

"Commander Hrozak, I would suggest—"

"It is already being done, Commander Kirk."

"If you can't bring it under control," Kirk offered, "we can take you aboard the *Enterprise* before any explosion."

For nearly a minute, only silence came from the Hoshan ship.

"Overload stabilizing once again, Captain," Spock announced. And then, a moment later: "Now decreasing. They appear to have reversed the sequence."

"We have," Hrozak said. And then, after a pause: "We would seem to be in your debt, even though we still cannot allow ourselves to fully trust you or your Destroyer friend."

"We don't ask that you trust us blindly," Kirk said. "We don't ask for the location of your home world. We only ask that you agree to take aboard the three Hoshan from the *Tromak*. And accept the translators that allow you to communicate, not only with us but with the Zeator. Speak with your leaders, tell them what we have told you, tell them what you have seen. Tell them that there is at least a small chance that the war that you have been carrying on for nearly two hundred years could be ended with no more bloodshed on either side."

"And the Destroyer? The Zeator, as you call him?"

"We will try to get his people to do the same. And whether or not we are successful, we will do whatever we can to get you and the Zeator to talking directly with each other."

Again there was only silence from the Hoshan ship. Spock continued to study his readouts, on the alert for any sudden change, while Kirk waited, as silently as the Hoshan commander. When Sulu turned from the helmsman's station as if to speak, Kirk held up a quieting hand.

Finally, after more than a minute, the Hoshan commander spoke. "The one thing we have not seen is your own firepower," Hrozak said. "If you are willing, expel one of the probes you say you carry. Allow us to take it within our own shields and inspect it with our own sensors. Then, if you are able, you can demonstrate your firepower by destroying the probe through our shields."

Kirk smiled faintly. "There might be some danger to you. How large a volume can your shields enclose?"

"Not so great as yours, but great enough. We are willing to take the risk."

Kirk turned to Scott, who had been on the bridge throughout the talks with the Hoshan. "How about it, Scotty? Can the phasers be set fine enough to take out a probe without damaging the Hoshan ship?"

"Without touching the ship, aye. However, I canna do anything about the secondary radiation from the phaser impact."

"You heard, Commander Hrozak?" Kirk asked.

"I heard. Our ships are built to withstand such radiation without our shields. We are still willing to take the risk to make sure that you are not all shell and no teeth."

"Yes," Kirk said, smiling faintly, "that very thought had crossed my own mind. Very well. Mr. Spock, transport a probe to the vicinity of the Hoshan ship."

"As you wish, Captain," Spock said, turning to the auxiliary control panel. "Probe launched," he said seconds later. "It is now five hundred meters from the Hoshan ship."

"We might as well make this as impressive as possible. Mr. Scott, can we perform this operation from a greater distance? Say from just beyond the effective range of the Hoshan lasers?"

"Their effective range now is zero, Captain."

"I know that, Scotty. Their original effective range."

"Aye, Captain, we can."

"Very well. Mr. Sulu, take us back, impulse power. Commander Hrozak, you heard what was said. Are you still willing to take the risk?"

"I am. And our sensors show nothing in the probe that you had not said was there. You may proceed whenever you wish."

"Beyond laser range, Captain," Sulu said a minute later.

"Excellent. Lock phasers onto the probe, Mr. Sulu, very carefully. How far is the probe from the Hoshan ship, Mr. Spock?"

"Fifteen hundred meters, Captain. A shield with that range would be consistent with the Hoshan technology."

"Ready, Commander Hrozak?"

"Ready, Commander Kirk."

"Very well. Phasers locked on, Mr. Sulu?"

"Phasers locked on, sir."

"Minimum-duration burst, Mr. Sulu. Fire."

Instantaneously, a single blue-white beam seared a path from the *Enterprise* to the probe, lancing through the Hoshan screens with virtually no lessening of intensity. Almost as quickly, the beam winked out, the only evidence of its brief existence a sparking, bubbling wound across half the face of the probe.

"Radiation levels, Mr. Spock?"

"One-eight-seven at the surface of the Hoshan ship, Captain, but less than one percent of that within the crew compartment. Well within safety limits."

"Commander Hrozak?"

Once again there was silence from the Hoshan ship, but this time for only fifteen seconds. "Very well, Commander Kirk," Hrozak's translated voice said, "you obviously have teeth as well as a shell. And no matter how hard I try, I can no longer see any persuasive reason for someone with your obvious capabilities to have to resort to the kind of trickery we have been discussing, or any other kind. Therefore, I will do as you ask. I will take your translators and your message and my records of what I have seen to my superiors. I will do what I can, but I can promise nothing."

"Thank you, Commander, that's all we ask. We will transport the crew of the *Tromak* and the translators whenever you're ready."

Cutting off the channel to the Hoshan ship, Kirk glanced around the bridge with a grim smile. "One down, gentlemen," he said, "one to go."

Chapter Fourteen

In many ways, the meeting—confrontation—with the Zeator was a replay of that with the Hoshan. Scotty, forced to watch not just one ship but four smother the *Enterprise* in wave after wave of unreturned fire, at first looked as pained as before, but finally, like Sulu's, his features took on a grimly prideful look.

The commander of one of the guard ships, however, despite all the logic Kirk could muster and all the pleas that Atragon could manage, refused to halt his ship's overload sequence. Its antimatter fuel vaporized the entire ship and disabled the nearby ship that Atragon had been on. Luckily it left the two more distant ships untouched. Also luckily for the crew of the disabled ship, Spock, having analyzed the signals needed to trigger the suicide implants, was able to override them long enough to allow McPhee, once again in the transporter room, to lock onto the survivors and pull them from the disabled ship before its automatic circuits took over and completed the overload sequence its commander had attempted to halt moments earlier, before the disabling of his ship had taken that option from him.

As a necessary precaution, the Zeator brought aboard the *Enterprise* were stunned by phaser fire as they materialized, but they were kept unconscious only long enough to take them to the medical section to confirm what Atragon had said about the implanted devices and to disable the auxiliary triggering mechanisms in their rings. Atragon, his words relayed directly to the bridge and from there via subspace radio to the two remaining Zeator ships, talked almost continually from the moment of the ship's explosion, explaining what was being done, and why, including an account of the Hoshan who had succeeded in detonating the Hoshan version of the implant, vaporizing himself and seriously injuring one of the humans.

The Zeator on the ships said little, only listened, waiting tensely for the five who had supposedly been snatched from their exploded sister ship to be allowed to regain consciousness. Like the Hoshan commander, neither reversed the overload sequence in his ship but held it steady at barely eight seconds to terminal overload. Kirk also remained largely silent, letting Atragon do the talking.

When the five from the destroyed ship were allowed to awaken, Atragon was standing in front of the cushioned examination tables they still lay on, unrestrained. Kirk, Spock, and McCoy stood behind Atragon, flanked by the same security team that had stunned the arriving Zeator in the transporter room. Here, the team's phasers, though immediately available, were not drawn.

Automatically, the fingers of each awakening Zeator darted to the trigger mechanism in his ring. None, however, actually attempted to activate it, although their fingers invariably remained close to the rings, as if ready to make the attempt at a moment's notice, despite Atragon's assurance that the mechanisms had been at least temporarily disabled and his repeated explanation of the reasons.

For the most part, they listened to Atragon's tale with an outward calmness, even passiveness, but when he suggested that the Hoshan, the so-called World Killers, might not be the ones responsible for the Slaughtered Worlds, that they might even be innocent victims of Zeator paranoia, they rebelled.

"Who are these creatures that you believe the fantasies they spin?" the one who appeared to be the commander asked, casting what was probably a malevolent look at the humans.

"Fantasy?" Atragon demanded. "Was your inability to touch this ship with your weapons a fantasy? Are these devices that let us speak with them a fantasy? Is it a fantasy that you are alive, here, when you should by all rights have been vaporized with your ship?"

"I grant that they have a technology superior to ours," the Zeator said. "That does not necessarily make them truthful! Who are they? Where are they from? Why are they here?"

"If it will help," Kirk interceded, "we will show you what we have already shown Atragon."

All six were then taken to the bridge, where, when the five new arrivals became unfrozen enough to assimilate new information, they were shown roughly the same sequence Atragon had been shown earlier, a brief summary of the *Enterprise*'s arrival and its subsequent encounters with the Hoshan and the Zeator. Atragon, seeing the images for a second time, explained as best he could to the other Zeator what they were seeing.

As with the Hoshan, however, it was the demonstration with the probe, with the *Enterprise*'s phasers piercing the Hoshan defensive screens in a split second, that seemed to impress them the most. In any event, it was then that the five halted their angry questioning of Atragon on virtually everything he said and even began suggesting to the commanders of the remaining two Zeator ships that they had nothing to lose by accepting the translators and at least speaking to other Zeator of what they had seen and heard.

Finally, reluctantly, the overload sequences were reversed on both ships. A half-hour later the six Zeator on the *Enterprise* were transported, three to each Zeator ship, along with a plentiful supply of translators.

Dr. Jason Crandall, who had been allowed to listen but not to participate in the meetings with the Hoshan and the Zeator, found himself wishing with ever-increasing intensity that the *Enterprise* possessed the same type of self-destruct mechanisms that the alien ships did. Such a device, if it existed, would be a ready solution, probably the only solution, to his problems. Even in his present state of desperation, he doubted that he could bring himself to commit suicide, individually and alone, even if he could find a quick and painless method. For one thing, suicide would mean that he had surrendered, and it would give Kirk an easy and unqualified victory over him. But if there were a lever somewhere, the kind of lever that apparently existed on the alien ships, a lever that would destroy not only himself but the *Enterprise* and everyone on board—pulling such a lever would not be surrender. It would, in fact, be a victory, the only victory that Crandall could, now, ever know.

In the first hours following his ill-conceived and abortive attempt to overthrow Kirk and his emotionless first officer, Crandall had felt a brief surge of relief, even gratitude, at the seeming leniency of Kirk's treatment. Such feelings, however, had quickly soured as he began to realize that he had little reason for relief, even less for gratitude. Perhaps not everyone on the *Enterprise* knew the precise details of what had happened on the bridge, but they knew enough. The expressions on the faces of every crew member he passed in the corridors or on the recreation decks, even in the turbolifts, told him that much and more. They knew. They knew, and now they saw him not only as an outsider who could never be allowed to enter their exclusive club but as an enemy as well.

Worse, they now saw him as a fool.

Behind their fleeting, superficial smiles now lurked derisive laughter. This ludicrous outsider, they thought whenever they saw him, had deluded himself so thoroughly that he actually thought he could become one of us. In his ignorance, he thought that he *understood* us, thought even that he could come between us.

Even Ensign Davis, the young woman he had once thought of as an ally, had turned against him, unwilling even to listen to the reasons for his action. Once he had seen her walking alone down one of the ship's endless corridors. For a moment, their eyes had met, and he had thought that, in her, there was at least one person on board who had some understanding of what he had done. But he had been wrong. The instant he turned toward her and opened his mouth to speak, her face reddened angrily, and, deliberately averting her eyes, she turned and virtually ran to the nearest turbolift, as if his very presence were poisoning the air.

Life under such conditions, Crandall had quickly realized, was intolerable, and every day he became more certain that conditions would never improve. For a time he had thought there was at least a chance that some day he might be put down on the Hoshan home world. The Hoshan might not be totally human, but they would almost certainly be less alien to him than the crew of the *Enterprise*.

And if only the *Enterprise* had entered the battle on the side of the Hoshan, making heroes of everyone on board, himself included, who knows how far he could have gone?

But now, with Kirk so enamored of his role as godlike bringer of peace, even that door was closed. Hoshan and Zeator might soon be talking to each other for the first time in their histories, but neither would ever fully trust the *Enterprise* or anyone on it. The Hoshan and Zeator worlds were both now out of Crandall's reach, probably forever, and the possibility of finding other civilizations in this no-man's land of devastation was virtually nonexistent. That had become ever more apparent with each new stellar system the *Enterprise* scanned.

Worst of all, however, was the soul-shriveling knowledge that, because of his own stupidity and miscalculations, earth and the Federation were now as lost to him as everything else. Even if the so-called gate reappeared tomorrow and deposited the *Enter-*

prise in a standard orbit around Starbase One, it would do Crandall no good. No matter how lenient Kirk played at being here on the *Enterprise*, Dr. Jason Crandall was, in Kirk's eyes, a criminal and a traitor, and there was absolutely no doubt in Crandall's mind that, if they ever did get back to Federation territory, he would instantly be brought up on charges. Kirk could afford to do nothing else, not there.

Here, far from the reach of the Council, Kirk was all-powerful, and he could afford to play whatever cat-and-mouse games he wanted with Crandall. In Federation territory, where he was only a starship captain, he would have no choice but to bring charges. Not that Kirk would want to keep Crandall's blunders a secret, of course. Doubtless he would take great pleasure in telling and retelling the story of the pitifully deluded outsider who had tried to instigate a mutiny.

Kirk's only reason for keeping it to himself would be if he thought that by so doing he could gain leverage over Crandall and his influential friends. He might think that a little blackmail would get him some extra gold braid or a plum post with Starfleet Command. Crandall had no doubt that Kirk would be more than willing to try it—if he thought he could get away with it. But blackmail with the entire crew of the *Enterprise* knowing the secret was obviously impossible. No matter how great their camaraderie, more than four hundred people, even the crew of a starship, were incapable of keeping a secret like this one.

No, even if by some miracle the *Enterprise* suddenly reappeared in Federation territory this very day, Crandall could see no acceptable future for himself, no future that he would choose to live through.

Lying back on the bed in his stateroom, from which he now rarely stirred, Dr. Jason Crandall continued to dream of levers and destruction.

"Captain Kirk! Ta' the bridge!" Lieutenant Commander Scott's voice crackled over the recreation deck intercom.

Kirk, sweating profusely from the calisthenics McCoy had insisted he start up again, dropped the medicine ball that Lieutenant Woida had almost floored him with and slapped the nearest intercom.

"Kirk here," he said between breaths. "What is it, Scotty?"

"Subspace contact, Captain, wi' both the Hoshan *and* the Zeator!"

"Where are they?"

"Both beyond our sensor range, Captain, and widely separated from each other. Both wish to speak wi' the commander of the *Enterprise*."

"On my way!"

Pausing only long enough to grab his uniform tunic, Kirk raced down the corridor to the elevator, slipping on the tunic as he ran. Less than a minute later, still breathing heavily, he emerged on the bridge.

"What—" he began, but the words froze as his eyes fell on the forward viewscreen, split to show two separate images, one in each half. On the left was a Hoshan, short and stocky in the same type of utilitarian, multipocketed outfit the others had worn, except that this one seemed somehow crisper, the pockets more numerous but more for display than for utility. Perhaps they were, Kirk thought briefly, a badge of rank for the Hoshan. He could remember no identifying markings on any of the Hoshan who had been on board the *Enterprise*.

On the right of the screen was a Zeator, tall and regal, his uniform a pale blue-green with white and yellow diamond-shaped markings on the breast, where the others had displayed similarly colored circles. A silvery streak ran down the center of his featherlike hair.

The two images had only two things in common. First, both Hoshan and Zeator held universal translators, and second, behind each of the aliens was a featureless bulkhead, revealing nothing of the interior of the ships.

"Their ships have always had a visual capability,

Captain," Spock said, even as Kirk darted a questioning glance at him, "but neither the Hoshan nor the Zeator have used it before except in the compressed subspace bursts."

"You are the Commander James Kirk we have been told of?" the Zeator said.

Suppressing a grimace, Kirk ran his fingers through his perspiration-damp hair and stepped forward. "I am Captain James Kirk, commanding the U.S.S. *Enterprise*, yes," he said as he slid into the command chair that Scott had vacated only moments be fore.

"I am Endrakon," the Zeator said, "in command of all ships patrolling the Slaughtered Worlds."

"And I am Belzhrokaz," the Hoshan said. "All Hoshan in the Zone of Destruction are my responsibility."

"I am pleased that you both have contacted us," Kirk said. "I am also pleased that our gifts have enabled you to speak with each other."

"Your devices are most helpful," the Zeator, Endrakon, said, raising his translator a fraction. "Had they existed a hundred years ago, many lives might have been saved."

"Many lives can still be saved," Kirk said, "if you will continue the contact you have begun."

"Yes," Endrakon said, "that is our hope. And that is why we have contacted you, Commander Kirk. We have need of your great ship."

Kirk hesitated a fraction, darting a glance at Spock and Scott, who volunteered nothing. "As we told your people when they were on board the *Enterprise*," he said, "we will do whatever we can to help. What is it you wish?"

"As I am sure you can understand, Commander Kirk," Belzhrokaz said, "a hundred years of all-out war cannot be ended in a day, nor can trust be built in a similar period. Both will take time, and both will require more direct contact between Hoshan and Zeator than can be accomplished through subspace links such as these. We must meet, face to face, if peace is ever to come."

"Understood," Kirk said. "Do you wish to meet, then, on neutral ground? On board the *Enterprise*?"

"Neutral ground, yes," Endrakon said, picking up where Belzhrokaz had left off as smoothly as if it had been rehearsed. "It is a concept neither of us has considered in hundreds of years, but that is what we wish. However, there is more."

"Again," Kirk said, "anything we can do to help, we will."

"The rest of what we need is more onerous, Commander Kirk," the Zeator continued, "and more dangerous. We need—we both need your great ship to guarantee the safety of our own ships when we meet."

"Could you not simply agree to disarm your ships?" Kirk asked slowly.

"Impossible!" the Zeator said and was echoed by the Hoshan.

"You could keep your ships separated, then," Kirk said, "as they are now. The *Enterprise* could collect representatives from both ships and—"

"No," Belzhrokaz interrupted. "We must face each other, not only individually on your *Enterprise* but with our ships. There is no other way if our efforts are to succeed."

"He is right," Endrakon said. "We must meet. Our forces must meet, peacefully. We must learn, after centuries of war, to trust each other, but during those first steps, we both must have your protection."

"From each other?" Kirk asked, frowning. "How can we protect you against each other?"

"We believe your presence alone will be enough," Belzhrokaz said. "We have both seen what your weapons can do, how they can penetrate our shields as if they did not exist. If either of us attacks the other, you must be prepared to destroy whatever ship fires the first shot."

"I wasn't aware," Kirk said slowly, "that either of you trusted *us* all that much."

"We do not trust you completely," the Hoshan continued, "but we trust you more than we trust each other at this point. And we have little choice. If we are to have even the slightest hope of ending these centuries of war, we have *no* choice."

"On that," the Zeator said, "we agree. Our worlds have lived in fear for centuries. We must take this chance to end that fear. Your presence and your gifts that allow us to communicate have given us that chance, and we must take it. With your great ship to ensure a peaceful first meeting, perhaps we will succeed."

Slowly, Kirk looked from the image of the Zeator to that of the Hoshan, trying to penetrate the barrier of their expressionless faces, as he had tried with the Hoshan earlier. But this time there was nothing, not even the tiniest clue in their features to guide him.

"Very well," he said finally, "it will be as you wish."

"Thank you, Commander Kirk," Endrakon said, echoed by Belzhrokaz. "If you will continue your subspace transmissions, we will both follow them to your ship."

A moment later, the images faded.

"Both ships are still transmitting, Captain," Uhura said, "but only a carrier. Shall I do as they said?"

Kirk nodded. "Continue to transmit," he said, "but do as they do. Only a carrier, no modulation."

"I dinna like it, Captain," Scott said, shaking his head. "I wouldna put it past either o' them to rig their own ships to blow and then try to blame it on the other."

"The thought had crossed my mind, Scotty. But we can monitor them for that sort of thing easily enough. And before they arrive, we'll *tell* them we can. We'll make it abundantly clear that we can tell the difference between another suicide and an attack." Kirk paused, frowning at the blank screens. "I only hope it's something that simple that they're up to."

Chapter Fifteen

ALWAYS IN THE past, once Dr. Jason Crandall's spirits hit rock bottom, once he came to fully accept the situation as it existed and began to make plans based on that newly accepted version of reality, his spirits would begin to lift. From despair would come the seeds of anticipation. It had happened in the wake of the Tajarhi disaster, when he had finally accepted the fact that, even though the accident had not been his fault, he would be the one to shoulder the blame. Once he had accepted that basic fact, no matter how unfair it might have been, and had begun to plan accordingly, he was on his way back up. He had, of course, had to leave Tajarhi and start fresh on another world parsecs away, but he had, eventually, regained much of what he had lost.

And it had happened here, on the *Enterprise*, when he had realized that, no matter what he did, he would never return to the Federation. He had once again started fresh, filled with optimism and enthusiasm. Unfortunately, his subsequent decisions and actions had been disastrous, largely because that very optimism had allowed him to see opportunities that did not, in reality, exist. His total misreading of McCoy's feelings, his willful obliviousness to the mindless nature and strength of the bonds that held this insular little group together, and finally his foolish attempt at mutiny had combined to make his situation even more hopeless than it had been before.

But he had been able, finally, to accept even that.

He had at last admitted to himself that he had no hope whatsoever of achieving any kind of tolerable life here on the *Enterprise*. He had realized that his only hope for *any* kind of victory over Kirk and the four-hundred-odd sycophants that made up this interstellar fraternity lay in the method of his own death.

For several days, however, he had done nothing about it, laid no plans. This time, because of the utter finality of his situation, his despair had not immediately begun its metamorphosis into anticipation, and for days he had simply indulged in pointless imaginings, fantasizing about what he could do if the *Enterprise* had self-destruct systems like the alien vessels. When he should have been out probing for an Achilles heel, when he should have been out among the crew, asking questions and talking and observing, no matter how much he was secretly ridiculed by them, he had been hiding in his stateroom virtually twenty-four hours a day, pointlessly dreaming of things that didn't exist.

But then, abruptly, when Kirk announced the return of the Hoshan and the Zeator, everything changed. In an instant, Crandall was jarred out of his fantasy world, and an instant later he realized that the *Enterprise* did indeed, under certain conditions, have the kind of self-destruct system he had been pointlessly fantasizing about for days.

A self-destruct system that, to his shame, he had already failed to use.

Twice.

Literally, he leaped to his feet in sudden exultation when the realization hit him, and in that instant he vowed that, no matter what, he would not fail the next time the opportunity arose.

He would finally have his victory.

"Never mind what the blasted machine says, Jim. Do *you* believe him?" McCoy, at his desk in the medical section, watched Kirk pace the length of the room.

"Bones," Kirk said, "there are times when you can evade medical questions almost as well as Spock can evade emotional ones. I'm the one who came down here to ask *you* if I *should* trust him. Could he have tricked the machine?"

"And that isn't a medical question, Jim. Medically speaking, Dr. Crandall appears to have recovered from the depression he went into after he tried to give me the *Enterprise* and found out I didn't want it. Also medically speaking, he appears to be healthy as a horse. As for whether or not he did—or could—get away with a lie while his hand is stuck in that computerized lie detector you call a Verifier . . ." McCoy's voice trailed off as his eyes widened in mock innocence. "Don't tell me you're losing faith in technology, Captain."

Kirk shook his head. "Hardly, Bones. However, after all the malfunctions I've seen, I don't trust it blindly, either. And out here, who knows how many millions or billions of parsecs from home, possibly in another universe altogether, with *everyone*—but particularly Crandall—in the middle of his or her own psychological crisis, nothing that depends on purely physiological reactions to determine truth or falsity can be one-hundred-percent reliable."

McCoy smiled faintly. "You know how I feel about the infallibility of machines, Jim, even under the best of circumstances, but it sounds to me as if you've already made up your mind. Now you're just trying to come up with a 'real' reason."

"You may be right, but I'd still like an evaluation from ship's chief medical officer."

"Without full-scale psychological tests, conducted under conditions a lot less stressful than the ones we're all living under now, there's no way of medically removing that last smidgin of doubt. Or confirming it, either."

"All right, then, what do your 'old country doctor' instincts tell you?"

"They don't apply to this sort of thing, Jim. How

would you like it if I asked you what your 'captain's instincts' told you when Crandall first suggested he might be able to help in the talks between the Hoshan and the Zeator?"

"I'd say that, logically, his suggestion made perfect sense. After all, he *is* a politician. According to the computer, before he let things get out of hand on Tajarhi, he'd been a middleman in several negotiations. None on this scale, but big enough. He'd successfully mediated half a dozen disputes on Tajarhi itself."

"That's Spock's logic, not your so-called instinct. What does *it* say?"

Kirk shook his head with a rueful smile. "My 'captain's instincts' tell me to be suspicious, even though I haven't been able to come up with a single reason other than his own previously erratic behavior. He's obviously not going to try another mutiny, not now that he understands the situation and knows he can't succeed. And he couldn't possibly think he could take over the *Enterprise* at phaser point and run it by himself. No one, not even Spock, could run it alone, and Crandall knows that. Logic—and the computer—tells me that, this time, he's finally come to his senses and is simply trying to make up for his earlier blunders by trying to be as helpful as he can."

"You're back to logic again. It and your machines tell you one thing, but your instinct tells you another?"

"Exactly, which is why I wanted your professional evaluation in the first place, Bones."

"And you've gotten it. My professional evaluation is that he's healthy. Probably healthier than you, if you don't stick to the diet and the exercise program I laid out for you. Personally and nonmedically speaking, I wouldn't trust him any farther than you could throw one of Lieutenant Woida's barbells, and I wouldn't let him anywhere near the bridge without a full security detail around him, one that's more alert than the one he got the drop on the first time."

Kirk smiled faintly. "Thank you for your candor, Doctor. I'll take it and my own prejudices into account. Now what about the rest of the crew?" he went on, his face sobering. "How are they holding up?"

McCoy settled back in his chair behind the desk. "As well as you could expect, considering the situation. A few more cases of psychosomatic illnesses than usual, but nothing spectacular yet. A few nightmares, a few people who have trouble sleeping. A half-dozen brawls for no reason but the tension everyone's under. But nothing we can't handle. Or rather, nothing the crew can't handle themselves, so far."

"But later, when—*if* it becomes clear that we have no chance of finding our way back to the Federation, ever?"

McCoy shook his head somberly. "I don't know, Jim, I just don't know. I guess we'll find out if what you said before, about the *Enterprise* being a sort of extended family, is really true. And if it is, if that's enough to make up for the real families and friends and homes they left behind."

Kirk was silent for a long moment. Then, pulling in a breath, he turned to the door. "It may have to be, Bones," he said as the door hissed open. "It may have to be."

When the Hoshan ships first came into sensor range, Crandall, ever under the watchful eye of Lieutenant Tomson, had been listening attentively to the subspace exchanges between Kirk and the Hoshan and the Zeator for more than an hour. Kirk had been explaining, among other things, why neither the Hoshan nor the Zeator could successfully fake being attacked by the other. So far, Crandall's only contribution had been a comment to the effect that he did not think that the Hoshan had believed Kirk's claim that the *Enterprise*'s sensors could detect the power buildup that preceded the firing of their lasers.

"You have demonstrated you can monitor their antimatter generators," Crandall had said when the communication link was broken, "but there was something in Belzhrokaz's face when he was listening to you that indicated, to me at least, that he was still skeptical."

Kirk had only nodded at the words, since he had reached essentially the same conclusion independently. The incident, however, had strengthened Kirk's logical conviction that Crandall was, in effect, trying to redeem himself and could indeed prove helpful when the two alien groups came together on the *Enterprise*. It had done nothing, however, to eliminate the instinctual distrust he had discussed with McCoy.

"Twenty-seven Hoshan ships, Captain," Spock said, moments after he had announced the arrival of the first ship within sensor range. "All appear to be essentially identical to those Hoshan vessels we encountered earlier."

Frowning, Kirk swung the command chair to face his first officer. "Twenty-seven?"

"Twenty-seven, Captain."

"Belzhrokaz didn't say anything about bringing an armada with him."

"Nor did he specifically state otherwise, Captain. Perhaps, like humans, the Hoshan believe that massive displays of force are the proper prelude to talks of peace."

Kirk scowled at the viewscreen, where the Hoshan ships were beginning to appear as faint dots. "And how many of their ships did you say our deflectors could withstand? Eleven?"

"For an extended period, that is correct. For brief periods, the number is higher."

"How much higher?"

"It depends on the definition of brief, Captain. Could you be more specific?"

"Let's say the period of time it would take the *Enterprise* to get out of range of their lasers, taking into account the power that you have to divert from the shields to the warp drive."

"The situation you postulate is even more complex,

Captain. There are too many variables to allow any specific number to be considered reliable."

"Some generalities, then. Anything to give me a feel for the situation."

"Very well, Captain. As I am sure you know, the more power that is diverted to the warp engines, the more the shields are weakened and the quicker they will fail. On the other hand, increased power to the warp engines will take us out of range of the lasers more quickly, thereby reducing the time the shields are required to hold. If the situation arises, a calculation of the optimum distribution of power for the specific circumstances that prevail will be a necessity. If the twenty-seven Hoshan ships just detected began simultaneous firing from one hundred kilometers, for example, full power to the shields would protect the *Enterprise* for approximately fifty-eight seconds."

Spock paused, leaning over his readouts. "If accomplished at the first moment of firing, optimum distribution of power between warp engines and deflectors would reduce that time to thirty-seven seconds but would take the *Enterprise* out of range within fifteen seconds. We would, however, be able to detect any potential laser firings at least ten seconds prior to the actual firing, which would give us an additional margin of safety."

"You're saying, then, that if we're on our toes, we don't have anything to worry about from the Hoshan ships, Mr. Spock?"

"I would not express it in those terms, precisely, Captain, but what you say is essentially true."

"And if the Zeator have just as many ships?"

Spock studied his readouts again. "If similar numbers of both Hoshan and Zeator fired simultaneously from a similar distance, we would still have sufficient time, but only if we initiated acceleration toward warp speed within one second of the attack."

"And the upper limit of the number of ships we could escape from in this way?"

"Theoretically, Captain, as long as we do not allow

ourselves to be encircled, there would be no limit. If all power were diverted from the shields to the warp engines within two seconds of the moment preparations to fire were detected—eight seconds before actual firing—we would be out of their effective range before their lasers could fire."

"Then we had better not let ourselves be encircled, gentlemen. And Mr. Spock, I assume you will have all the necessary calculations ready for immediate implementation by the helm."

"Of course, Captain."

The Zeator, coming within sensor range an hour later, had thirty-one ships.

When Kirk had finally, reluctantly, allowed Dr. Jason Crandall onto the bridge, Crandall had been elated, albeit a bit surprised. On his good days, he had always had a fifty-fifty chance of faking out any lie detector that relied on physiological reactions, whether it was computerized or not, but even after he had apparently succeeded with the so-called Verifier, Kirk had still held back. Obviously, like everyone on board except perhaps Dr. McCoy, Kirk had a rigid faith in the capabilities of his ship and its gadgets, but even so, he had delayed for more than a day before accepting Crandall's offer to help in the upcoming negotiations, by which time Crandall had almost given up all hope of ever getting onto the bridge again.

And the bridge was where he would have to be, if he were going to have any chance of winning his final victory, either now or at some time in the future. For the immediate future, his primary hope centered on the excessively suspicious nature that both Hoshan and Zeator had so far displayed. Neither Belzhrokaz nor Endrakon, he was sure, would blindly accept their subordinates' claims of the *Enterprise*'s powers, particularly its seeming invulnerability to their weapons. They would, Crandall suspected and hoped, ask for another demonstration, and that would be all the chance he would need.

But then, as the messages flew back and forth through subspace prior to the aliens' coming within sensor range, his hopes dwindled. To his surprise, and perhaps to that of Kirk as well, neither of the aliens so much as mentioned the demonstrations of the *Enterprise*'s capabilities, let alone asked for new ones. For whatever reason, there seemed to be an air of resigned acceptance in their attitudes toward the humans.

As they had indicated during the first communications, they trusted the humans only slightly more than they trusted each other, but neither Belzhrokaz nor Endrakon, unlike the earlier, lower-ranking aliens, seemed inclined to challenge, or even question, anything Kirk said. Even when it had seemed, at least to Crandall, that the Zeator commander had doubted Kirk's claims of what the instruments on the *Enterprise* were capable of detecting, Endrakon had said nothing, had asked for no proof. And proof of that particular claim would have been far easier to supply than the proofs Kirk had originally supplied in regard to the *Enterprise*'s deflectors and weaponry. A simple thirty-second demonstration would have proven it beyond a doubt, but no proof was requested.

It was, Crandall soon began to think, as if both the Hoshan and the Zeator were simply trying not to rock the boat, and that in itself made Crandall suspicious, though he was careful not to mention this to Kirk. The two alien commanders were, he was increasingly convinced, up to something, and each new development, each new uncertainty, only strengthened that suspicion and therefore strengthened Crandall's own regenerating optimism.

Finally, then, both fleets of ships came to a stop just inside transporter range. A pair of Hoshan and Zeator subordinates shared the viewscreen, maintaining communications with each other and with the *Enterprise* while the two commanders left to join their respective delegations, which would be transported to the *Enterprise* as soon as they were ready.

"It is understood," Kirk repeated, "that for your

safety and our own, all delegates will be rendered unconscious briefly so that we can verify your claim that all personal self-destruct devices have been deactivated."

"Of course, Commander Kirk," the Hoshan subordinate said, as Belzhrokaz had said earlier, and the Zeator quickly agreed.

"Very well. We have a conference room prepared. As requested, it is equipped to allow the delegates to be in constant, virtually instantaneous visual contact with their own ships. Transport can begin whenever you give us the exact coordinates of your delegations."

"Hoshan coordinates already received, Captain," McPhee's voice came from the transporter room. And, a moment later: "Zeator coordinates also received. Ready to transport on your order."

"Security?"

"Ready, Captain," Lieutenant Tomson acknowledged, also from the transporter room.

"Mr. Spock?"

"Ready to neutralize the devices if necessary, Captain."

For a moment, Kirk was silent, his eyes going again to the two aliens sharing the forward viewscreen. As their commanders had been, the two were firmly expressionless.

"Your delegations are ready?"

"They are, Commander Kirk," both aliens said.

"Very well." With a last glance at Spock and Crandall, Kirk swung the command chair to face the helm. "Mr. Sulu, prepare to lower deflectors for transport."

"Ready, Captain."

"Mr. McPhee, take the Hoshan first, and don't waste any time."

"Of course, Captain."

"Mr. Sulu, lower deflectors. Bring them back to full power the moment you hear from McPhee."

"Aye-aye, Captain."

One eye on the aliens on the screen, Sulu tapped in

the code that lowered the deflectors, leaving his fingers poised above the keys that would restore them.

For a moment there was total silence. Then McPhee's voice came from the transporter room.

"Having trouble locking on, sir. The coordinates don't—"

"Lasers on all ships preparing to fire, Captain!" Spock said sharply.

"Deflectors up, Mr. Sulu!" Kirk snapped. "Get us out of here!"

Even before Kirk had voiced the order, however, Crandall, his eyes fixed on the controls beneath Sulu's fingers, was lunging forward, slamming past Kirk, sending the command chair spinning. An instant later, he crashed against Sulu, knocking him from his chair before the helmsman had the chance to carry out either order. At the very moment Sulu was sprawling to the deck, Crandall felt the numbing sting of a phaser, but before consciousness faded he knew that it had come too late to help Kirk and his beloved *Enterprise*.

Chapter Sixteen

TO A GREAT EXTENT, it was Spock's Vulcan mental discipline, his ability to accommodate dozens of sensory inputs simultaneously and to integrate them into logical patterns, that allowed him to so rapidly interpret the countless readings his science station instruments supplied. To Spock's bemusement, Kirk had once compared it to the ability of a great symphony conductor to instantly absorb the mass of musical notations from the sheets in front of him, integrate them into the total sound the orchestra should produce, and then, with his baton, draw the required combination of sounds from the dozens of players, confident that, if even a single horn or string hit a wrong note, he would be able to detect it and pinpoint its source.

It was an aspect of this same ability that now saved the *Enterprise* from total disaster.

Even as he was announcing that the alien ships were preparing to fire, Spock heard a sudden intake of breath somewhere behind him, and as the captain began to issue his curt orders, the science officer heard a sudden motion, a motion that did not fit the expected pattern of response to his announcement.

Darting a look over his shoulder, he saw Crandall charging forward, lunging toward the helm and Mr. Sulu.

Without hesitation, Spock turned and vaulted over the handrail. As his booted feet hit the deck behind the navigator's station, Crandall was already crashing into

Sulu, knocking the helmsman from his chair. In the same instant, Ensign Reems, leaping to one side to get a clear shot past Kirk in the spinning command chair, fired his phaser, hitting Crandall squarely, sending him sprawling limply onto Sulu, who was struggling to get to his feet and back to the helm.

Spock, taking one long step, leaned over Sulu's empty chair and stabbed at the buttons that would implement the program to raise the deflectors and initiate acceleration to warp speed.

In that same instant, the first of the Hoshan lasers fired.

A fraction of a second later, the deflectors only starting to build, the first Zeator lasers fired.

Within two seconds, all lasers in both fleets were firing, and the *Enterprise* shook violently as the deflectors absorbed what energy they could and the engines strove to accelerate out of range.

Within fifteen seconds, they were in warp drive and it was over.

A comprehensive damage report took a bit longer. Safely at the edge of sensor range, listening on all subspace frequencies but broadcasting on none, the *Enterprise* rested, waiting for the verdict.

"We're no' quite defenseless, Captain," Chief Engineer Scott said from the engineering deck, "but almost. The deflectors were seriously overloaded, trying to build up while under attack. Repairs are possible, but they'll take a wee bit o' time."

"How much, Scotty?"

"Several days, Captain. Each generator has to be torn down and rebuilt from scratch. But that's not the worst o' the problems."

"What's the worst, then?"

"The dilithium crystals, Captain, the one thing we canna replace or repair. They're on the ragged edge. We can use them, but only sparingly. If ye need more than warp four or more than half power from the phaser banks, they'll be gone."

"Warp four should be enough to keep us out of reach."

"Aye, provided they don't gi' up the ghost altogether."

"See that they don't, Scotty."

"Aye, Captain, I'll do what I can."

"Dr. McCoy?"

"One broken arm, already being set. Beyond that, some bumps and bruises, but nothing serious."

"Lieutenant Uhura?"

"All subspace channels functional, sir."

"And the Hoshan and Zeator?"

"No longer broadcasting on any frequency."

"Mr. Spock, what are they doing?"

"They have formed a single formation, Captain. They appear to be trying to follow us at their maximum speed, warp two-point-five."

"Appear to be following?"

"They are duplicating our own departing heading almost precisely."

Kirk grimaced. "And this time, we don't dare let them catch us. Mr. Sulu, lay in a course to our original point of entry into this sector."

"Aye-aye, sir. We're going to look for the gate again?"

"If that's what it was, yes. We don't appear to be in a position to do much good around here, or to look very far afield for whoever built it, unless Mr. Scott can do something about the dilithium crystals. Security?"

"Tomson here, Captain. Dr. Crandall is confined to a detention cell, as ordered."

"Any trouble getting him there?"

"He offered no resistance, sir, but some of the crew got a little ugly when they saw him."

"I'm not surprised. Keep a close watch on him, just to make sure no one tries to do something foolish."

"Very good, sir. I'll see that no one gets to him."

"Thank you, Lieutenant. Now, Mr. Spock, Dr. McCoy, Mr. Scott, as soon as you can spare the time, I think we'd better have a few words about our options."

Dr. Leonard McCoy shook his head and scowled, not at any of the other three around the briefing-room table but at himself. "I'm not saying I should have predicted what happened," he said, "but I *should* have guessed that something like it *could* have happened."

"No more than I, Bones," Kirk said. "None of us had any way of knowing what was going on inside his head, not even the computer. From all indications, he was the last person you would expect to turn suicidal, least of all the way he did." He shrugged. "Maybe it was all the self-destruction he saw in the Hoshan and Zeator. Maybe it's contagious in some way."

"Maybe for people like Crandall!" McCoy growled.

"Be on the alert anyway, Bones."

"Blast it, Jim—" McCoy began but then subsided. "You're right. I'll have my staff keep an eye out for symptoms. So far, there's nothing beyond the tension you could expect, given the circumstances."

"Yes, gentlemen," Kirk said, looking briefly at each of the three, "the circumstances. Any thoughts as to why we were attacked?"

"Only the obvious one, Captain," Spock said. "As you yourself have pointed out, the methods by which many of the worlds in this sector were destroyed are beyond the technology of either Hoshan or Zeator. Apparently the significance of this fact was not lost on them, and their actions, viewed in a narrow perspective, were only logical."

Kirk sighed in agreement. "Once we proved that neither of *them* could have destroyed those worlds, they jumped to the conclusion that, since we had a superior technology, *we* were the ones responsible. Yes, Spock, the thought had crossed my mind even before the attack, but I tried to keep an open mind. Scotty? Bones? You agree?"

"For all the good it does, I do," McCoy said, and Scott nodded.

"Which still leaves the question of who *did* destroy all those worlds," Kirk said. "And whoever it was, are they still around? Are they the same ones who built the gate? *If*, that is, the gates were indeed built and are not, after all, a natural phenomenon. I know we've been over this ground before, but the condition of the *Enterprise* and the presence of the Hoshan and Zeator lynch mob change the picture somewhat. Before, we were free to conduct a search throughout hundreds of thousands of cubic parsecs with full power available to the warp engines and the deflectors. Now, unless we find a source of dilithium, we're severely limited in both range and safety."

"Aye," Scott said, "and I canna guarantee the crystals will hold up forever, even under limited use."

"But even if they fail," Kirk said, "we would still have warp drive."

"Aye, up to about warp two-point-five, but no' immediately. Until I could pull the crystals and wire around them, we would have no' but impulse power."

"So, gentlemen, you see the situation. Any thoughts?"

"Obviously," McCoy said, "we see if the gate has come back."

"Agreed. Anything else? I can't be sure, of course, but I'd be willing to bet that, once our two warring friends can't locate us back there where we left them, they'll come back to the area where the gate was and keep watch for us."

"Logical," Spock said. "And once they establish a sufficiently dense perimeter around it, we could not, in our present condition, penetrate it unharmed."

McCoy's scowl deepened. "You're saying it could be now or never? If we don't find the gate now, we'll never find it?"

"Precisely, Doctor," Spock said. "However, the odds of finding our way back to known space have never been favorable. Recent developments have only increased already high odds against us. However, there is one possibility that has not yet been mentioned."

"Yes, Mr. Spock?" Kirk prompted.

"You will recall that, during our initial explorations in the immediate region of our arrival point, there was one planet from which anomalous readings were obtained. Deep underground, our sensors gave readings that, while not indicative of true life, at least proved that something was there—a sophisticated power source as well as something that, conceivably, could have been some unknown form of organic computer."

"I remember," Kirk said. "I also remember that you were as puzzled as I have ever seen you. And that there was no way to get more information except by beaming down into totally sealed-off areas through miles of solid rock. With the options we had then, it wasn't that attractive an alternative. With the more limited options now before us, are you suggesting it warrants a second look? Including beaming down?"

"Precisely, Captain. The planet does not lie far from the course we must take to return to our arrival point, so we will lose little time. In addition, considering the relative proximity of such a totally inexplicable phenomenon to the equally inexplicable phenomenon of the gate itself, it is only logical to assume at least the possibility of a connection."

"A control center of some kind?" Kirk asked. "Customs point for new arrivals? Automated ticket dispenser?"

"As I have said before, Captain, with no more information than we currently have, anything is possible."

"And considering the luck we've had trying to locate the gate on our own so far," Kirk said with a grimace, "even the remotest possibility of gaining new information would be worth the risk."

"My thoughts exactly, Captain. I must admit, however, that those readings have never been far from my mind. Whatever produced them has been, from the beginning, a most intriguing and frustrating phenomenon."

McCoy shook his head, a faint smile appearing for the first time since the four had entered the room. "Spock, you could be being eaten alive, and you'd spend your last minutes trying to analyze the creature's digestive juices."

"Just because one's life may soon end, Doctor, is no reason to cease all attempts to learn."

Kirk laughed. "He's right, Bones. You never know what you'll find that might be useful. We'd all be dead ten times over if—"

"Captain." Sulu's voice came over the intercom. "Hoshan and Zeator ships coming into sensor range from ahead. It looks as if they've been waiting for us to come back this way."

"How many, Mr. Sulu?" Kirk shot back.

"Three so far, sir, one Zeator and two Hoshan."

"Can we slip past them without being detected?"

"Without knowing the precise range of their sensors, there's no way to tell. From the way they're separated—fourth ship, another Zeator, just came within sensor range."

"You were saying?"

"I was saying, they appear to be evenly spaced. If their sensor fields overlap, there's no way we can get through undetected."

"But even if they detect us, we can still outrun them."

"We can—as long as the crystals hold out."

"Assuming they detect us and follow, how much time would we have in the vicinity of the gate before they arrive?"

"At the maximum warp Mr. Scott says we're capable of, we would have roughly one standard day."

Standing abruptly, Kirk said, "We're on our way, Mr. Sulu. Scotty, get below and keep your fingers on the crystals' pulse. Mr. Spock, get back to your station and locate any gaps that exist in that sensor net. And if none exists, find the weakest spots and we'll see what we can do."

"I feel obliged to point out, Captain," Spock said as they left the room and strode toward the turbolift, "that even if we successfully penetrate the perimeter the Hoshan and Zeator have apparently established, we could be less successful in finding our way back out."

"Point taken, Mr. Spock. If it comes down to it, however, we are not totally helpless. Even with the phasers at only half power, we can still punch a hole through any perimeter they set up."

"We canna take them all on at once, Captain," Scott interrupted.

"Understood, Mr. Scott. With any luck, we won't have to. Just keep those crystals alive as long as you can."

Twenty minutes later, Spock looked up from his instruments. "They know *something* passed through their perimeter, Captain," he said, "but at the range we maintained, their sensors could not distinguish between a starship coasting with all drives shut down and a small asteroid. Even so, one ship has broken formation and is approaching us. To avoid them, we will have to engage warp drive, which, at this distance, they will be able to detect."

Kirk grimaced. "It was a good try. And we'll still have at least twenty-four hours. Ahead, Mr. Sulu, at maximum attainable warp factor. And Scotty—" He stopped, the grimace turning to a faint grin. "You know the drill, Scotty."

"Aye, Captain, I do." Scott's voice came from the engineering deck. "I'll do what I can."

Even before the *Enterprise* dropped out of warp drive, it was obvious there had been changes on the planet in their absence.

"The antimatter power source detected earlier is now fully operational, Captain," Spock announced.

"Weapons?"

"None detected as yet, Captain."

"Mr. Sulu, put up what deflectors we have and proceed on impulse power."

"Aye-aye, sir."

"Lieutenant Uhura, any subspace activity?"

"None, Captain."

"Continue monitoring all frequencies but maintain radio silence. Mr. Sulu, maximum magnification. Zero in on the spot directly above the energy source."

"Done, sir."

On the screen, the planet looked no different from before, no different from dozens of the other devastated worlds they had seen. Virtually airless and drenched in radiation, its surface was fused like something that had long ago emerged from some cosmic blast furnace. Not a trace of the original surface was visible through the planetwide scar tissue.

"Sensor activity, Captain," Spock said, leaning closer over his instruments. "We are being scanned by devices at least as sensitive as our own."

"All stop, Mr. Sulu! Spock, still no indication of weapons?"

"None, Captain."

"Could they be shielded? If their technology is superior to ours, could they have phasers or other weapons, undetectable behind shields?"

"Possible, Captain, but I detect no shielding of any kind at this time. Nor can I detect any openings in the five kilometers of rock above the power source. However, the sensors are now picking up definite life form readings."

"Similar to your earlier readings?"

"Negative, Captain. Those readings would not have registered at this distance. The present ones are quite—normal."

"How many? What type?"

"Impossible to tell at this range, Captain."

"And the sensors that are scanning *us*—whatever is down there is definitely aware of us?"

"Definitely, Captain."

"The gate people, sir?" Chekov wondered, glancing up from the navigation board.

"Or the ones who destroyed these worlds in the first place," Kirk murmured.

"Or both, Captain," Spock said. "Anyone possessing the technology to build the gates would in all probability also possess the technology to obliterate those worlds."

"Ever the optimist. Very well, they know we're here, so we might as well see if they want to talk. Lieutenant Uhura?"

"Transmitting on all frequencies, sir. No immediate response."

"Sensor scans strengthening, Captain," Spock said and then paused, his eyebrows arching minutely. "Their sensors appear to be affecting our own."

"What? In what way?"

"Our own readings are becoming more precise, Captain. It is as if our sensor probes were, in some way I cannot explain, being enhanced by theirs. Or, perhaps more accurately, ours may actually be riding on theirs to some extent."

"Could it be a trick? Could they be modifying our sensor probes? Feeding us false information?"

"It is conceivable, Captain, if their level of sophistication is sufficiently greater than our own. None of the enhanced readings, however, contradicts any information in the original readings."

"What *do* they tell us, then?"

"Nearly one thousand life forms are currently indicated, all roughly humanoid. There is still no evidence of weapons, nor of any shielding that might hide any weapons with which I am familiar."

"But it would at least be possible for them to hide weapons, not by shielding perhaps, but by falsifying the information our sensors are supposedly picking up?"

"Anything is possible, Captain," Spock said, not taking his eyes from his readouts. "And I now detect transporter activity, originating on the planet ahead."

"What?" Kirk's eyes darted toward his first officer. "We're still far beyond transporter range, Mr. Spock."

"Far beyond *our* transporter range, Captain."

"Mr. Sulu, get us out of here!" Kirk snapped, realizing angrily that he had wasted valuable, perhaps crucial seconds with his almost automatic response to Spock's announcement.

"Aye-aye, sir."

But even as Sulu's fingers danced across the controls, Kirk knew that, this time, the seconds he might have gained would not have made any difference. These transporters, whoever was operating them, could not be escaped so easily. They must have been locked on virtually the instant Spock had detected them. Already he could feel not only the beginnings of the all-over tingle that indicated the transporting process itself had begun but something else, a chilling dampness he had never experienced before. And in front of him, the forms of Sulu and Chekov were already beginning to fade.

A moment later the entire bridge vanished into a swirling haze.

Chapter Seventeen

THE COMMAND CHAIR no longer beneath him, Kirk tumbled to an all-too-solid, plastic-smooth floor, only inches away from Sulu and a pair of crewmen he didn't recognize. Catching himself, he leaped to his feet, grasping for his communicator even as images of the huge, cavernous room that now surrounded him registered in his mind.

But the communicator was gone, as was the universal translator which, since the first encounter with the Hoshan, he had kept clipped to his belt as well.

In front of him, Sulu and the two crew members were scrambling to their feet, but even as they did, more began to materialize, but not in the silvery snowfall that was the trademark of Federation transporters. Instead, they appeared first as a hazy swirl of smoke, not unlike a condensed or focused version of the billowing mists that had marked the appearances and disappearances of Gary Seven, and for a moment the thought darted through Kirk's mind that perhaps the still unknown race that had trained Seven and sent him on his benevolent mission to twentieth-century earth might be involved here, not only with whomever or whatever was doing the transporting but with the gate that had brought them here in the first place.

But that possibility, he realized an instant later, was only speculation, something to blunt the shock of what he was seeing. A dozen feet away, Spock was slowly solidifying, and beyond him, Lieutenant Uhura, and to the left, Scott and Chekov. And in all the space between, dozens more of the crew were appearing, many lurching and crashing into one another as they tried to keep their balance. Just to Kirk's left, an ensign from security appeared, his empty hand extended in front of him as if holding a phaser, and in the distance, before his view was obscured by dozens more of the materializations, he spotted Lieutenant Tomson.

Virtually the entire crew was being snatched from the *Enterprise,* leaving it a derelict! Or, worse, under the control of whomever was operating these transporters!

Automatically, Kirk took in his new surroundings, hoping against hope there would be something he could use, something that would give him even a hint about who was doing this and what he could do to counteract it.

Overhead, in the center of the otherwise featureless, arched ceiling nearly a hundred feet high, was a circular, faintly glowing formation that might have been part of the transporter equipment. Other than that glow, he couldn't locate the source of the relatively dim light that filled the entire room. Everything was visible, but, as if it were an overcast day on a planet's surface, there was no single source of light and not a single shadow anywhere.

"Spock!" Kirk called loudly while most of the massive room was still gripped by stunned silence. "McCoy! Uhura! Chekov! Scott! Tomson! Over here!" There was, he noted automatically, virtually no echo or reverberation, despite the hugeness of the room and the high, arched ceiling.

Everywhere in the room, faces turned toward Kirk's voice, but for the moment, except for those whose names he had called, there was only dazed silence in response. Spock and the others threaded their way through the disoriented crowd toward him,

Spock slowing once to more closely observe another crew member—Ensign McPhee, it turned out—as he materialized less than a yard in front of him.

"Do any of you have a communicator?" Kirk asked when they had all gathered around him. "A phaser? A translator? Tricorder? Any equipment at all?"

Hands darted to belts but came away empty. Apprehensive or angry frowns creased all brows but Spock's, whose arched eyebrow was as eloquent as any of the other words or expressions.

"We seem to be on the receiving end this time, gentlemen," Kirk said when it became obvious that none of them had retained a single piece of equipment through the transport operation. "Whoever brought us here has separated us very neatly not only from the *Enterprise* but from anything we could use to defend ourselves, analyze our surroundings, or communicate with anything or anyone other than ourselves."

"Apparently, Captain," Spock said, looking slowly around. By now, the materializations seemed to have stopped, and the faint glow had disappeared from the massive transporterlike formation in the ceiling. The crew members—the entire four-hundred-plus ships' complement, from the look of it—were beginning to regain their voices.

"The question is," Spock went on, raising his voice to be heard above the growing din of hundreds of other incredulous and puzzled voices, "where are the ones who brought us here? Who are they, and what do they want? And of even more immediate concern, are they now controlling the *Enterprise*, and if so, are they aware that its damaged deflectors make it virtually defenseless or that portions of the Hoshan and the Zeator fleets will in all likelihood arrive within less than one standard day?"

"Brilliant, Spock," McCoy grated. "I don't suppose you've got any answers to go along with the questions."

"Not at this point, Doctor, but if you will be patient—"

From somewhere in the mass of milling people, an angry, incoherent shout cut Spock off in midsentence. Kirk, frowning as he turned toward the sound, heard a second shout, and then a scream.

Suddenly, there was silence everywhere except for the continued shouting—the cursing, Kirk now realized—from the one area. Wordlessly, he strode toward the distant voices, Spock and the others following, the crowd largely evaporating from his path as they recognized him.

As he neared the site of the disturbance, he caught the word "Crandall," sounding very much like an epithet itself, and he increased his pace. Crandall must have been picked off the *Enterprise* along with the regular crew members, and now, deprived of the protection of his detention cell, he was obviously fair game for those who, rightly or wrongly, blamed him for their present predicament. Within seconds, Kirk and Lieutenant Tomson were forcing their way through a tightly packed ring of more than a dozen angry men.

"Break it up, gentlemen!" Kirk snapped, and at the sound of his voice there was sudden silence.

Inside the ring, two ensigns had a flushed and battered Crandall between them. One was gripping Crandall's green tunic front and lifting him until he stood on tiptoes. "This yellow son of a—" the other began, his voice stiff with fury, his balled fist drawn back to strike again, but Kirk cut him off sharply.

"That's enough, mister! Both of you, let him go! Now!"

"But Captain—"

"I said *now!*"

With obvious reluctance, the one lowered his fist and the other untwined his fingers from the crushed fabric of Crandall's tunic front.

"We will deal with Dr. Crandall once we are safely out of here," Kirk went on, "and not before. For the moment, he is in the same boat as the rest of us, and I won't have any more of this undisciplined behavior!

All our efforts—repeat, *all* our efforts and concentration must be focused on understanding the situation we're in. Otherwise, we may never have a chance to get safely out of here and back to the *Enterprise*. Is that understood, gentlemen?"

"But he's the one who got us into this mess in the first place! What if he—"

"Dr. Crandall has acted foolishly, perhaps maliciously, and he's caused us problems, including damage to the ship. He is not, however, solely responsible for our being here, perhaps not even partially responsible. *We* will keep an eye on him from now on. *You*—all of you!" he said, raising his voice to a shout that carried throughout the huge room. "All of you will observe and listen and, above all, *think!* Is that clear?"

For a long moment there was total silence, but then, first from the two men directly in front of him and finally, like a rush of murmuring echoes, from everywhere in the room: "Yes, Captain, we understand."

Grasping Crandall's arm, Kirk marched him out of the now dissolving knot of spectators, bringing him to a halt in the middle of the group of officers a dozen yards away.

"As for you, Dr. Crandall—"

"Why didn't you let them finish me?" Crandall asked, an odd tone of defiance in his voice, anger in his bruised features. "It would have saved you a lot of trouble!"

"You may be right, Dr. Crandall," Kirk said coldly, "and if you try to pull anything else, I *will* let them finish you. In any way they see fit. Understood?"

For a moment, the defiance from Crandall's voice seemed to glitter from his eyes, but then he slumped and averted his gaze. "I understand, Captain," he said, his voice as subdued as his new posture.

"I hope you do, Crandall, I sincerely hope you do," Kirk said. "Lieutenant Tomson, don't let him out of your sight."

"Captain!" A single voice, high-pitched and excited, pierced the newly rising hum of voices that was beginning to fill the room. "Our phasers and communicators—everything's over here!"

The one who had called—a young ensign, her assignment on the *Enterprise* her first post out of the Academy, Kirk remembered as he saw her—was waiting eagerly at the edge of the huge circle of *Enterprise* personnel. Beyond her—beyond an edge defined by the transporterlike circle in the ceiling—the cavernous room extended another fifty even more dimly lit feet. "Ensign Davis, isn't it?" he said automatically.

"Yes, sir," she said, freezing under his gaze, momentarily positive that, somehow, by just looking at her, he would become aware of her earlier disloyalty, her foolishness in believing, even for a few days, the insidious hints and half truths that Crandall had tricked her with.

"There," she said, breaking the grip of the guilty delusion as she turned abruptly and pointed into the dimly lit emptiness. "They're out there, but I can't get at them! There's some kind of barrier!"

"Good work, Ensign," he said as he looked in the direction she was pointing and saw, in a recessed area of one wall, where the light was the dimmest of all, hundreds of pieces of equipment—communicators, phasers, tricorders, medikits, planetary survival equipment, universal translators, virtually every portable item from the *Enterprise* and some never meant to be portable. They appeared to be suspended in midair in the recessed area, as if lying on invisible shelves.

Frowning, Kirk took a cautious step toward the equipment.

Immediately, he felt the barrier. Obviously a force field of some kind, it felt not like a wall but, at first, like a gentle wind in his face.

"Keep back," he said, motioning the others away. "Spock, be ready to pull me out of this thing, if it looks like I'm in trouble. I'll keep up a running account as I go."

"As you wish, Captain," Spock said, experimentally extending one arm to reach past Kirk, deeply into the field, then withdrawing it.

"Jim!" McCoy protested, but fell silent as he saw the determined look on Kirk's face. "All right," he said after a second, "but just remember, all my medical equipment is back on the *Enterprise*. Except for the tricorders and medikits, which appear to be on the other side of this invisible wall."

Nodding his acknowledgment, Kirk moved another short step forward and began talking.

The wind, no longer a gentle breeze, mounted with each inch, until it was no longer a wind but a steadily increasing pressure, mounting until it felt like a smooth, nonviolent version of the pressure air exerts against a hand that's extended out through the window of a moving vehicle. The pressure was not against any single point or group of points, but uniformly against every square centimeter of the front of his body. Getting enough breath to describe the sensations became harder with each inch he moved forward.

Abruptly, he stopped trying to move, and in the instant that he did, the pressure vanished. "It's gone," he said. "The pressure, whatever it is, went away as soon as I stopped pushing against it."

"Fascinating," Spock said. "Obviously it does not work on the same principle as our tractor or repulsor beams."

Slowly, Kirk lifted his arms, but when he tried to reach forward with one hand, the pressure returned abruptly and fully, not just against his hand and arm but his entire body. With each inch his hand was extended, the greater the pressure became; and as the pressure increased, he began to have even more difficulty breathing, as if it really were a perfectly steady but extremely strong wind blowing in his face, taking his breath away.

"Fascinating," Spock repeated. "And, Captain, notice that your sleeve is apparently not affected, nor is the material of the rest of your uniform. The force would appear to act directly on one's body but not on one's clothing."

Spock was right, Kirk realized instantly. Otherwise the sleeve of the extended arm would have been forced halfway back up his arm. Lowering his arm but continuing to lean into the pressure, he looked down at his uniform and saw that the folds in the material, the trouser legs that flared out over his boot tops were likewise untouched by the pressure.

For a long moment, he stood still, relieving the pressure and catching his breath. Finally, he sat down and removed one boot and, pushing against the sole, slowly slid it top first along the floor into the barrier. As before, the pressure built up against his hand and body, but not against the boot, the top of which extended a good thirty centimeters beyond the farthest point he could force his hand.

Retrieving his boot, he started to slip it on. "Any thoughts, Spock? Anyone?"

"If I had a good old Georgia fly rod," McCoy said, "I might be able to snag some of that stuff. Unless there's a field around *it* that blocks out *in*animate objects."

"They're obviously supported by a force field of some sort," Spock said, "or perhaps embedded in it."

"Yes, but—" Kirk, still seated on the hard, plastic-like floor, frowned, stopping in the middle of pulling his boot back on. For a moment, he ran his fingers over the insulating inner lining.

"Something happened to this boot while it was in the barrier," he said. "Or on the other side."

The others leaned closer as he removed the boot again. The inner surface, instead of being smooth and seamless, was rough, as if it had been scraped by some harsh abrasive. It was still soft, like the dark foam rubber it resembled, but the surface texture was totally changed.

"Let me see your hand, Jim," McCoy said quickly. "If it was something in the barrier—"

Still frowning, Kirk withdrew his hand from the boot and looked at it with McCoy. It was, as far as either could tell, unchanged.

Meanwhile, Spock had leaned down and picked up the boot and was examining it. After a second, one eyebrow arched slightly and he glanced briefly through the barrier.

"A vacuum, Captain," he said. "There would appear to be a vacuum on the other side of the barrier or, at the very least, extremely low air pressure."

"How can you know *that?*" McCoy asked skeptically.

"It's quite simple, Doctor. As you know, the insulation in our boots contains, as does most insulation, thousands of minute bubbles of inert gas. Many of those bubbles appear to have burst, as they would do if exposed to a vacuum. The rupturing of those bubbles is the cause of the surface roughness."

Kirk took the boot back and examined the inner surface again. "At least," he said after a second, "it's still wearable. However," he went on, resuming the task of replacing the boot, "escaping through the barrier would not appear to be a viable option."

"I fear not, Captain. Nonetheless, I would suggest a close inspection of the entire perimeter. We do not yet know what conditions prevail in other areas, nor even that openings do not exist."

Standing, Kirk nodded. "Quite right, Mr. Spock. Scotty, Chekov, Sulu, you go that way. Spock and Uhura and I will go the other and meet you on the far side. Lieutenant Tomson, you bring Crandall and come—"

Abruptly, Kirk's words were cut off as he felt the clammy tingle of a transporter beam gripping him.

"Spock!" he snapped. "It's happening again! If I don't return—"

Again his words were chopped off, this time by the

momentary paralysis that precedes the actual transporting process.

And then, with the same quickness he had noted before, the room and everyone around him faded into nothingness, and he waited tensely to see what would replace them.

Chapter Eighteen

ONCE AGAIN, KIRK had little time to wait. Within fractions of a second, his new surroundings leaped into view.

For just an instant, the thought flashed through his mind that he had been somehow returned to the *Enterprise*'s transporter room, so similar was the dimly lit area he found himself in, but the illusion quickly faded as he saw the dark-skinned, bearded man who stood at the transporter controls, his shadowy eyes fixed on a metallic, switch-laden box that looked remarkably jury-rigged. It was, however, perched on the edge of a control panel whose levers and buttons vaguely resembled the *Enterprise*'s transporter controls.

The platform on which Kirk stood on was also different, higher than the one on the *Enterprise* and equipped with only three transport units, not six. And, like the giant circle in the ceiling of the room he had just been snatched from, a faint red glow hovered around the upper, overhead section of each unit.

Cautiously, he tried to move and found that, for all intents and purposes, he was rooted to the spot. It was as if, he thought helplessly, he had been dumped into the middle of one of the barriers, one that kept him not only from moving forward but from moving more than two or three inches in any direction. He could breathe easily enough, and move his limbs and his head, but that was all.

Returning his attention to the operator, Kirk saw that he was wearing a dark, starkly plain tunic and trousers. If it was a uniform, there was no visible insignia of rank. His fingers cautiously worked a half-dozen of the switches on the jury-rigged box and then worked the other controls.

A moment later, one of the other two transport units glowed more brightly, and the air above it filled with a tightly contained volume of swirling fog that quickly metamorphosed into the shape of a woman, dark-skinned and short-haired like the operator, and dressed in the same featureless tunic and trousers. In her hands, she carried a small device that in general appearance reminded Kirk of a tricorder, except that it, too, had a jury-rigged look about it.

Unrestrained by whatever held Kirk, she stepped off and went to stand at the edge of the transporter platform. As she motioned with one hand, a panel slid up in one of the walls, revealing a window or viewscreen of some kind. Watching the screen, she tapped a series of instructions into the tricorderlike device she held.

As she did, an image appeared on the screen—an image of herself. A moment later, she spoke. Her voice was deep but somehow melodic, and the sound she made sounded to Kirk's ear like "Aragos." At the same time, what could have been a graphic representation of the sound appeared on the screen below her image, and a series of previously unseen, multicolored lights next to the screen flickered briefly.

Another series of instructions was tapped into the tricorderlike device, and her image vanished, only to be replaced by one of Kirk himself. Instead of speaking again, the woman turned to look at Kirk directly, with an expression that very well could have been eager expectancy.

Had she been introducing herself? he wondered with a frown.

"James Kirk," he said, watching the screen's graphics form and fade and the lights next to the screen flicker. "I am captain of—" he started to continue, but a sharply upraised hand silenced him.

Hastily, she tapped something else into the device, accompanied by more graphics and flickering lights, and he couldn't help but wonder if she were somehow erasing what he had said.

Then another image appeared, this time of the device she was holding, and again she spoke and again the graphics appeared and the lights flickered. When they faded, she nodded to the operator, and a moment later the air above the third of the transport units clouded and then cleared, revealing one of the *Enterprise*'s medical tricorders suspended in midair. Simultaneously, its image appeared on the screen, and the woman looked expectantly toward Kirk once again.

And finally it dawned on him.

A language lesson!

Hope flooded through him. His captors, whoever they were, wanted to talk, not kill! In the same way he had wanted to communicate with the Hoshan and Zeator brought aboard the *Enterprise*, these people wanted to communicate with *him!* And that screen with its graphics and flickering lights must be a crude form of translator. Obviously, it did not have the ability, as did the universal translators, to read and map the corresponding neuronic activity of the speakers' minds, so the process would be long and tedious.

Far *too* long to save the *Enterprise* from the combined Hoshan and Zeator fleet that was at this moment probably less than twenty standard hours distant.

If only he could get his hands on a translator!

On the screen, the image was flashing, as if to get his attention, and the woman was looking at him, obviously urging him to speak.

"Medical tricorder," he said, stimulating another set of graphics and flickering lights.

Ironically, the next item that appeared in the air above the transporter and on the screen was a translator, but, other than naming it, there was nothing Kirk could do.

* * *

An hour after he had been snatched away, Captain Kirk reappeared in the cavernous room, at almost the precise point from which he had originally been taken. Alerted by the billowing precursors of the transport beam, Spock and McCoy and a half-dozen others were hurrying toward him the instant he was completely materialized.

"They want to talk," Kirk snapped out while they were still approaching him. "They have a crude computer translator, and they appear to be simply trying to learn the language."

Before he could say more, Dr. McCoy and Lieutenant Commander Scott vanished in twin pillars of swirling transporter smoke.

"Captain," Spock said, barely missing a beat as his two companions disappeared, "you saw our captors?"

"I saw them," he said and went on to briefly describe the scene he had been snatched into. "Either they call themselves Aragos, or that's the name of the one who was trying to communicate with me."

"Aragos, Captain?" Spock said. "I am sure I have heard that word before."

"I know," Kirk said. "It sounds familiar to me, too, now that I have the time to think about it." He grimaced. "If we could just get in touch with the computer, or get our hands on a translator! Spock, no one's come up with a substitute for Bones's fly rod idea?"

"Negative, Captain. We have literally nothing but the clothing we wear. However, it was observed during your absence that several of the objects from the *Enterprise* were apparently transported somewhere and returned, one at a time."

Kirk nodded. "I'm not surprised. They were using them as part of the language lesson. In fact, that might be the main reason they brought them all down here. They transported them to the room I was in, showed them to me, and had me name them. They ran through one of everything, I think, and then started showing me pictures of the *Enterprise*'s controls."

Turning to look out through the barrier, he saw one of the objects from the *Enterprise* turn momentarily to smoke and then vanish as he watched. "They seem to be running Bones and Scotty through the same routine," he said with a frown. "Apparently they didn't believe what I told them."

"Perhaps it is just as well, Captain."

"You sound as if you have an idea, Mr. Spock."

"I do, but it cannot be implemented unless they repeat their procedures again with me. If they do, I can attempt to influence them mentally."

"A mind touch? Without physical contact?"

"I can guarantee nothing, Captain. If I am given the chance, I can only try. If, as you say, they are anxious to communicate with us, they may be more receptive than they would be under other circumstances."

"Let's hope so. If we don't establish some kind of communication before the Hoshan and the Zeator get here, it probably means the end of the *Enterprise*. And the end of any chance to return to the Federation."

He broke off, shaking his head. "Even if these people have the technology to defend it, I don't think they're in control enough to use it effectively," he said and went on to describe the seemingly jury-rigged auxiliary controls for the transporter and the tricorderlike device the woman had used. "Whoever they are," he finished, "I don't think they're the ones who built this place originally. Their ancestors, perhaps, but not them."

For nearly an hour, then, the two of them talked, with Uhura, Sulu, and Chekov alternately listening and volunteering comments. Kirk described the transporter room and its controls in as much detail as he could remember, and even as he did, the items beyond the barrier continued to appear and disappear. Finally, as they were discussing the earlier, lower-level life form readings the *Enterprise* had detected, Spock suggested they might have been generated not by organic computers but by the same humanoids the later sensor readings detected.

"Suspended animation?" Kirk asked. "You're saying these people may have built this place as a sort of ultimate bomb shelter? A place to survive until whatever destroyed their world went away and it was safe to come out again?"

"Possible, Captain, even though the readings were not entirely consistent with suspended animation. Both the Hoshan and the Zeator told us they themselves constructed massive defenses for their own worlds, which apparently are outside this zone where all worlds have been destroyed. Here, directly in the path of whatever was destroying the worlds, this subsurface vault and the possibility of outliving their enemies may well have been their only hope for survival."

"But why would they awaken now, just in time to snatch us off the *Enterprise?*"

"Pure chance, perhaps. Or our earlier approach could have triggered some revival mechanism. There was, you will remember, an operating power source. I detected no sensor probes at the time, but that does not mean none was present. Or our own sensor probes might have been the triggering mechanism, reviving the people in order that they could defend themselves."

"Or find out if the war was over. Unlike everyone else we've run into here, this bunch at least wants to talk, so—"

Kirk broke off sharply as, a few feet away, the smoky forms of Scott and McCoy began to materialize.

Hurrying toward them, Kirk wondered who, if anyone, would be next.

"Bones! Scotty!" he said quickly. "A transporter room? Language lesson?"

"Aye," Scott said, "I think so."

But before he could say more or McCoy could do more than nod, Spock broke in.

"I am next, I believe, Captain," he said, and as Kirk turned sharply toward him, the swirling smoke of the alien transport system began to form.

"Spock!" Kirk shouted, as if raising his voice could penetrate the clouds and reach the Vulcan's now transparent ears. "Get that translator!"

Maybe, he thought, we have a chance after all, and he wondered if they were being watched, if even the fact that it was Spock he had conferred with after his return was what had prompted the aliens to take the Vulcan next.

"Captain!"

Lieutenant Tomson's shout jerked Kirk's attention away from the fading column of smoke that had been Spock. Turning abruptly, Kirk saw why she had yelled.

Someone else was disappearing in a swirl of smoke, the last someone Kirk had hoped would be taken.

If anyone could throw a monkey wrench into Spock's attempt to communicate with the aliens, it was Dr. Jason Crandall.

Chapter Nineteen

SPOCK'S VULCAN EYES, more accustomed to sudden or extreme variations in light than most humans, took in the dimly lit transporter room at a glance and then centered his gaze on the controls. The auxiliary controls, as the captain had said, looked jury-rigged, but to Spock's analytical eyes, the setup was more indicative of ingenuity than imperfection or any lack of understanding or skill. In some ways it reminded him of devices he and Chief Engineer Scott had improvised to work around failed equipment on the *Enterprise* or to make a piece of equipment perform an emergency service that its original designers had never intended it to do.

As he studied the controls, still relegating the humanoid forms in the room to the background of his thoughts, one of the other transport units was activated. Looking around, he saw that Dr. Crandall was materializing, and for a moment he wondered what logical reason the aliens could have had to select Crandall. If they had been observing the *Enterprise* crew where they were being held, they could well have determined, as had the first Hoshan brought aboard the *Enterprise*, that Captain Kirk was the leader and was therefore the first individual with whom to attempt contact. Knowledge of the language was obviously not required for such deductions to be made. Similarly, because McCoy and Scott and Spock himself were among those the captain had first gathered around him, the aliens could have selected from that group for their subsequent attempts at contact. However, he quickly realized, they would also have seen Crandall being rescued by Kirk, and that alone could have caused them to assume he was an individual of importance.

Satisfied with the logic of the situation, Spock turned his attention to the two dark-skinned humanoids. They were as the captain had described: a female and a bearded male, both dressed in simple, dark outfits with no indication of rank or authority. As his eyes took in their shadowy features, however, he detected something else, something in the way they stood, tensely waiting.

But it was more than that, he realized a moment later. Already, even before attempting any form of mental contact, he could detect something beyond the physical tension. Behind it, he could feel the mental tension and a trace of the fear that generated it. These humanoids, as the captain had hoped, were not enemies. They were not the ones who had destroyed these worlds tens of thousands of years ago. In emptying the *Enterprise,* they had not acted out of hostility. Nor had they acted solely out of fear of the *Enterprise,* although fear—fear not only of the *Enterprise* but of something ill defined and deliberately forced out of their conscious minds—had undoubtedly been a part of their motivation.

As it still was.

From Crandall, now fully materialized and looking about with frantic eyes, Spock felt nothing, but that was not surprising. During Crandall's time on the *Enterprise,* Spock had observed that Crandall, even more so than most humans, had the ability to conceal his true emotions and generate the illusion of other, totally false ones. Unlike Vulcans, whose emotions were rigorously controlled by logic, Crandall and others of his type were able only to repress and disguise their emotions. Behind the ever-changing and deceptive facades that they maintained, they were in truth controlled by their constant and illogical inner turmoil. Where Vulcans were masters of their emotions, Crandall was a slave to his, no matter how it could sometimes appear to other humans.

As Spock considered what effect Crandall's presence might have on his efforts to obtain a translator, the first image appeared on the screen in the far wall. As it had been for the captain, it was an image of the woman who stood next to the transporter platform, controlling the screen through the device she held.

"Aragos," Spock said before she could speak, and as he spoke the name, the same frustrating sense of familiarity that had troubled him before flickered through his thoughts. Turning his eyes on the bearded male at the transporter controls, he repeated the word, this time with a questioning intonation, though he doubted that the tone would have any meaning to them.

The woman's features, however, did undergo a change, and she hastily keyed something into the device she held. A moment later, the man's image appeared on the screen, and the woman repeated the word slowly.

Next, the captain's image appeared.

"Human," Spock said.

"The noble captain," Crandall said with obvious sarcasm.

Spock's own image replaced the captain's.

"Vulcan," he said.

"The captain's loyal and logical first toady," Crandall said.

McCoy and Scott appeared in rapid succession, remaining on the screen only long enough for Spock to pronounce them human and Crandall to provide derisive comments. Then Crandall's image took shape, and Crandall laughed sharply.

"The prisoner!" he said, his words overlapping Spock's repeated, "Human."

Meanwhile, even as the series of images and Crandall's illogical remarks had occupied one small segment of Spock's consciousness, the greater part of the Vulcan's mind had been reaching out in an attempt to strengthen the ephemeral bridge that had seemed to exist between himself and the Aragos woman from the moment their eyes had met. Even with that initial link, however, he knew that anything deep enough to be meaningful would be difficult without physical contact.

He had occasionally achieved such contact in the past, as when he and the captain and several others had been taken prisoner on Eminiar VII. At that time he had been able to influence the guard outside the room in which they were being held, but the actions he had induced the guard to take had been simple and not far removed from his assigned duties. A touch of initial mental confusion, an impression that all was not as it should have been within the room he was guarding, a slight damping of the wariness that went with the guard's natural curiosity were all that had been required. His disruptor drawn but his watchfulness and caution blunted, the man had entered the room and had been instantly subdued.

Here, however, it would take much more. It would not be a matter of simply making one of the Aragos step closer to him. Unless he could also force them to release him from the restraining field, he could take no physical action himself. When and if the translator again appeared in the transporter, the woman would have to be prompted to take it from the transporter and turn it on.

And leave it on, not just for a few moments but possibly for hours.

But even then, the plan might fail. Turning the translator on would automatically link it to the *Enterprise*'s computer, provided the *Enterprise* was within range. If it were not, the limited capacity of the translator itself, even with its ability to detect and map the Aragos's neuronic activity as they spoke, would not allow it to build up a usable vocabulary in a totally unknown language for hours, perhaps days.

The plan did, however, offer the best chance for success of any he had been able to devise, so it was only logical to make an attempt. If it did not work, he would try whatever then appeared to have the next best chance of being successful.

While that same small corner of his mind continued to attend to naming the objects as they appeared on the screen, another portion observed and recorded in detail every move the two aliens made, every control they touched, both on the transporter and on the device the woman held. At the same time, Spock continued to reach out mentally. In an attempt to compensate for the lack of actual physical contact, he visualized his hands reaching toward her, their immaterial fingers splayed out and bent as they would be if he were actually touching her. At his sides, his own hands assumed the same position, their raised tendons the only visible sign of the strain he was undergoing.

Slowly, the visualization became more real, until it was almost as if his hands were physically there, coming together to cup the woman's head between them. He could not only see them but feel them, feel the physical texture of her dark, smooth skin, the whispering touch of her hair where the tips of his fingers reached beyond the hairline above her temples and pressed against the warmth of her scalp.

And the link itself became stronger, as if she, too, were reaching out, unconsciously grasping for his mind, pulling it toward her own.

For a moment, her eyes flickered toward him, and he felt fear surge through her, as if she suspected what was happening and distrusted it.

Instead of withdrawing, he tightened the link, forcing his own inner calmness and rationality on her mind like a warm, comforting blanket on a shivering child.

And as he did, as the link solidified even more, he felt something else.

Distant and faint at first, it was touching not Spock's mind but the woman's, but through her, he experienced it. She herself, he realized, was not aware of it, but it was there, and as he probed, he began to understand her lack of awareness.

Unlike his own mind, this *other* was not an independent, questing intelligence, reaching out to touch and grip her mind. Instead, it was something that had been there for a long period of time. It was virtually a part of her, so intimate was its link to her mind. But it was also somehow lifeless, artificial, similar in a way to a computer but more nearly alive. Perhaps, Spock thought, it was similar to Nomad, a freak cross between machine and organic intelligence, or perhaps even the organic computer that he had first suspected of being the source of the anomalous life form readings detected on this planet.

And with the thought came confirmation.

Not the confirmation of an actual reply, but a confirmation born of his own logical analysis of the seemingly countless inputs he was receiving and had received. The pattern of the original sensor readings suddenly made sense. They had reflected, he now realized, *both* the organic heart of the computer and the hundreds of living beings over whose sleeping minds and frozen bodies it watched. Both had been linked so closely together—even more closely than they were now—that the readings had been inseparable and hence impossible to analyze individually.

But that in itself was only logical. In order to care for hundreds of living beings whose life processes had been slowed so drastically that they could survive not just hundreds but thousands, even tens of thousands of years, the system that monitored them and cared for them would *have* to be intimately linked to them, not only to their physical bodies but to their minds, for the minds would require as much care as the bodies. The caretaker would have to be, in effect, virtually an extension of those individual minds.

And so it had been.

And now, through the woman, Spock suddenly found himself in contact, not only with the organic heart of the computer but with the hundreds of others of her race. In the instant that he fully comprehended its nature, the barriers fell and he found himself face to face with a thousand-headed Hydra, each head with its own memories and dreams and hates and terrors.

In the instant full contact was made, a torrent of impressions and emotions descended on him, overwhelming even his capacity to observe and analyze, his ability even to remain aloof and unentangled.

But there was still more.

What Spock had intended to be a mind touch was, suddenly, through the power of what he had contacted, verging on a full-fledged mind fusion, not with a single mind but with hundreds.

And not only with the Aragos, still unconsciously linked as they were through the organic computer, but also with the crew of the *Enterprise*, each and every one. The thing that Spock had initiated had taken on a life of its own. Like the process that can instantly freeze an entire container of supercooled water when a grain of sand is dropped in to act as a "seed," it reached out and absorbed every mind, every memory within reach.

From the captain and McCoy, it took the shared agony that had wrenched at them as, to safeguard their entire world, they had been forced to stand helplessly by and watch Edith Keeler's brutal death under the wheels of a speeding car back in the Depression-era United States. And from their days on Yonada, it drew more shared suffering, this time mixed with the bittersweet joy that came when McCoy himself, though miraculously reprieved from his own self-diagnosed terminal illness, was forced to part from Natira, the woman for whom he had been prepared to forsake his last days on the *Enterprise*.

From the captain himself radiated the unsharable elation he had felt when he first realized he was about to achieve his life's ambition of commanding a starship, but mixed with that elation was the later pain not only of Edith Keeler's death but that of his brother on Deneva and the deaths of dozens of friends and crewmen under his command over the years.

And from Spock's own depths emerged the personal hell he had experienced at his first sight of the paralyzed remains of his one-time commander and lifelong friend, Fleet Captain Christopher Pike, a hell that had forced him, logically and inevitably, into mutiny against Starfleet itself.

These and thousands—millions—of other images and memories and emotions flooded over Spock, threatening to absorb him, threatening to take his mind and, in the fusion, dilute it and weaken it like a drop of blood being dissolved in an ocean of water.

Desperately, yet with an icy methodicalness, Spock tried to pull away. The first link in the chain was that between himself and the woman with him in the alien transporter room. If the fusion was to be overcome, that was the link that had to be broken. Even in the midst of this mind-wrenching turmoil, Spock realized that it was the combination of his own Vulcan telepathic ability and the ability of the organic computer to monitor its charges that enabled this all-encompassing fusion to exist. If the link to either was broken, the fusion would dissolve. The other links would decay to their normal strength or go out of existence altogether.

Mustering all the mental strength he could summon, Spock pulled back, struggling against the vortex that held him. In his mind's eye, he once again visualized his hands gripping the woman's head, realizing with fascination that his fingers seemed to have acutally penetrated her skull. Slowly, finger by finger, he loosened his grip, withdrawing the immaterial but painfully real-seeming fingers from her skull, pulling them backward, seeing her flesh and hair reform in their wake. Then the hands were no longer touching even that, but were cupped in the air about her head, but still the vortex swirled about him, sucked at his imagined hands like the vacuum of space sucked air from a punctured ship.

But then, suddenly, the link was broken. His imagined hands did not withdraw but simply vanished, as if all resistance to his efforts to pull back had been instantaneously removed. At the same moment, the raging tide of other minds receded. The hundreds of Aragos and their thousands of years of dreams and nightmares, the crew of the *Enterprise* and their countless joys and terrors, all were gone in the instant the one single link snapped, allowing Spock's mind to recoil with all the tremendous force he had been using to break that link.

All were gone.

Except—

In the sudden silence and isolation, there was a scream, and as that part of his mind that had been trapped in the maelstrom of the fusion emerged and reunited with that small portion that, through it all, had somehow continued to observe his true physical surroundings, Spock realized that the scream had been going on for several seconds, that it was, in all probability, the reason for the sudden breaking of the link.

It was Crandall.

But even as that information imprinted itself in his once again fully integrated mind, he saw the Aragos moving.

The woman dropped the tricorderlike device and lurched backwards, away from the transporter platform, a look of terror on her face.

The man, Spock now realized, had himself been rigidly immobilized by the effect of the fusion, but now he had a similar look on his face and was bringing his hands back to the transporter controls, preparing to banish Spock and Crandall back to their cavernous prison.

And in that instant of observation, a new plan sprang into being in Spock's mind. It was a plan that had little chance of success. And even if it did succeed, there was even less chance that either he or Dr. Crandall would survive to share in its success.

It was, however, the only plan that, so far as Spock

was aware, had any chance at all. He would spare Crandall if he were able, but he saw no way in which it could be done. With further analysis, it might be possible, but there was barely time to act, certainly no time for additional observations and deductions. In any event, neither his own life nor Crandall's could be considered significant when weighed against the possible salvation of the *Enterprise* and its four-hundred-odd officers and crew.

Without hesitation, he reached out with his mind. In the aftermath of the chaotic and momentary fusion, the barriers were still low, the resistance almost non-existent. It was as if he were actually in physical contact with the man at the transporter controls, so quickly was the mental contact established.

In the same instant, however, Spock felt the other, the organic core of the computer and the hundreds of minds it still touched. It, too, was reaching out, blindly trying to reestablish its links to those hundreds of new minds that had been snatched from it.

But this time Spock was prepared, and he concentrated solely on the man, excluding all else. Unlike the first time, when his own curiosity had helped open the doors that had allowed the fusion, he resisted all other influences, all other probings. Instead of an image of hands grasping the other's face and head, there formed almost automatically in Spock's mind the image of a wall shutting the two of them in, the rest of the universe out.

And his task this time was immeasurably easier than what he had set for himself before. Instead of a series of actions, all of which would have gone directly against both the woman's logic and her instincts, he needed this time only to divert the man's attention, to cause one move out of a half-dozen he would make, all in panic-driven haste, to be in error.

If, that is, he could trust the accuracy of the memories supplied by that portion of his mind that had observed the man's actions as he had transported item after item to and from the third transport unit. And if

Spock's own hurried analysis of those actions, of the functions of the switches and dials, were correct.

But there was no time for doubts, no time for further observation or analysis. Already the man's fingers were darting across the controls, and within a second—

Concentrating so intensely he could almost see the controls as if through the eyes of the operator, Spock willed the man's fingers to an even more rapid pace, all the while centering his thoughts on the one, critical switch.

For an instant, just an instant, the man's fingers hesitated, as if he, like the woman before him, had become aware of Spock's intrusion, and the man's eyes blinked. But in the wake of the massive intrusion of only moments before, the man could be sure of nothing, and the new suspicion only increased his haste as he resumed his movements.

And the switch was thrown.

The switch that, Spock believed, controlled the destination to which he would be transported, was thrown.

Not daring to withdraw for fear that the man would, even under these conditions, notice his mistake, Spock could only wait and try to maintain the wall that separated him from the distressing chaos of another uncontrolled fusion. He could only wait and watch as Crandall's transport unit energized seconds before his own and the man dissolved into swirling smoke.

Finally, after a half-dozen seconds that seemed to Spock's tension-heightened awareness like twice that number of minutes, he felt the tingling chill of the transporter grip him.

Filling his lungs with a last intake of breath, narrowing his eyes to slits to give them as much protection as possible, he blocked his mind against the pain he knew was coming and watched the transporter room fade from around him.

An instant later—though he knew that in reality the transport process took several seconds—his body felt as if it were about to explode as the vacuum took him in its grip.

Beyond the barrier, apparently only inches away, dozens of faces turned toward him, their eyes widening in shock, their mouths opening in soundless shouts. Ignoring the sharp prickling in his ears, the only portion of the pain his mind had yet allowed to reach his consciousness, Spock turned from the barrier.

He had, as he had hoped, materialized outside the barrier, but he was a good fifty feet from the array of *Enterprise* equipment, fifty feet from the translator he needed to snare from its invisible support and throw through the barrier to the captain. Both humans and Vulcans had survived for brief periods of total exposure to a vacuum, but whether either could function usefully for more than fractions of a second was unknown. Would the blood vessels in his eyes rupture, blinding him? How long could he withstand the sudden unbearable pressure of the air of that last deep breath before he was forced to release it, letting the vacuum in to tear directly at his lungs? How long could he block out the violently cramping pains imposed on every joint by the sudden reduction of external pressure? Even for a Vulcan with a full complement of mental and physical disciplines, to function under such conditions for more than a few seconds would not be easy.

And as he completed the turn away from the barrier, he saw that the task would be even more difficult than he had imagined.

Standing virtually in the midst of the *Enterprise*'s equipment, blood trickling from his ears, a set of survival gear already on his face, was Dr. Crandall.

Chapter Twenty

LITTLE MORE THAN two hours ago, Dr. Jason Crandall's world had once more been turned upside down.

One moment he had been lying in despair in an *Enterprise* detention cell, reliving again and again his bungled attempt to keep the deflectors from being raised, knowing that it had undoubtedly been his final chance to achieve any kind of victory over Kirk and his hateful disciples. The next moment, he found himself snatched from the cell and dumped in the midst of what appeared at first to be nothing more than a vastly larger cell.

But this one, he realized in an almost instantaneous burst of elation, looked as if it contained not just himself but every single person who had been on board the *Enterprise*.

No longer was he the only prisoner, the only one helpless to do anything but bemoan his fate! Now, suddenly, his enemies were prisoners as well! They were *all* prisoners, he no more helpless than any of the others, even that insufferable captain! Even if he was never able to gain the victory he had hoped for by destroying the *Enterprise*, he could at least no longer be defeated. He could still be killed—probably *would* be killed—but he could not be defeated, not by death! He could now die gladly, secure in the knowledge that Kirk and his four hundred sycophants were no better off than he himself. Their precious starship, their exclusive spacegoing fraternity, their vaunted loyalty to each other—in the position they were now in, none of it meant a thing!

It no longer mattered, Crandall told himself with something that bordered on glee, that the *Enterprise* had somehow saved itself from the Hoshan and Zeator lasers for which he had attempted to lower the deflectors. It no longer mattered that he was helpless. The others were equally as helpless as he, and for two hours he had reveled in that knowledge, enjoying the anger and frustration and fear he saw in the faces around him. Even the attack on him, so quickly stopped by Kirk for whatever his perverted reasons, had only added to Crandall's manic enthusiasm, proving as it did that they credited him with at least some of the responsibility for their downfall.

But then, snatched away to that dimly lit transporter room, as he had elatedly watched the total helplessness of even the supposedly superhuman Vulcan, something happened that made all the previous upheavals in his life fade into nothingness by comparison.

In less than a minute, his mind, his entire life, was literally turned inside out.

In one eternity-long minute, everything changed.

He had often undergone changes before, not only in his evaluation of the world around him but in his evaluation of himself, but never had he experienced anything like this. His mind suddenly lost all its barriers, all its privacy, and the thoughts and feelings of hundreds of others came pouring in, filling his mind as if it were their own, overwhelming and absorbing and blending with his own memories and emotions.

And, to his utter amazement, he found himself experiencing not revulsion or hatred or even fear, but understanding.

And then, an instant later, an overwhelming shame.

Through a hundred different pairs of eyes, he saw what others saw.

Through a hundred different minds, he felt what others felt.

He saw Captain Kirk's early efforts to befriend him,

to make him feel welcome in spite of his own hostility and overbearing demands.

He saw the remnants of Ensign Davis's admiration for what she thought he had been, her sorrow at what she saw as his irrationality, his betrayals.

He saw the hundreds of honest smiles that officers and crew alike had, despite his lack of response, bestowed on him, smiles he had interpreted as a sarcastic surface, concealing only contempt.

But most of all, from hundreds of different viewpoints, he saw—himself.

And he cringed.

He had been wrong.

Virtually every thought and every motive he had attributed to the officers and crew of the *Enterprise* had been wrong, painfully and shamefully wrong.

Under impossible circumstances, they had tried their best to understand and help him, and he had, at every turn, done *his* best to destroy them.

Had his whole life been lived the same way?

Had his brother, all those long years ago, truly meant to help him, not, as he had assumed, trick him into making a fool of himself in front of the class?

Had that negotiator on Tajarhi—Crandall couldn't even remember his name now—been sincere in that out-of-channels, late-night warning? Had the resultant disaster, the loss of life and all the rest, actually been Crandall's fault? Had his distrust of the man, his assumption that the call was part of a desperate, last-minute scheme to win a better settlement, been the true cause?

Had his whole life been, as these weeks on the *Enterprise* had been, a series of disastrous misunderstandings, all growing out of his own egocentric—and horribly wrong!—imaginings? Had he, in assigning to others the motives he himself was driven by, ruined not only his own life but the lives of countless others?

The only possible answer, the answer he saw in the suffocating torrent of revelations that had descended upon him, was a soul-rending YES!

But now—

Now, in the final moments of his life, he had one last chance to redeem himself.

Even as his transport unit had begun to operate, he realized that he knew what the Vulcan hoped to do. The Vulcan's thoughts, not in words but in images, had leaped into his suddenly receptive mind, and he knew what was going to happen.

As, too late, he tried to suck in a final breath, he felt the transporter take hold, and, suddenly, he was in the vacuum virtually in the middle of the array of *Enterprise* equipment.

For an instant it was as if every nerve in his body had gone dead, and in that instant, before he felt his lungs begin to burst, his joints to cramp, he saw and grasped the survival gear that hung only inches in front of him.

But a translator—a translator was what he needed!

As he lifted the survival gear to his face, as his entire body erupted in an explosion of pain, he saw Spock. The Vulcan had appeared next to the barrier, and already he was moving toward Crandall.

But he wouldn't make it.

Even a Vulcan could not do miracles.

For an instant, the old Jason Crandall surged up inside him, and pleasure flared through him at Spock's helplessness.

But it was gone as quickly as it had come, buried not only by the volcanic pain in every part of his body but, more completely, by a renewed wave of shame.

Abruptly, not giving himself a chance to think, he forced his violently cramping muscles to obey one last command and rip the survival gear from his face and, with a gut-wrenching effort he wouldn't have thought possible only seconds before, throw it through the deadly vacuum to the Vulcan.

As Spock, himself moving in a series almost of twitches, caught it, Crandall, all control gone, felt the air that remained being ripped from his lungs, felt his joints freeze in agony, his body begin to topple.

His last, pain-shrouded sight was Spock slipping on the survival gear and lurching toward him.

Somehow, Spock caught the survival gear and instantly fastened it over his face. Instinct cried out for him to simply suck in the life-giving air, but he knew he did not have the time. The gear was not intended for use in a vacuum, only in hostile atmospheres on planetary surfaces, and, while it would give him air to breathe, it would do nothing for the violent, cramping pains that would, he knew, render him helpless the moment the barriers his mind had set up crumbled. And, of equally immediate concern, the operator of the transporter might discover his mistake any second, and that would be the end of Spock's chance to reach a translator.

At least, he thought as he hobbled forward, there is no barrier around the equipment, as they had feared there might be. Crandall had proven that. Those in charge undoubtedly considered the vacuum and the barrier around the prisoners sufficient protection.

As Spock moved, his slitted eyes scanned the equipment, but it was only as he was passing Crandall's crumpled, bleeding body that he located a translator.

Lurching to one side, he grasped it from its invisible shelf.

Turning, seeing the captain and Dr. McCoy and Mr. Scott pressing against the barrier, he raised his arm to throw.

But even as he did, he realized it was too late.

Without the preliminary clammy tingle—had it, too, been blocked from his mind along with the havoc being wreaked upon his body by the vaccum?—the momentary paralysis of the transporter-beam lock-on gripped him.

And he was back in the alien transporter room.

The shock of the sudden return of normal air pressure hit him almost as hard as had its removal less than a minute before, but the instant he could move, he flicked on the translator, grimacing mentally as the faint pulsing light that indicated the *Enterprise*'s computer was out of range came on. A moment later, as the sound of the Aragos voices came to him, he realized with some slight relief that, while his ears were badly plugged, the eardrums had not burst. He also realized that, if the field he was embedded in had not held him upright, he would have fallen.

On the second transport unit, the collapsed form of Dr. Crandall, blood now running freely from nose and ears and even eyes, took shape.

Unable even to lower his arm, so tightly did the field grip him, Spock waited helplessly, expecting the woman to step up and take the translator and the survival gear from him or the man to do something with his transporter controls that would send the two items back to join the rest of the *Enterprise*'s equipment.

But the woman did not move toward him.

Nor did the man do anything to the transporter controls, though his fingers hovered closely over them.

The woman, now standing next to the man, was talking to him, gesturing angrily.

Suddenly, to Spock's amazement, the translator began speaking.

"It is not a weapon!" it said, apparently translating the woman's words. "Did you not see it in his thoughts?"

It was, of course, impossible, but it was happening. It took hours or days for the translator, isolated from the main computer on the *Enterprise*, to analyze a new language. The language, therefore, was not new. It was one already in the translator's own memory. The Aragos, therefore—

And he remembered.

Even as the blocks he had established against the pain began to dissolve and his mind threatened to retreat into oblivion before the assault, the reason for the nagging familiarity of the name and for the performance of the translator came to him. Aragos was the name of one of dozens of races—planetbound humanoid races—discovered by earlier expeditions into the Sagittarius arm of the Milky Way galaxy, where the gate had been. As with most planets that did not have space travel, particularly those at such great distances, there had been no contact beyond the gathering of data, including languages. Distance and the Federation's noninterference policy virtually forbade anything more.

But here, countless light-years from that planet, was incontrovertible evidence that, at some unknown time in the past, this particular race had had not just space travel but interstellar travel.

They had found the gate, and they had passed through it.

But those thoughts flashed through Spock's besieged mind in an instant, and almost before the translator's last words faded, he was forcing himself to call out to the Aragos.

"She is right!" he said, the words slurred from the strain and from the effects of the vacuum on his throat and tongue and lips. "It is a translator, to allow us to speak with each other!"

Virtually simultaneously, the alien words issued from the translator.

The woman fell silent, spinning to face him. The man's jaw dropped as his eyes darted to the translator.

"We mean no harm," Spock said, "as I know now that you mean none to us. We need your help, as I suspect you need ours."

The woman's eyes widened as the translation came, but then, abruptly, she turned to the man.

"Release them!" she said.

The man hesitated, his eyes darting from the woman to Spock and back, but then his fingers moved across the controls.

A moment later, deprived of the support of the restraining field, Spock crumpled, unconscious, to the floor.

Chapter Twenty-One

"DATA TRANSFER TO auxiliary memory complete, Captain."

Spock, a greenish-red tinge to his eyes and an odd raspiness in his voice the only outward signs that remained of his ordeal after Dr. McCoy's hurried and harried ministrations, tapped a final code into the science station controls as he spoke. Standing by the padded handrail behind Spock, the leader of the Aragos—Ckeita, the woman from the transporter room—watched, as interested in the Vulcan's apparent recuperative powers as in the *Enterprise*'s equipment. Below on the engineering deck, a half-dozen of her scientists and technicians were working with Scotty to jury-rig the modifications that would enable the sensors to pinpoint the location of the gate.

"Analysis for relevant information underway," Spock said a moment later. "We will soon know if the pattern for the gate's behavior can be extrapolated to the present time with sufficient precision.

"Excellent, Mr. Spock," Kirk said, "but how soon is soon?"

"Impossible to make a reliable estimate, Captain. There are thousands of years of data to be sifted and analyzed."

"Understood, Mr. Spock. Just see that it's completed before the Hoshan and Zeator are able to cut us off from the gate."

"I will do what I can, Captain," Spock said. "I must

point out, however, that they may well possess far more ships than the ones we have already encountered. If so, such additional ships may already have been deployed in the area of the gate, the approximate location of which we had supplied to both parties."

"I know," Kirk said, grimacing as he looked away and then punched the button that activated the engineering deck intercom. "Progress, Mr. Scott?"

"Aye, Captain. Wi' those six down here, I dinna think Starfleet will recognize the sensor circuits when we get back, but if what they're doing does get us back, I'll no' complain."

"And the dilithium they supplied us with? Is it compatible with our own?"

"Aye, it can be used to replace our own crystals, but we would have only impulse power while the replacement was being carried out. And new dilithium crystals will do no' a thing for the damaged deflectors. Those still need several days for a complete overhaul of the generators."

"What you're saying, then, Scotty, is that we're better off sticking with the damaged crystals and hoping for the best?"

"Aye, Captain, unless ye want to take the chance o' being dead in the water for more than a standard day."

"All right, Mr. Scott, so be it. Be prepared to replace them the moment we're safely through the gate. We'd be years from the Federation without them. Mr. Sulu, take us to the gate, maximum warp that's consistent with the condition of our crystals."

"Aye-aye, sir."

"And Scotty, how are the life support systems holding up under the demands of our nine-hundred-odd hitchhikers?"

"The air might get a wee bit thin in a few months, but there'll be no problems before."

"If we're all still on the *Enterprise* then, that will be the least of our problems." Kirk paused just long enough to activate the sick bay intercom. "Bones, what's the prognosis for Crandall? Will he make it?"

"If we can get him to a starbase hospital, he will," McCoy's voice grated from the speakers, "but otherwise it's doubtful. He's on full support, and that will keep him alive, but he needs too many new parts for me to reassemble him here. And tell Spock—again!—that I want him back down here in no more than one hour! No matter how tough his Vulcan hide is, I want to keep very close tabs on all that chemical baling wire I used to keep his numerous loose parts from falling off."

"All right, Bones. Now, if—"

"Thirty ships have just come into sensor range, Captain," Chekov broke in. "They are both Hoshan and Zeator, and they are not fighting with each other."

"Heading?"

"They are moving directly toward the planet we just visited ourselves, sir. They must be following our original course."

"On our present course, will we come within *their* sensor range?"

"No, sir."

"Steady as she goes, then, Mr. Sulu."

Ckeita looked around. "Are these the ships of the ones who destroyed these worlds? The ones who attacked us and stranded us here?"

Kirk shook his head as the words emerged from the translator. "No," he said. "They've only had interstellar flight a few hundred years."

"Then who—" the Aragos began.

"I don't know," Kirk said, "but from what the Hoshan and Zeator told us and from what you say happened to you more than five thousand years ago, I'm beginning to have a theory. You said that, like us, you came here through the gate at that time and were attacked without warning?"

"Five thousand years . . ." For a moment, Ckeita stood perfectly still, her gaze focusing on something none of the others could see. "That is the hardest fact of all to accept. To us, it is no more than five years, even less to those who were put under first and were not awakened for any of the false alarms."

Shaking her head in a very human gesture, she seemed to force that train of thought away. "What you say is correct, Captain Kirk," she went on. "We were attacked with something very much like your phasers. We were a scientific expedition, not a military one, so all we could do was run. It was only sheer luck that the ones who attacked us were themselves attacked, and further luck that the two were evenly matched and totally destroyed each other."

"Each other or themselves," Kirk said. "If the ones you ran into are anything like the current combatants, they may have simply disabled each other. Then, each fearing what the other—or you—would do or learn if they were captured, they may have done the final job of destruction, not on each other but on themselves. Mutual suicide."

The woman was silent a moment, as if trying to remember. Then she nodded, not quite the human up-and-down motion but a circular bobbing of her head. "I find such actions difficult to credit, but little more difficult than the mindless attacks they subjected us to. And it would, if true, explain why the ships were destroyed some time after the battle appeared to be over. We assumed some internal damage had been done during the battle, damage that only after an interval resulted in the explosions of their antimatter engines. But to purposely destroy *themselves*—" She shivered.

"You've explained how you avoided destruction by the two ships," Kirk said, "but how did you end up where we found you? Or, more accurately," he added with a faint smile, "where you were when you found us. And how your expedition came to be here at all, for that matter."

"More luck, I fear, Captain Kirk," she said with a grimace, "as was virtually everything associated with our expedition. The gates themselves had been discovered purely by accident."

"As we discovered them ourselves," Kirk said.

Ckeita nodded, the same almost circular bobbing motion she had used before. "Yes, they are the product of a science far beyond yours or mine, Captain Kirk, so accident is the only way those of our level *could* discover them. As you know, however, once we were aware of their existence, we were able to devise methods of locating them—and observing them in a limited way. We studied the shorter-range ones for years, both those with surrounding gravitational turbulence and those without. But we had only marginal success in calculating the patterns they followed and a total failure to learn anything at all about the one that brought us here, except that, like the others, it varied in size and was, on average, by far the smallest of the lot. From our fragmentary findings on the others, there seemed to be an inverse relationship between a gate's size and the distance it transported an object, so we assumed—guessed, really—that the smallest one possessed a much greater range than the others.

"Finally, curiosity won out over caution, and a group of us committed ourselves to a full-scale expedition to try to satisfy that curiosity. We didn't know where it would take us, except that it would probably be millions of parsecs from our homes. Nor did we have any guarantee that we could return. Some of the shorter-range gates operated in both directions, but not nearly all, and not with any consistency. It was this possibility—probability, even—that we would never return that prompted us to make our expedition so large. If, as many of us suspected, we found ourselves stranded in another galaxy or even another time, we would be a large enough group to survive, even to colonize any habitable worlds we were lucky enough to find. If we had suspected even the *possibility* of the existence of the kind of madness we encountered—"

Ckeita broke off, shaking her head again. "Once we recovered from the shock of the incredible density of the star population," she resumed, "we began exploring. But we found only dead worlds—*devastated* worlds, by the hundreds—and soon we were ready to return to the gate. It might not return us to our home, but it might at least let us escape whatever madness existed here.

"But we were too late. We had barely begun our return when the first attack came. When it was over, even though all we had left was impulse power, we fled. What else could we do? But then a third ship appeared and began pursuing us. Fortunately, we were within sensor and transporter range of the planet you found us on, and by the time the attack finally came, our instruments had detected the artificial caverns, the power sources, and the breathable atmosphere. Even as our ship was being destroyed, we transported ourselves down, along with whatever equipment and material we had time for, including the dilithium from the already useless warp-drive engines. Whoever was attacking us apparently did not possess transporter technology, so they did not know we were no longer in the ship when it was finally totally destroyed.

"In any event, we found ourselves in the retreat, much as it is today. Since we were virtually all scientists and engineers, we were able to discover the uses of some small portion of the retreat's contents, including the suspended animation chambers and that part of the computer that controlled them. And the transporters and sensors, as you know. They were, again perhaps by luck, perhaps by scientific necessity, very similar to our own, though far superior, so it was not as difficult as you might imagine.

"Nor was it that difficult to recognize and understand much of the equipment we found set up in the caverns to monitor the gate. It, too, was similar to ours, except that it was much more advanced, apparently able to monitor not only the gate's activity and size but its strength and several other characteristics we were never able to fully understand. We even found that certain of the monitoring equipment was linked to the computer's suspended animation control circuits, so that, whenever something came through the gate, someone would be awakened. We had no idea why this was so, but it suited our purposes as well as if it had been designed for us. If we were ever to be rescued, it would have to be by our own people coming through the gate, and this computer was already set to awaken us if that happened."

"So that was why you awakened not long after we came through," Kirk said. "I didn't think it could be a coincidence."

"No, not a coincidence. Some of us have been awakened a half-dozen times in what you tell me is the past five thousand years, but yours is the first living ship. One derelict, completely alien but also completely useless, its warp-drive engines dead for hundreds of years, came through two hundred years ago. The other arrivals were all simply debris, rocks that happened to drift through."

Ckeita paused, glancing at the forward viewscreen and then at Kirk again. "But you said you had a theory, Captain. A theory to account for all this madness."

He nodded. "One that's already been at least partially borne out," he said, going on to outline what the Hoshan and Zeator had said, that each had first entered space peacefully only to be attacked blindly and ferociously by unidentified ships that refused all attempts at communication.

"It's possible," he concluded, "that these attacks are only a small part of what could be, literally, a millennia-spanning chain, including not just the Hoshan and the Zeator but every race that's come out into space in this sector in the past several thousand years. Each one is attacked and each one, of course, retaliates, until, eventually, they reach the state the Hoshan and the Zeator were in when we arrived. They trust no one, and anyone who is unable to respond to their own specific recognition code is automatically assumed to be the enemy and attacked without warning, without mercy."

"But something had to start it, Captain Kirk. How could something so terrible ever *begin?*"

"I don't know about your people," Kirk said, "but on my own planet, earth, there was a time when something very like it would have been all too easy to start. Even with constant communications between nations, hardly a day went by for centuries when there wasn't a war going on *somewhere*. In space, where fear of the unknown is always a factor, and where communication between races just discovering each other is difficult under the best of circumstances—"

He shook his head again. "No, at first I didn't want to admit it, even to myself, but the more I've thought of it, the more I've realized that such a thing is easily possible. All it would take would be one purely evil force to start the chain reaction. Earth had its Hitlers. The Federation has the Klingons. Or it could have started simply with a misunderstanding, the way it almost did between the Federation and the Gorns.

"But however something like that starts, unless communications are somehow established between the two factions, it can end only with the total destruction of one side or the other. But with all of space for an enemy to hide in, how could the victor be positive that his enemy's destruction was total, that the enemy was truly gone? Were there colonies that survived? Could there be fleets of enemy warships returning from a conquest a thousand parsecs away?

"So the supposed victors, understandably paranoid after tens or hundreds or thousands of years of seemingly mindless attacks, keep their defenses up, and one day a new race ventures into their territory. Like you, like us, the newcomers are attacked, their ships destroyed because the survivors of that earlier war are unwilling—or unable—to take a chance that the newcomers might not be their old enemy, either resurrected or reincarnated."

Ckeita shivered. "You paint a grim picture of your species and your Federation, Captain Kirk, if you feel such things are possible."

"Both have had their grim aspects, their grim times," Kirk said with the faint beginnings of a smile, "but both on earth and in the Federation there have always been a few people—enough, so far—who were willing to take a chance, not for war but for peace. Like Spock back there in your transporter room. He was ready to die for the chance of establishing communications between us."

Ckeita nodded, closing her eyes for a moment. "You have spoken of your Federation," she said, opening them and looking directly into Kirk's eyes, "and its enemies. But you have not spoken of my people. I know that, after five thousand years, their world would no longer be mine, but I would like to know—do the Aragos still exist?"

"They exist," Kirk said, exchanging a glance with Spock, "but we know little of them. They no longer travel among the stars, that we do know, but little else."

"But you can take us there? To their world? Our world?"

"If we get back through the gate successfully, yes, we could take you. Not immediately, but in time."

"That is understood, Captain Kirk."

"I also imagine that the Federation would establish a relationship with your world, perhaps help you learn what happened to make your people retreat from space."

"Yes, that is something we would very much like to know. I cannot imagine that they did it willingly. Not all Aragos were as curious or as adventurous as those who volunteered for our expedition, but there was no lack of either trait."

"I'm sure there wasn't," Kirk said. "But if most of your ships were geared for scientific exploration, with little or no defenses—"

"The Klingons you mentioned before, Captain Kirk?"

"It's possible, though we have seen no evidence of

them in your part of the galaxy. Unfortunately, however, others probably exist who are equally as ruthless, and if one of them—"

"Your theory would appear to have further confirmation, Captain," Spock broke in, looking up from the science station instruments. "The computer records are even more extensive than I at first believed. They cover more than forty thousand standard years, and they include the log of one who would appear to be the computer's designer."

"Fascinating, I'm sure," Kirk said, "but the workings of the gate—"

"Are of paramount importance. Of course, Captain. The analysis is still underway."

"Very well. Now, you were saying? About the designer's log?"

"To summarize, Captain, the computer and the caverns that contained it were, as you suggested, constructed by one of the races who, after moving peacefully out into space, were attacked by unknown enemies. The world in question, however, was not that race's home world. The home world's location is, of course, not given, but it was at least a hundred parsecs distant, perhaps much more."

"Then why there? Why would they build their bunker there?"

"Two reasons, Captain. First, that world was one of their colony worlds, one with the facilities to do the job. Though it is not specifically indicated, it is possible that similar retreats—bunkers, if you prefer that terminology—existed on other colony worlds, perhaps on the home world as well. This one, however, was built not only as a retreat but as a monitoring station, possibly a guard station, to observe the gate."

"The gate? Why did they want to guard the gate?"

"Unfortunately, the log does not contain specifics. However, it appears that they arrived at the same theory concerning the attacks that you yourself suggested. In addition, they apparently had reason to believe that whoever initiated the chain of attacks had come through the gate several thousand years before and had quite possibly retreated through it rather than having been destroyed."

Kirk nodded thoughtfully. "If nothing else," he said, "this would explain why their transport system was designed to be capable of snatching every living thing off an approaching ship and separating them from their weapons and communicators."

"Affirmative, Captain. It is a most efficient method of gaining control of any attacking ships. However, the fact that their computer included the program the Aragos were using to attempt to learn our language would indicate that the builders, like the Aragos, were interested in establishing communications with their captives, not simply imprisoning them and confiscating their ships."

"But if they knew all this," Ckeita said, "why could they not stop this chain of madness you describe?"

"Unknown," Spock said, obviously still feeling the effects of the vacuum as he paused uncharacteristically to clear his throat. "The log ends with the construction of the computer and the retreat. The builders' plans included continuous monitoring of all aspects of the gate for an indefinite period as well as provisions for placing all fifty thousand of that world's colonists into suspended animation in case of attack. However, except for the activation of the monitoring system, which was designed to awaken them whenever anything came through the gate, none of those plans appears to have been carried out. Or if they were, there was no record of them in the log, although there may well be further relevant information that has not yet come to light. The builders of the retreat may have been wiped out during the attack that destroyed the planet's surface, or they may have retreated to other of their worlds. If they were right about the original attackers coming through the gate, their observational instruments may even have brought the attackers back and led them to the planet before the people there were ready for them. Or they may simply have decided they were wrong about the gate and abandoned the project. At this stage, unless further information is located in the computer, there is no way of knowing. We—and the Aragos—can only be grateful that the instruments designed to observe the gate were activated before the end, however that end may have come."

Ckeita shivered again. "Had we known all that you now tell us," she said, "I suspect we would have let the final ship destroy us."

Spock looked at her. "You took the only logical course open to you," he said, and after a moment she nodded her agreement.

Two hours later, Spock, his battered body reinforced by still more of Dr. McCoy's "chemical baling wire," looked up sharply from his instruments.

"I have the pattern, Captain," he said. "With sufficient precision, we will be able to utilize the gate."

"'Sufficient' precision?"

"The gate should be currently operating on a cycle of approximately eight-point-six-nine-three hours. During that time, it varies in size and destination continuously. Each transmitting window is approximately seven-point-two seconds in length. During the window which will allow us to return to our own galaxy, the gate itself will be approximately point-seven-two-nine kilometer in diameter. It is approximately this size for much of each cycle, which explains why we were unsuccessful in our efforts to locate it before."

"Less than one *kilometer*?" Kirk strode from the command chair to scowl over Spock's shoulder at the readouts, then turned to Ckeita. "You said that before you came through you had been able to monitor the size of the gate. Did you know it could become this small?"

"We did not. We had not established any recurrent pattern in its changes, nor could we measure its size with any precision. We knew only where its center was and that its size appeared to vary continually. The shorter-range ones, we are quite sure, were rarely less than several thousand kilometers in diameter."

"And the modifications your people are making to our sensors will enable us to pinpoint the center of the gate? Even when it is that small?"

When Ckeita did not reply, Spock said, "The modifications are based on the monitoring equipment found in the caverns, Captain, and it is that monitoring equipment which has given us the information to establish both the cycle and the size of the gate. Simply locating the gate should therefore present no insurmountable difficulty."

"I don't suppose you've found anything that explains *how* these things work?"

"Not specifically, Captain. However, according to readings taken by instruments the *Enterprise* unfortunately does not possess, the gate's energy would appear to be constant. It would be logical to assume that the more compressed that energy is—that is to say, the smaller the gate at any given moment in its cycle—the farther an object is transmitted. It could be considered analogous to a sun and its gravity. When one is huge and diffuse, the gravity is comparatively small, but when it contracts—"

"I know, Spock," Kirk broke in. "It becomes a neutron star and then a black hole, and the gravity is enough to rip atoms to shreds. What I would really like to know is, when is *our* window coming around next?"

"In approximately five-point-two-four hours, Captain. At our current warp factor, we will arrive in approximately four-point-one-seven hours."

"Which gives us slightly more than one hour to spare," Kirk said.

"Or to penetrate the perimeter the Hoshan and

Zeator may have established," Spock said, not looking up from his instruments.

Once again, the Hoshan and Zeator commanders, Belzhrokaz and Endrakon, shared the *Enterprise*'s viewscreen.

As Spock had feared, the nearly day-long delay on the Aragos planet had enabled their combined fleet, forty ships strong, to be waiting, spread out directly across the *Enterprise*'s path less than a million kilometers from the gate. At least they had not opened fire the instant the *Enterprise* eased into their sensor range. Neither, however, had they shown any indication of letting the *Enterprise* pass without a battle. They had established communications almost immediately and appeared to be willing to talk virtually forever, although Kirk suspected this willingness was largely to give the remaining thirty ships, already on their way from the Aragos planet, time to arrive.

"You speak of trust," Belzhrokaz was saying for what must have been the hundredth time. "If you truly wish us to trust you and believe this story you tell us of an enemy that was the source of all our troubles many thousands of years ago, surrender your ship. If everything is as you say, we will return it to you unharmed."

"If everything we have done so far hasn't convinced you that we mean you no harm," Kirk said, unable any longer to totally suppress his irritation at the Hoshan's repeated suggestion, "I can't imagine what would. As for the beings who may have triggered at least four hundred centuries of war, we have transmitted to you as much of the data as your computers will handle, and we have given you the coordinates of the retreat. Even without transporters to allow you direct access, your sensors will confirm its existence, and your own computers will, with very few improvements, be able to link up with the computer in the retreat."

"All very reasonable," Endrakon said, "but how

can we be positive that you yourself are not this enemy you speak of? How can we know that you have not simply manufactured all this data in your own computer?"

"The very fact that we didn't wipe you out when we had the chance should be *some* indication!" Kirk snapped, his patience suddenly reaching the breaking point. "Even now, the odds are excellent that we can, if you force us, punch a very bloody hole right through the middle of your fleet! That was, in fact, the recommendation of the leader of the Aragos nearly an hour ago. They have been trapped here for several thousand years and are understandably even more impatient than *we* are!"

Cutting off the sound to the two alien commanders, Kirk turned sharply to Spock. "How much time?"

"Five-point-seven minutes, Captain. And the thirty ships that were following us to the Aragos planet have just entered our sensor range. Based on their current course and formation, they appear to be attempting to cut us off from any possible retreat."

Kirk shook his head in an angry grimace. "So it's now or never. If we wait around for the next window, we'll be surrounded, and with the deflectors and the dilithium crystals in the shape they're in—"

Restoring the sound, Kirk stood and faced the images of the two commanders directly. "Thirty more of your ships have just been detected," he said. "They are approaching us from the rear, apparently in an attempt to surround us."

Kirk paused, watching the two for any sign of reaction, but there was none he could detect.

"Very well," he said, still facing them directly, "you leave us no choice. I will repeat once more: Everything we have said is true. We have demonstrated our good faith again and again. We have taken a chance and trusted you, apparently too often and too far. You have the evidence in your computers. You have the testimony of Bolduc and Atragon and the others who were aboard our ship. There's nothing more we can do to convince you."

Again he paused, and this time he saw a sideways flicker of Belzhrokaz's eyes, as if someone were trying to get his attention. Kirk waited another second, and when nothing further happened, he continued.

"We are coming through," he said flatly. "As we have demonstrated, our weapons are easily capable of destroying your ships. Our deflectors, unfortunately, are no longer capable of standing up to the kind of fire we allowed you to direct at us before. Therefore, we have no choice but to fire on any ship that attempts to fire at us. We will not fire, however, unless we detect indications that you are about to fire. Remember, our instruments can monitor your weapons. We will know which ones are about to fire, and we will *stop* them from firing the only way we are able—by destroying them and the ships in which they are contained. We don't want to, but we will—unless you let us through. It's up to you."

Abruptly, he signaled to Lieutenant Uhura, who cut the link, blanking the screen. A moment later, the dense star field in front of them replaced the image of the two commanders. A half-dozen Hoshan and Zeator ships—the ones closest to the course the *Enterprise* must follow to the gate—were also scattered about the screen.

"Ahead, Mr. Sulu, impulse power, and keep that gate in your sights. All phasers, lock onto targets closest to our path and prepare to fire on Mr. Spock's command."

More tense than he had ever been at the beginning of any normal battle, Kirk settled back in the command chair, his darting eyes fixing alternately on Spock and the forward viewscreen, where the alien ships' images grew larger with each second. Despite his confident words to the alien commanders, he knew that the *Enterprise*'s chances were not good in any battle that might come. Even before they had first detected the waiting fleet, Scotty had told him that the dilithium crystals had been pushed even closer to the ragged edge by their trip from the Aragos planet. The drain caused by engaging the warp drive even one more time could finish them altogether, and the deflectors were essentially useless. A single burst by one of the aliens' brute-force lasers could disable the *Enterprise* entirely, and with a dozen alien ships within range and more approaching, it would be virtually impossible for the phasers to take them all out in time to prevent them from firing.

Ahead, the ships continued closing in on the *Enterprise*'s path. There were now more than a dozen visible on the screen.

"Time, Mr. Spock."

"Three-point-three minutes, Captain. At our present speed, we will enter the gate two-point-five seconds into the window."

For another fifteen seconds, there was only silence.

"Lasers activated on two ships, Captain, but they are not beginning the buildup toward firing."

"Hold fire until they do, Mr. Sulu."

"Three—five more, Captain. Closest approach to enemy ships in eighty-three seconds. And all weapons on all ships are now activated."

"Be ready, Mr. Sulu."

"Ready, sir. Phasers locked onto nearest targets and programmed to shift to new targets after minimum effective period of fire."

"Captain," Uhura called loudly, "the Hoshan commander is—*both* commanders are attempting to reestablish contact."

"Put them on the secondary screen."

An instant later, the two commanders appeared on the screen above the science station. This time, neither was in the purposely neutral set from which they had spoken before. Both were in what appeared to be the command centers of their ships, and next to the Hoshan commander stood Bolduc.

"What is it?" Kirk snapped. "Have you decided to opt for sanity and let us through?"

"Yes," the Hoshan commander began, but before he could say more, Spock's still raspy voice cut in.

"Laser on nearest Hoshan ship, bearing one-zero-five, mark eighteen, initiating firing sequence, Captain."

Chapter Twenty-Two

"MR. SULU," KIRK snapped, "you have your orders!"

"No, wait!" the Hoshan commander shouted, and an instant later he was snapping out desperate orders of his own for the seemingly renegade ship to hold its fire.

But it was too late, except for Kirk to snap to Sulu, "Minimum burst, only the one ship!"

An instant later, less than a second before the laser would have fired, the *Enterprise*'s phasers lashed out, but only for an instant.

For another moment, there was total silence. Then Spock's voice: "No casualties, Captain, but self-destruct overload sequence has been initiated."

"No other ships preparing to fire?"

"None, Captain."

"Belzhrokaz! Can the sequence be stopped?" Kirk shot at the Hoshan, but the commander only shook his head despairingly as he continued to repeat his own order not to fire.

"Get your other ships out of range, Commanders!" Kirk snapped. "Time, Mr. Spock!"

"One-point-two-three minutes to the gate, Captain. Twenty-seven seconds to terminal overload in the Hoshan ship."

"Transporter room! Get everyone off that ship! Now! Keep them in the transporter matrix until we can arrange to have someone waiting to deactivate their personal self-destruct devices."

"Keptin!" Chekov, his eyes wide, darted a look toward Kirk. "The gate will—"

"Will have to wait until next time, Mr. Chekov," Kirk said. "Transporter room, are you—"

"Locked on, sir!" came McPhee's voice.

"Excellent! Get them out of there!"

"Already on their way, sir."

"Warp speed, Mr. Sulu!"

The helmsman's darting fingers answered, and an instant later the forward viewscreen was filled with the kaleidoscopic brilliance of the relativistic starbow.

Then, for just a moment, the computer-generated image of the surrounding star field filled the screen, but within seconds it shimmered, replaced once again by the sublight image.

"The crystals are gone, Captain!" Scotty's voice almost wailed from the intercom.

But they had lasted long enough. Behind them, the Hoshan ship flared into a miniature nova, but the *Enterprise* was out of reach.

"The other ships—" Kirk began.

"None seriously enough damaged by the explosion to trigger a terminal overload sequence, Captain," Spock said. "And the lasers on all other ships are being deactivated."

Suddenly, as if a flood valve had been opened somewhere inside him, the tension drained out of Kirk, leaving him almost limp.

"Thank you, Commanders," he said softly into the silence that had suddenly enveloped all the ships, "for finally taking a chance on something besides more killing."

The next window was only minutes away. The Hoshan and Zeator ships, now including the thirty that had come by way of the Aragos planet, watched from a distance as Sulu once more began the approach.

"Will it last, sir?" Chekov asked over his shoulder. "Do you really think they will not begin shooting at each other the minute we are gone? There is an old Russian proverb—"

"I know," Dr. McCoy said as he continued to watch the viewscreen from his vantage point next to the command chair. "When the cat's away, the mice will go back to war?"

"Mice, Dr. McCoy? The proverb has to do with a wolverine, but the idea is perhaps the same. Keptin?"

"I don't know, gentlemen," Kirk said, still watching the screen with its nearly seventy ships hovering only tens of thousands of kilometers away. "But even the six that we picked off the disabled ship didn't seem too disturbed at finding out they were still alive. And both commanders—"

"Dr. McCoy." Nurse Chapel's voice came over the bridge intercom. "Dr. Crandall appears to be regaining consciousness."

"What?" McCoy frowned as Kirk punched the button that would allow him to answer. "Keep him under. In his condition, *any* activity could make the damage even worse than it already is. I'll be right down!"

Turning, McCoy headed for the turbolift.

"Just a second, Bones," Kirk called, slipping out of the command chair and striding toward the doctor.

"What is it, Jim? I don't have all day. You heard—"

"I heard, Bones, I heard. I also heard a few things during that—that whatever it was that Spock triggered back there on the Aragos planet. Mentally heard a few things, that is, and 'felt' a lot more."

"We all did, Jim," McCoy said impatiently.

"But you didn't happen to be looking in the same direction I was a minute later, Bones. When Spock and Crandall were transported into the vacuum, I was watching. I saw Crandall. I saw what he did. I saw his face when he did it. And I felt just a little of what had happened to him, of how he had been changed—*really* changed—in the last sixty seconds."

"And now you don't have any doubts about him?"

McCoy said, a touch of sarcasm joining the impatience in his voice. "Your 'captain's instinct'—"

Kirk shook his head with a faint smile. "This time my 'captain's instinct' is on his side."

"If it's working that well, then it should also tell you that, unless you let me go take care of him, he won't survive long enough to ever find out how you feel about him."

"That is precisely what I'm afraid of, Bones, and I want to do something to help the odds."

"Keeping me standing here—" McCoy began, but Kirk continued, speaking rapidly.

"You've always said that a patient's state of mind, even when he's unconscious or in a coma, has a lot to do with his recovery. So, what would happen if he were allowed to regain consciousness for just a minute, just long enough, say, for you to tell him something that would stick with him when he goes back under? Something that might help him hang on until we can get him to a starbase hospital? Even with the new dilithium crystals, it's going to be a long haul."

"All right, Jim, I'll thank him for saving us. Now if—"

"Make it something more concrete than that, something that'll be sure to register. For instance, I've been thinking that the Aragos world back in our own galaxy will be in line for an ambassador once the Federation has established formal contact. Considering Crandall's experience—and the change he's undergone—he's someone I could recommend for such a post."

Somehow, McCoy managed to scowl and smile at the same time. "I'll tell him," he said. Turning to enter the turbolift, he added with a shake of his head, "You know, Jim, there are times when I think my country doctor routine has rubbed off on you. Now if you can just pass a little of it on to Spock, you might—"

The closing door cut off whatever else he was going to say.

"Two minutes to the gate, Captain," Spock said as Kirk returned to the command chair.

"Captain," Lieutenant Uhura said sharply, "both commanders are trying to reestablish contact."

"Put them on the secondary screen, Lieutenant."

Abruptly, the Hoshan and Zeator commanders appeared, once again in their respective control rooms. What, Kirk wondered, did they want now? They had said their curt good-byes hours ago, when the rescued Hoshan had been beamed aboard Belzhrokaz's ship.

"We had to speak to you again, Commander Kirk," Belzhrokaz said without preamble. "Neither of us can guarantee that our own superiors will not overrule us, but do know this: We, Endrakon and myself and all those who now observe your departure, will do our best to see that you will be given a better welcome when you return."

"*If* you return," Endrakon added, and in that moment Kirk saw in the alien's slim, avian face a flash of the same guilt that had filled Atragon's face when he had first been told that his people had for more than a century been warring against a people who had, originally, been as innocent as they themselves had been when they had first been attacked three centuries earlier.

A moment later, something similar darted across the Hoshan's face, settling in his deepest, shadowed eyes.

And in that moment, much of the doubt that Kirk had felt about this uneasy alliance faded, and he smiled.

"We'll be back," he said. "I'm sure, now, that we'll be back someday."

"Gate in ten seconds, Captain," Spock announced.

Mentally counting down, Kirk watched not the forward screen but the images of the alien commanders, themselves watching wordlessly until, in a sudden flare of color not at all characteristic of normal subspace signal loss, the images vanished.

Simultaneously, the clouds of stars on the forward viewscreen flickered out and were replaced by the comparative emptiness of the Sagittarius arm of the Milky Way galaxy. The only sound, if sound it was,

was that of four-hundred-odd officers and crew and nearly a thousand Aragos suddenly relaxing.

"Transition successful, Captain," Spock said.

"Excellent, Mr. Spock. Mr. Scott?"

"Aye, Captain," Scott's voice came immediately from the intercom, "the dilithium crystals. We're on it already. And the deflectors."

"Of course, Mr. Scott. I assumed you would be." Pausing, Kirk turned toward Spock. "And now that we're safely home, Mr. Spock, I would suggest you take the rest of the watch off, in fact, the next two or three, and that, unless you have other plans, you let Dr. McCoy check your baling wire again and see what can be done about something more permanent."

"I have no other plans," Spock said, for once not protesting the suggestion that he rest for a time. "Thank you, Captain."

"No," Kirk said, more conscious than ever of the evidence of the Vulcan's ordeal, the gravelly quality that still coated his voice and the greenish-red tinge still visible in his eyes, "thank *you*, Mr. Spock."

THE

STAR TREK

PHENOMENON